# Decade
# The 1940s

edited by Brian W. Aldiss and Harry Harrison

Pan Books in association with Macmillan London

First published 1975 by Macmillan London Ltd
This edition published 1977 by Pan Books Ltd,
Cavaye Place, London SW10 9PG,
in association with Macmillan London Ltd
Introduction and Selection © SF Horizons Ltd 1975
ISBN 0 330 25033 7
Printed in Great Britain by
Hunt Barnard Printing Ltd, Aylesbury, Bucks.

# Contents

# Acknowledgements

'Co-operate – or Else!' by A. E. Van Vogt, Copyright © 1942 by Street & Smith Publications, Inc: reprinted by permission of the author and his agent, Forrest J. Ackerman.

'Reason' by Isaac Asimov, Copyright © 1941 by Street & Smith Publications, Inc: reprinted by permission of the author.

'Arena' by Fredric Brown, Copyright © 1944 by Street & Smith Publications, Inc: reprinted by permission of the author's estate.

'Fireproof' by Hal Clement, Copyright © 1959 by Street & Smith Publications, Inc: reprinted by permission of the author.

'The Last Objective' by Paul Carter, Copyright © 1946 by Street & Smith Publications, Inc: reprinted by permission of Street & Smith Publications, Inc.

'Huddling Place' by Clifford D. Simak, Copyright © 1944 by Street & Smith Publications, Inc; Copyright renewed 1972 by Clifford D. Simak: reprinted by permission of the author.

'Hobbyist' by Eric Frank Russell, Copyright © 1947 by Street & Smith Publications, Inc: reprinted by permission of the author and the author's agents, Scott Meredith Literary Agency, Inc.

'The Xi Effect' by Philip Latham, Copyright © 1949 by Street & Smith Publications, Inc: reprinted by permission of the author and the author's agents, Scott Meredith Literary Agency, Inc.

# Introduction

Nowadays, a student's room may be cluttered with glossies of pop stars, LP artwork by Roger Dean, close-ups of Diana Ross or Robert Redford, left-wing slogans, posters advertising progressive groups, Earthsea maps, pages from Sunday colour supplements, Incredible Hulks, moon landings from magazines, postcards from Italy, a nudie calendar, portraits of Mao or engravings by Beardsley and Escher, poems by Leonard Cohen, polystyrene patterns, stills from *Tommy*, and similar assorted cultural debris. In the forties, we had only *Astounding*.

The world has proliferated since then. People, ideas, objects, images, cram our conceptual world of the seventies. If the science fiction of the forties appears simple and naïve now, that is for two reasons, two reasons which render it of more than mere nostalgic interest: firstly, it in part reflected the world in which it was written and, secondly, it reached out towards – and thus helped to establish – the conceptual world in which we now live.

This series of *Decade* science fiction anthologies takes as one of its basic premises the fact that science fiction has changed and is changing all the time. However, it may be said that it does not change greatly in its fundamentals: at its best, it deals with conceptual rather than 'real' worlds. In this respect, it differs from an ordinary story or novel.

It would be hard to find a sentence that more typically embodies what SF still stands for in many people's minds than the opening sentence of the first story in this volume: 'As the spaceship vanished into the steamy mists of Eristan II, Professor Jamieson drew his gun.'

There's one of SF's prime symbols, the spaceship. There's a

mysterious planet. And there's a professor – hardly likely to be a professor of Eng. Lit. – toting a weapon.

Well, it is not all like that now, and indeed it never was, as many of the other stories in this collection show. Nevertheless, there are certain hallmarks of the forties, some of which point towards the past, some towards the future.

It is easy to forget that there were two, not one, inaugural epochs for magazine science fiction. One commenced in 1926 when Hugo Gernsback launched *Amazing Stories*, the first magazine devoted entirely to SF. The other epoch was the eighteen nineties, with such magazines flourishing as *The Strand*, *Pearson's*, *Argosy*, and *All-Story*. These magazines generally carried something recognizable as science fiction; they carried H. G. Wells's seminal short stories which in many ways mark the birth of SF – not because they were necessarily the first such stories, but because they were the first memorable ones.

Many of the stories featuring in that first epoch were variations on an old theme, the Lost Race tale. H. Rider Haggard and Arthur Conan Doyle were both notable exponents of such romances.

Lost Race stories still cropped up, *mutatis mutandis*, but by and large the early Gernsbackian SF relied upon three grand and basic ideas, which may be categorized as 1) the perfectability and proliferation of machines, 2) the struggle for the evolution and survival of species, and 3) the second law of thermodynamics which, in stating that energy tends always to equal distribution, carries with it the message that suns and planets will grow cold and die.

These lofty ideas are meat for much speculation, and they are not new. They rank, indeed, amid the ideas which caused much of the pessimism among some of our more distinguished Victorian forebears, including Matthew Arnold, Leslie Stephen, Hartmann, Schopenhauer, Tennyson and Thomas Hardy, whose Tess knew she lived on a 'blighted' world. Writing in 1898, the novelist Joseph Conrad said, 'If you believe in improvement, you must weep, for the attained perfection must end in cold, darkness, and silence.' These same ideas were new to the class of readership – young and underprivileged – who laid hands on their first SF magazines during the late twenties and thirties.

Incidentally, another First Award must go to Mr H. G. Wells, since his novella *The Time Machine* embodies in near-perfect form these three strands of thought. The perfection of the time vehicle enables his time-traveller to go forward and see firstly how mankind evolves, and then how it dies out when the sun itself begins to grow cool. The novella embodies to perfection that cosmic dilemma of which Conrad spoke.

What of course was new about SF was a kind of fiction in which these lofty ideas could be easily discussed or dramatized. Another strand of Victorian thought was useful here: the tremendous expansion of the terrestrial time-scale which went on continuously throughout the nineteenth century, as Earth history was unrolled like a great dusty carpet. The Future became SF's chief playground. Here, robots could plausibly threaten to take over; here, man could battle with alien races on other planets; here – or *there* to be more precise – planets could be as young or as ancient as necessary, and time could run dramatically out, to end in cold, darkness, and silence.

Most of the stories in this collection fall within these parameters, framed within the questioning of post-Victorian thought. But for them, too, time can be seen in retrospect to be running out.

One reason for this was that a major war, the great SF war of the twentieth century, was being fought during the first half of the decade. The vast scale of this war, the countless individuals and nations embroiled in it, the numerous organizations as well as weapons, constituted virtually a new experience, a global convulsion. It had a maturing effect upon many SF writers, as they saw their prophecies – many of them lightly enough made – becoming flesh in unexpected ways.

The battle of the species was played out before their eyes. Here too was an enormous proliferation of machines. The distances involved, the mobility, were also far greater than ever before. To strike a personal note, one of the present anthologists was an instructor in automated rear-turret guns for Flying Fortresses, while the other travelled something like fifty thousand miles from one trouble spot to another (whereas his father, in the previous world war, had travelled three hundred miles to spend three years in a muddy trench). Some of the grimmer stories in our collection carry direct echoes of the second war. 'Arena' is an ironic comment on it and on supernatural intervention.

The war was concluded with the most dramatic demonstration ever staged of the powers of science, technology, and superorganization working in conjunction, the dropping of atomic bombs on Japan. It was an omen that SF, which had long predicted such an event, was to be taken seriously – an omen, that is, to the readers more than the writers. The writers already took themselves seriously, seeing themselves as men, largely disregarded, who had begun to speak a new conceptual language.

From this period on, what we have categorized as the three grand ideas of SF play a less important part. The question of control – the old Frankenstein problem of what society does after the scientist has invented his new thing – is increasingly dominant. It arises, for instance, in Asimov's 'Reason'.

All of Van Vogt's and Isaac Asimov's and most of Heinlein's major SF work was written during the forties. Their payments were low, their readership small. It is the usual penalty of the prophet; their mass audiences lay in wait in the age of the paperback, two or more decades ahead. As with Heinlein, Van Vogt and Asimov, so with other writers. A similar neglect attends other works of science fiction written outside the magazine field, such as Aldous Huxley's astringent *Ape and Essence* which, with its emphasis on ecology and weird cults, portrays with such prophetic force the action of a later date that it was widely dismissed as hysterical at the time of publication.

Inevitably one generalizes when speaking of a whole decade. Tendencies make for good discussions. To particularize about our authors. Eric Frank Russell was a licensed jester in *Astound-*

*ing* for many years; one of his favourite stories is here reprinted. A Liverpudlian, Russell hid his Englishness under an American idiom. British markets for SF hardly existed in the forties.

Fredric Brown is another humorist. We have preferred his more serious 'Arena' to the better-known 'Placet Is a Crazy Place'.

Asimov's is a curious career. He turned to scientific popular-isation in the fifties and has returned only rarely to SF. Yet his early stories find a larger market now than ever before. Hal Clement is another author with a scientific background; his novels, of which *Mission of Gravity* is best-known, show sym-pathetic understanding of an alien point of view.

Philip Latham forms our third writer whose authorship takes second place to a scientific career. Under his real name (Latham, like Clement, is a pen-name), he is an astronomer. 'The Xi Effect' well reflects his professional interests.

Paul Carter's is the only name on our Contents page which has not established itself in the halls of fame. Mr Carter wrote all too little. For that reason, his grim tale may come as a sur-prise to many who are otherwise familiar with forties SF.

All of these stories are culled from the pages of only one magazine. Many SF magazines flourished during the forties but, by common comment, one of them stood head and horns above the others: *Astounding Science Fiction*, later to evolve into *Analog*. This pre-eminence was due to the talents of its editor, John W. Campbell. His genius has been lauded too often for repetition to be necessary here, but it may be remarked that Campbell's great gift to the magazine field lay not in bringing new authors to it but in bringing new topics for discussion.

There is no denying that the situations and styles of many of these stories appear melodramatic to the taste of today. They were part – some believe the most lasting part – of a great pulp empire, now vanished, which preferred vivid action to analysis, cliches to new mintings, surprise to characterization.

During this decade, diverse magazines like *Amazing, Fantastic Adventures, Thrilling Wonder, Unknown, Planet Stories* and

*Startling* enjoyed a lively existence. Yet the material they were producing was, in the main, only a more sophisticated repetition of what had been going on in the thirties. Such influences as H. P. Lovecraft and Edgar Rice Burroughs remained strong. It was to *Astounding* that you had to go, for instance, to read Simak's quiet piece on the nature of a city, 'Huddling Place'. Its ideas came over freshly in the war-torn cities of the forties. 'Huddling Place' formed part of a series of stories all dealing with the same characters or world-picture. They were later published together as Simak's best-loved book, *City*. The Asimov and Van Vogt stories also became parts of series. Such 'series' stories were very popular; and there were other economic reasons for their continuance.

The forties are, in publishing terms, part of prehistory. There was almost no hardbound SF as such, and the days of paperbacks lay ahead (although in England Olaf Stapledon's seminal *Last and First Men* had already appeared in two volumes in Pelican Books, a branch of Penguins which otherwise never carried fiction). Anything that happened happened in the magazines – which have been extensively dredged in these last two decades to satisfy the paperback demand for SF. So it was a great age for series, and serials. *Astounding* in the forties ran several novels in this form, by such writers as Henry Kuttner, Hal Clement, Jack Williamson, E. E. Smith, Russell, Asimov, Heinlein, Hubbard, Van Vogt, and other distinguished names. They, even more than the short stories, define the ambience of Campbell's *Astounding*.

The other magazines also ran novels, among them many perennial favourites, such as Leigh Brackett's *The Sword of Rhiannon*, Charles Harness's *The Paradox Men*, and Fredric Brown's *What Mad Universe*. These titles convey effectively the distinction between *Astounding* and the other magazines; serial titles in *Astounding* tended to greater seriousness: *Fury*, *The End Is Not Yet*, *World of Nul-A*, *Methuselah's Children*.

It is idle to attempt to sum up the forties, since one of its pleasures is its diversity. For many SF fans, it remains the Golden Age. For others, the Golden Age was earlier; for others, yet to come. Perhaps it all depends when you start reading. And Now is always as good a time as any.

B.W.A.

# A. E. Van Vogt
# Co-operate – or else!

As the spaceship vanished into the steamy mists of Eristan II, Professor Jamieson drew his gun. He felt physically sick, battered, by the way he had been carried for so many long moments in the furious wind-stream of the great ship. But the sense of danger held him tense there in the harness that was attached by metal cables to the now gently swaying anti-gravity plate above him. With narrowed eyes, he stared up at the ezwal which was peering cautiously down at him over the edge of the anti-gravity plate.

Its three-in-line eyes, grey as dully polished steel, gazed at him, unwinking; its massive blue head poised there alertly and – Jamieson knew – ready to jerk back the instant it read in his thoughts an intention of shooting.

'Well,' said Jamieson harshly, 'here we are, both of us about a hundred thousand years from our respective home planets. And we're falling down into a primitive jungle hell that you, with only your isolated life on Carson's Planet to judge by, cannot begin to imagine despite your ability to read my thoughts. Even a six-thousand-pound ezwal hasn't got a chance down there – alone!'

A great, long-fingered, claw-studded paw edged gingerly over the side of the raft, flicked down at one of the four metal cables that supported Jamieson's harness. There was a bright, steely *ping*. The cable parted like rotted twine from the impact of that one cutting blow.

Like a streak of blurred light, the enormous arm jerked back out of sight. And then there was only the great head and the calm, unwinking eyes peering down at him. Finally, a thought penetrated to Jamieson, a thought cool and unhurried:

'You and I, Professor Jamieson, understand each other very well. Of the hundred-odd men on your ship, only you remain alive. Out of all the human race, therefore, only you know that the ezwals of what you call Carson's Planet are not senseless beasts, but intelligent beings. I could have stayed on the ship, and so eventually reached home. But rather than take the slightest risk of your escaping the jungle dangers below I took the desperate chance of jumping on top of this anti-gravity raft just as you were launching yourself out of the lock. What I cannot clearly understand is why you didn't escape while I was still battering down the control-room door. There is a blurred fear-picture in your mind, but—'

Jamieson was laughing, a jarring sound in his own ears, but there was genuine amusement in the grim thoughts that accompanied it. 'You poor fool!' he choked at last. 'You still don't realize what you're falling down to. While you were hammering away at that door, the ship was flying over the biggest ocean on this planet. All those glints of water down there are really continuation of the ocean, and every pool is swarming with malignant beasts. And, somewhere ahead of us, are the Demon Straits, a body of water about fifty miles wide that separates this ocean-jungle from the mainland beyond. Our ship will crash on that mainland, about a thousand miles from here, I should say. To reach it, we've got to cross that fifty miles of *thing*-infested area. Now you know why I was waiting, and why you had a chance to jump on to that anti-gravity plate. I—'

His voice collapsed with an '*ugh*' of amazement as, with the speed of a striking snake, the ezwal twisted up, a rearing, monstrous blue shape of frightful fangs and claws that reached with hideous power at a gigantic bird. The bird was diving straight down at the shining surface of the anti-gravity raft.

It did not swoop aside. Jamieson had a brief, terrifying glimpse of its merciless, protruding, glassy eyes, and of the massive, hooked, pitchfork-long claws, tensing for the thrust at the ezwal; and then—

The crash set the raft tossing like a chip in stormy waters. Jamieson swung with dizzy speed from side to side. The roar of the wind from the smashing power of those mighty wings was like thunder that stunned his brain. With a gasp, he raised his gun. The red flame of it reached hungrily at one of those wings. The wing turned a streaky black, collapsed; and, simultaneously, the bird was literally flung from the raft by the raging strength of the ezwal.

It plunged down, down, became a blurred dot in the mist, and was lost against the dark background of the land mass below.

Above Jamieson, the ezwal, dangerously off balance, hung poised over the edge of the raft. Four of its combination leg-arms pawed the air uselessly; the remaining two fought with bitter effort at the metal bars on top of the raft – and won. The great body drew back, until, once again, only the massive blue head was visible. Jamieson lowered his gun in grim good humour.

'You see,' he said, 'even a bird was almost too much for us – and I could have burned your belly open. I didn't because maybe it's beginning to penetrate your head that we've got to postpone our private quarrel, and fight together if we ever hope to get out of the hell of jungle and swamp below.'

The answering thought was as cold as the sleet-grey eyes that stared down at him so steadily:

'Professor Jamieson, what you *could* have done was unimportant to me who knew what you *would* do. As for your kind offer to ally yourself with me, I repeat that I am here to see you dead, not to protect your pitiful body. You will, therefore, refrain from further desperate appeals, and meet your fate with the dignity becoming a scientist.'

Jamieson was silent. A thin, warm, wet wind breathed against his body, bringing the first faint, obscene odours from below. The raft was still at an immense height, but the steamy mists that clung with a limp, yet obscuring strength to this primeval land had yielded some of their opaqueness. Patches of jungle and sea that, a few minutes before, had been blurred by that all-pervading fog, showed clearer now, a terrible, patternless sprawl of dark trees alternating with water that shone and flashed in the probing sunlight.

Fantastic, incredible scene. As far as the eye could see into the remote mists to the north, there was steaming jungle and foggy, glittering ocean – the endless, deadly reality that was Eristan II. And, somewhere out there, somewhere in the dimness beyond the concealing weight of steam, those apparently interminable jungles ended abruptly in the dark, ugly swell of water that was the Demon Straits!

'So,' said Jamieson at last, softly, 'you think you're going to get through. All your long life, all the long generations of your ancestors, you and your kind have depended entirely on your magnificent bodies for survival. While men herded fearfully in their caves, discovering fire as a partial protection, desperately creating weapons that had never before existed, always a bare jump ahead of violent death – all those millions of years, the ezwal of Carson's Planet roamed his great, fertile continents, unafraid, matchless in strength as in intellect, needing no homes, no fires, no clothing, no weapons, no—'

'You will agree,' the ezwal interrupted coolly, 'that adaptation to a difficult environment must be one of the goals of the superior being. Human beings have created what they call civilization, which is actually merely a material barrier between themselves and their environment, so vast and unwieldy that keeping it going occupies the entire existence of the race. Individually, man is a frivolous, fragile, inconsequential *slave*, who tugs his mite at the wheel, and dies wretchedly of some flaw in his disease-ridden body. Unfortunately, this monstrous, built-up weakling with his power lusts and murderous instincts is the greatest danger extant to the sane, healthy races of the Universe. He must be prevented from contaminating his betters.'

Jamieson laughed curtly. 'But you will agree, I hope, that there is something wonderful about an insignificant, fearful jetsam of life fighting successfully against all odds, aspiring to all knowledge, finally attaining the very stars!'

'Nonsense!' The answer held overtones of brittle impatience.

'Man and his thoughts constitute a disease. As proof during the past few minutes you have been offering specious arguments, apparently unbiased, actually designed to lead once more to an appeal for my assistance, an intolerable form of dishonesty. As further evidence I need but anticipate intellectually the moment of our landing. Assuming that I make no attempt to harm you, nevertheless your pitiful body will be instantly and, thereafter, continuously in deadly danger, while I – you must admit that, though there are beasts below physically stronger than I, the difference is not so great that my intelligence, even if it took the form of cunning flight, would more than balance the weakness. You will admit furthermore—'

'I admit nothing!' Jamieson snapped. 'Except that you're going to get the surprise of your life. And you're going to regret beyond all your present capacity for emotionalism the lack of those very artificialities you despise in man. I do not mean material weapons, but—'

'What you mean is unimportant. I can see that you intend to persist in this useless, mendacious type of reasoning, and you have convinced me that you will never emerge alive from that island jungle below. Therefore—'

The same, tremendous arm that a few minutes before had torn steel chain flashed into sight and downward in a single co-ordinated gesture.

The two remaining cables attached to Jamieson's harness parted like wet paper; and so great was the force of the blow that Jamieson was jerked a hundred feet parallel to the distant ground before his long, clenched body curved downward for its terrific fall.

A thought, cool with grim irony, struck after him:

'I notice that you are a very cautious man, professor, in that you have not only a packsack, but a parachute strapped to your back. This will enable you to reach ground safely, but your landing will be largely governed by chance. Your logical mind will doubtless enable you to visualize the situation. Good-bye and – bad luck!'

Jamieson strained at the thin, strong ropes of his parachute, his gaze narrowed on the scene below. Through the now almost transparent mist, and somewhat to the north, was a green-brown blaze of jungle. If he could get there—

He tugged again at the ropes, and with icy speculation watched the effect, calculated the mathematical possibilities. He was falling slowly; that would be the effect of the heavy air of this planet: pressure eighteen pounds per square inch at sea level.

Sea level! He smiled wryly, without humour. Sea level was approximately where he would be in a very few minutes. There was, he saw, no sea immediately beneath him. A few splotches of water, yes, and a straggle of trees. The rest was a sort of clearing, except that it wasn't exactly. It had a strange, greyish, repellent appearance like—

The terrible shock of recognition drained the blood from his cheeks. His mind shrank as from an unthinkably lecherous thought. In panic he tore at the ropes, as if by sheer physical strength he would draw the tantalizingly near jungle to him. That jungle, that precious jungle! It might contain horrors, but at least they were of the future, while that hellish stuff directly below held no future, nothing but a grey, quagmire trap, thick mud choking—

Abruptly, he saw that the solid mass of trees was beyond his reach. The parachute was less than five hundred feet above that deadly, unclean spread of mud. The jungle itself – stinking, horrible jungle, blatantly exuding the sharp, evil odours of rotting vegetation, yet suddenly the most desirable of places – was about the same distance to the north-west.

To make it would require a forty-five-degree descent. Carefully, he manipulated the rope controls of the parachute. It caught the wind like a glider; the jungle drew closer, closer—

He landed triumphantly in a tiny straggle of trees, a little island separated from the main bulk of forest by less than a hundred and fifty feet.

The island was ten feet long by eight wide; four trees, the longest about fifty feet tall, maintained a precarious existence on its soggy, wet, comparatively firm base.

Four trees, representing a total of about a hundred and eighty feet. Definitely enough length. But – his first glow of triumph began to fade – without a crane to manipulate three of those trees into place, the knowledge that they represented safety was utterly useless.

Jamieson sat down, conscious for the first time of the dull ache in his shoulders, the strained tenseness of his whole body, a sense of depressing heat. He could see the sun, a white blob barely visible through the white mists that formed the atmosphere of this deadly, fantastic land.

The blur of the sun seemed to fade into remoteness; a vague darkness formed in his mind; and then a sharp, conscious thought that he had been asleep.

He opened his eyes with a start. The sun was much lower in the eastern sky and—

His mind stopped from the sheer shock of discovery. Instantly, however, it came alive, steady, cool, despite the vast, first shock of his amazement.

What had happened was like some fantasy out of a fairy story. The four trees, with the tattered remains of his parachute still clinging to them, towered above him. But his plan for them had taken form while he slept.

A bridge of trees, thicker, more solid than any the little island could have produced, stretched straight and strong from the island to the mainland. There was no doubt, of course, as to who had performed that colossal feat: the ezwal was standing unconcernedly on two of its six legs, leaning manlike against the thick trunk of a gigantic tree. Its thought came:

'You need have no fear, Professor Jamieson. I have come to your point of view. I am prepared to assist you to reach the mainland and to co-operate with you thereafter. I—'

Jamieson's deep, ungracious laughter cut off the thought. 'You damned liar!' the scientist said finally. 'What you mean is that you've run up against something you couldn't handle. Well, that's all right with me. So long as we understand each other, we'll get along.'

The snake slid heavily out of the jungle, ten feet from the

mainland end of the bridge of trees, thirty feet to the right of the ezwal. Jamieson, scraping cautiously towards the centre of the bridge, saw the first violent swaying of the long, luscious jungle grass – and froze where he was as the vicious, fantastic head reared into sight, followed by the first twenty feet of that thick, menacing body.

Briefly, the great head, in its swaying movement, was turned directly at him. The little pig eyes seemed to glare straight into his own stunned, brown eyes. Shock held him, sheer, unadulterated shock at the incredibly bad luck that had allowed this deadly creature to find him in such an immeasurably helpless position.

His paralysis there, under those blazing eyes, was a living, agonizing thing. Tautness struck like fire into every muscle of his body. It was an instinctive straining for rigidity, unnormal and terrible – but it worked.

The fearsome head whipped aside, fixed in eager fascination on the ezwal, and took on a rigidity all its own.

Jamieson relaxed; his brief fear changed to brief, violent anger; he projected a scathing thought at the ezwal:

'I understood you could sense the approach of dangerous beasts by reading their minds.'

No answering thought came into his brain. The giant snake flowed farther into the clearing; and before that towering, horned head rearing monstrously from the long, titanically powerful body, the ezwal backed slowly, yielding with a grim reluctance to the obvious conviction that it was no match for this vast creature.

Cool again, Jamieson directed an ironic thought at the ezwal:

'It may interest you to know that as chief scientist of the Interstellar Military Commission, I reported Eristan II unusable as a military base for our fleet; and there were two main reasons: one of the damnedest flesh-eating plants you ever saw, and this pretty little baby. There's millions of both of them. Each snake breeds hundreds in its lifetime, so they can't be stamped out. They're bisexual, attain a length of about a hundred and fifty feet and a weight of ten tons.'

The ezwal, now some fifty feet away from the snake, stopped and, without looking at Jamieson, sent him a tight, swift thought.

'Its appearance did surprise me, but the reason is that its mind held only a vague curiosity about some sounds it had heard, no clear, sharp thought such as an intention to murder. But that's unimportant. It's here; it's dangerous. It hasn't seen you yet, so act accordingly. It doesn't think it can get me, but it's considering the situation. In spite of its desire for me, the problem remains essentially yours; the danger is *all* yours.'

The ezwal concluded almost indifferently: 'I am willing to give you limited aid in any plan you might have, but please don't offer any more nonsense about our interdependence. So far there's been only one dependant. I think you know who it is.'

Jamieson was grim. 'Don't be too sure that you're not in danger. That fellow looks muscle bound, but when he starts moving, he's like a steel spring for the first three or four hundred feet – and you haven't got that much space behind you.'

'What do you mean? I can run four hundred feet in three seconds, Earth time.'

Coldly, the scientist whipped out: 'You could, *if you had four hundred feet in which to run*. But you haven't. I've just been forming a mental picture of this edge of jungle, as I saw it before I landed.

'There's about a hundred and fifty feet of jungle, then a curving shore of mud plain, a continuation of this mud here. The curve swings back this way, and cuts you off neatly on this little outjutting of jungle. To get clear of the snake, you've got to dart past him. Roughly, your clearance is a hundred and fifty feet all around – and it isn't enough! Interdependent? You're damned right we are. Things like this will happen a thousand times a year on Eristan II.'

There was startled silence; finally: 'Why don't you turn your atomic gun on it – burn it?'

'And have it come out here, while I'm helpless? These big snakes are born in this mud, and live half their lives in it. It would take five minutes to burn off that tough head. By that time I'd be swallowed and digested.'

The brief seconds that passed then were pregnant with reluctant desperation. But there could be no delay. Swiftly the grudging request came:

'Professor Jamieson, I am open to suggestions – and *hurry*!'

The depressing realization came to Jamieson that the ezwal was once more asking for his assistance, *knowing* that it would be given; and yet it itself was giving no promise in return.

And there was no time for bargaining. Curtly, he projected:

'It's the purest case of our acting as a team. The snake has no real weakness – except possibly this: Before it attacks its head will start swaying. That's almost a universal snake method of hypnotizing victims into paralysis. Actually, the motion is also partially self-hypnotizing. At the earliest possible moment after it begins to sway, I'll burn its eyes out – and you get on its back, *and hang on*. Its brain is located just behind that great horn. Claw your way there, and eat in while I burn.'

The thought scattered like a chaff, as the tremendous head began to move. With a trembling jerk, Jamieson snatched his gun—

It was not so much, then, that the snake put up a fight, as that it wouldn't die. Its smoking remains were still twisting half an hour later when Jamieson scrambled weakly from the bridge of trees and collapsed on to the ground.

When finally he climbed to his feet, the ezwal was sitting fifty feet away under a clump of trees, its middle legs also on the ground, its forelegs folded across its chest – and it was contemplating him.

It looked strangely sleek and beautiful in its blue coat and in the very massiveness of its form. And there was comfort for him in the knowledge that, for the time being at least, the mighty muscles that rippled underneath that silk-smooth skin were on his side.

Jamieson returned the ezwal's stare steadily; finally he said:

'What happened to the anti-gravity raft?'

'I abandoned it thirty-five miles north of here.'

Jamieson hesitated; then: 'We'll have to go to it. I practically depowered my gun on that snake. It needs metal for recharging; and that raft is the only metal in bulk that I know of.'

He was silent again; then softly: 'One more thing. I want your word of honour that you won't even attempt to harm me until we are safely on the other side of the Demon Straits!'

'You'd accept my word?' The steel-grey, three-in-line eyes meditated on him curiously.

'Yes.'

'Very well, I give it.'

Jamieson shook his head, smiling darkly. 'Oh, no, you don't, not as easily as that.'

'I thought you said you'd accept my word.' Peevishly.

'I will, but in the following phraseology.' Jamieson stared with grim intentness at his mighty and deadly enemy. 'I want you to swear by the sun that rises and by the green, fruitful earth, by the joys of the contemplative mind and the glory of immortal life—'

He paused. 'Well?'

There was a grey fire in the ezwal's gaze, and its thought had a ferocious quality when finally it replied: 'You are, Professor Jamieson, even more dangerous than I thought. It is clear there can be no compromise between us.'

'But you'll make the limited promise I ask for?'

The grey eyes dulled strangely; long, thin lips parted in a snarl that showed great, dark fangs.

'No!' Curtly.

'I thought,' said Jamieson softly, 'I ought to get that clear.'

No answer. The ezwal simply sat there, its gaze fixed on him.

'Another thing,' Jamieson went on. 'Stop pretending you can read all my thoughts. You didn't know that I knew about your religion. I'll wager you can only catch my sharpest idea-forms, and those particularly when my mind is focused on speech.'

'I made no pretences,' the ezwal replied coolly. 'I shall continue to keep you as much in the dark as possible.'

'The doubt will, of course, harass my mind,' said Jamieson,

'but not too much. Once I accept a theory, I act accordingly. If I should prove wrong, there remains the final arbiter of my atomic gun against your strength. I wouldn't bet on the victor.

'But now' – he hunched his long body, and strode forward – 'let's get going. The swiftest method, I believe, would be for me to ride on your back. I could tie a rope from my parachute around your body just in front of your middle legs and by hanging on to the rope keep myself from falling off. My only qualification is that you must promise to let me off before making any hostile move. Agreeable?'

The ezwal hesitated, then nodded: 'For the time being.'

Jamieson was smiling, his long, spare, yet strong, face ironical.

'That leaves only one thing: What did you run up against that made you change your mind about killing me immediately? Could it have been something entirely beyond the isolated, static, aristocratic existence of the ezwal?'

'Get on my back!' came the snarling thought. 'I desire no lectures, nor any further sounds from your rasping voice. I fear nothing on this planet. My reasons for coming back have no connection with any of your pitiful ideas; and it would not take much to make me change my mind. Take warning!'

Jamieson was silent, startled. It had not been his intention to provoke the ezwal. He'd have to be more cautious in the future, or this great animal, bigger than eight lions, deadlier than a hundred, might turn on him long before it itself intended.

It was an hour later that the long, fish-shaped spaceship swung out of the steamy mists that patrolled the skies of Eristan II. It coasted along less than a thousand feet up, cruel-looking as a swordfish with its finely pointed nose.

The explosive thought of the ezwal cut into Jamieson's brain: 'Professor Jamieson, if you make so much as a single effort at signalling, you die.'

Jamieson was silent, his mind held stiff and blank, after one mental leap. As he watched, the great, half-mile-long ship sank visibly lower and, as it vanished beyond the rim of the jungle ahead, there was no doubt that it was going to land.

And then the ezwal's thoughts came again, sly now, almost

exultant: 'It's no use trying to hide it – because now that the actuality is here I remember that your dead companions had awareness of another spaceship in the back of their minds.'

Jamieson swallowed the hard lump in his throat. There was a sickness in him, and vast rage at the incredibly bad luck of this ship coming here – now!

Miserably, he gave himself to the demanding rhythm of the ezwal's smooth gallop; and for a while there was only that odour-tainted wind, and the pad of six paws, a dull, flat flow of sound. Around him the dark jungle, the occasional, queer *lap, lap* of treacherous, unseen waters. And it was all there, the strangeness, the terribleness of this wild ride of a man on the back of a blue-tinted, beast-like being that hated him – and knew about that ship.

At last, grudgingly, he yielded. He said snappishly, as if his words might yet snatch victory from defeat: 'Now I know, anyway, that your thought-reading ability is a damned sketchy thing. You didn't begin to suspect why you were able to conquer my ship so easily.'

'Why should I?' The ezwal was impatient. 'I remember now there was a long period when I caught no thoughts, only an excess of energy tension, abnormally more than were customary from your engines. That must have been when you speeded up. Then I noticed the cage door was ajar – and forgot everything else.'

The scientist nodded, gloom a sickish weight on him. 'We received some awful buffeting, nothing palpable, of course, because the interstellars were full on. But, somewhere, there must have been a blow that knocked our innards out of alignment.

'Afterwards, we watched for dangers from outside; and so you, on the inside, got your chance to kill a hundred men, most of them sleeping.'

He tensed his body ever so carefully, eyes vaguely as possible on the limb of the tree just ahead, concentrating with enormous casualness on the idea of ducking under it. Somehow, his real purpose leaked from his straining brain.

In a single convulsion of movement, like a bucking horse, the ezwal reared. Shattering violence of movement! Like a shot from a gun, Jamieson was flung forward *bang* against that steel-hard back. Stunned, dizzy, he fought for balance – and then it was over.

The great animal plunged aside into a thick pattern of jungle, completely away from the protruding limb that had momentarily offered such sweet promise of safety. It twisted skilfully between two giant trees, and emerged a moment later on to the beach of a long, glittering bay of ocean.

Fleet as the wind, it raced along the deserted sands, and then on into the thickening jungles beyond. No thought came from it, not a tendril of triumph, no indication of the tremendous victory it had just won.

Jamieson said sickly: 'I made that attempt because I know what you're going to do. I admit we had a running fight with that Rull cruiser. But you're crazy if you think they mean advantage for you. Rulls are different. They come from another galaxy. They're—'

'Professor!' The interrupting thought was like metal in the sheer, vibrating force of it. 'Don't dare try to draw your gun to kill yourself. One false move, and I'll show you how violently and painfully a man can be disarmed.'

'You promised,' Jamieson also mumbled, 'to make no hostile move—'

'And I'll keep that promise – to the letter, after man's own fashion, *in my own good time*. But now – I gathered from your mind that you think these creatures landed because they detected the minute energy discharge of the anti-gravity raft.'

'Pure deduction.' Curtly. 'There must be some logical reason, and unless you shut off the power as I did on the spaceship—'

'I didn't. Therefore, that is why they landed. Their instruments probably also registered your use of the gun on the snake. Therefore they definitely know someone is here. My best bet, accordingly, is to head straight for them before they kill me accidentally. I have no doubt of the welcome I shall receive when they see my captive, and I tell them that I and my fellow

ezwals are prepared to help drive man from Carson's Planet.
And you will have gotten off my back unharmed – thus my
promise.'

The scientist licked dry lips. 'That's bestial,' he said finally.
'You know damned well from reading my mind that Rulls eat
human beings. Earth is one of the eight planets in this galaxy
whose flesh is palatable to these hell-creatures—'

The ezwal said coldly: 'I have seen men on Carson's Planet
eat ezwals with relish. Why shouldn't men in turn be eaten by
other beings?'

Jamieson was silent, a shocked silence at the hatred that was
here. The flintlike thought of the other finished:

'You may not realize how important it is that no word of
ezwal intelligence get back to Earth during the next few months,
but we ezwals know. I want you dead!'

And still there was hope in him. He recognized it for what it
was: That mad, senseless hope of a man still alive, refusing to
acknowledge death till its grey chill lay cold on his bones.

A crash of brush roused him out of himself. Great branches
of greater trees broke with wheezing unwillingness. A monstrous
reptile head peered at them over a tall tree.

Jamieson had a spine-cooling glimpse of a scaly, glittering
body; eyes as red as fire blazed at him – and then that lumber-
ing nightmare was far behind, as the ezwal raced on, contemptuous, terrible in its unheeding strength.

And after a moment, then, in spite of hideous danger, in spite
of his desperate conviction that he must convince the ezwal how
wrong it was – admiration flared inside him, a wild, fascinated
admiration.

'By God!' he exclaimed, 'I wouldn't be surprised if you really
could evade the terrors of this world. In all my journeys through
space, I've never seen such a perfect combination of mind and
magnificent muscle.'

'Save your praise,' sneered the ezwal.

Jamieson hardly heard. He was frowning in genuine thought-
fulness: 'There's a sabre-toothed, furred creature about your

size and speed that might damage you, but I think you can out-run or outfight all the other furred animals. Then there are the malignant plants, particularly a horrible creeper affair – it's not the only intelligent plant in the galaxy, but it's the smartest. You'd need my gun if you got tangled up with one of those.

'You could evade them, of course, but that implies ability to recognize that one's in the vicinity. There are signposts of their presence but' – he held his mind as dim as possible, and smiled grimly – 'I'll leave that subject before you read the details in my brain.

'That leaves the great reptiles; they can probably catch you only in the water. That's where the Demon Straits would be a mortal handicap.'

'I can swim,' the ezwal snapped, 'fifty miles in three hours with you on my back.'

'Go on!' The scientist's voice was scathing. 'If you could do all these things – if you could cross oceans and a thousand miles of jungle, why did you return for me, knowing, as you must now know, that I could never reach my ship alone? Why?'

'It's dark where you're going,' the ezwal said impatiently, 'and knowledge is not a requirement for death. All these fears of yours are but proof that man will yield to unfriendly environment where he would be unflinching in the face of intelligent opposition.

'And that is why your people must not learn of ezwal intelligence. Literally, we have created on Carson's Planet a dumb, beast-like atmosphere where men would eventually feel that nature was too strong for them. The fact that you have refused to face the nature-environment of this jungle planet of Eristan II and that the psycho-friction on Carson's Planet is already at the factual of point 135 is proof that—'

'Eh?' Jamieson stared at the gleaming, blue, rhythmically bobbing head. 'You're crazy. Why, 135 would mean – twenty-five – thirty million. The limit is point 38.'

'Exactly,' glowed the ezwal, 'thirty million dead.'

A gulf was opening before Jamieson's brain, a black realiza-tion of where this – monstrous – creature's thoughts were leading. He said violently:

'It's a damned lie. My reports show—'

'Thirty million!' repeated the ezwal with a deadly satisfaction. 'And I know exactly what that means in your terms of psycho-friction: point 135 as compared to a maximum safety tension limit of point 38. That limit, of course, obtains when nature is the opponent. If your people discovered the cause of their agony was an intelligent race, the resistance would go up to point 184 – and we'd lose. You didn't know we'd studied your psychology so thoroughly.'

Whitely, shakily, Jamieson replied: 'In five years, we'll have a billion population on Carson's Planet, and the few ezwals that will have escaped will be a small, scattered, demoralized—'

'In five *months*,' interrupted the ezwal coldly, 'man will figuratively explode from our planet. Revolution, a blind mob impulse to get into the interstellar transports at any cost, mad flight from intolerable dangers. And, added to everything, the sudden arrivals of the Rull warships to assist us. It will be the greatest disaster in the long, brutal history of conquering man.'

With a terrible effort, Jamieson caught himself into a tight matter-of-factness: 'Assuming all this, assuming that machines yield to muscle, what will you do with the Rulls after we're gone?'

'Just let them dare remain!'

Jamieson's brief, titanic effort at casualness collapsed into a wave of fury: 'Why, you blasted fools, a man beat the Rulls to Carson's Planet by less than two years. While you stupid idiots interfered with us on the ground, we fought long, delaying actions in the deeps of space, protecting you from the most murderous, ruthless, unreasonable things that the Universe ever spawned.'

He stopped, fought for control, said finally with a grim effort at rational argument, 'We've never been able to drive the Rull from any planet where he has established himself. And he drove us from three major bases before we realized the enormousness of the danger, and stood firm everywhere regardless of military losses.'

He stopped again, conscious of the blank, obstinate, contemptuous wall that was the mind of this ezwal.

'Thirty million!' he said almost softly, half to himself. 'Wives, husbands, children, lovers—'

A black anger blotted out his conscious thought. With a single, lightning-swift jerk on his arm, he drew his atomic gun, pressed its muzzle hard against the great blue-ridged backbone.

'By Heaven, at least you're not going to get the Rulls in on anything that happens.'

His finger closed hard on that yielding trigger; there was a white blaze of fire that – missed! Amazingly – it missed.

Instants passed before his brain grasped the startling fact that he was flying through the air, flung clear by one incredibly swift jerk of that vast, blue body.

He struck brush. Grasping fingers of sticky jungle vine wrenched at his clothes, ripped his hands, and tore at the gun, that precious, all-valuable gun.

His clothes shredded, blood came in red, ugly streaks – everything yielded to that desperate environment but the one, all-important thing. With a bitter, enduring singleness of purpose, he clung to the gun.

He landed on his side, rolled over in a flash – and twisted up his gun, finger once more on the trigger. Three feet from that deadly muzzle, the ezwal drew up with a hideous snarl of its great, square face, jumped thirty feet to one side, and vanished, a streak of amazing blue, behind a thick bole of steel-hard jungle fungi.

Shaky, almost ill, Jamieson sat up and surveyed the extent of his defeat, the limits of his victory.

All around was a curious, treeless jungle. Giant, ugly, yellow fungi towered thirty, fifty, eighty feet against a red-brown-green sky-line of tangled brown vines, green lichens, and bulbous, incredibly long, strong, reddish grass.

The ezwal had raged through other such dense matted wilderness with a solid, irresistible strength. For a man on foot, who dared not waste more than a fraction of the waning power of his gun, it was pathless, a major obstacle to the simplest progress – the last place in the world he would have chosen for a fight against anything. And yet—

In losing his temper he had hit on the only possible method of drawing his gun without giving the ezwal advance warning thoughts. At least, he was not being borne helpless along to a great warship loaded with slimy, white Rulls.

Rulls!

With a gasp, Jamieson leaped to his feet. There was a treacherous sagging of the ground under his feet, but instinctively he stepped on to a dead patch of fungi; and the harsh, urgent tones of his voice were loud in his ears, as he said swiftly:

'We've got to act fast. The discharge of my gun must have registered on Rull instruments, and they'll be here in minutes. You've got to believe me when I tell you that your scheme of enlisting the Rulls as allies is madness.

'Listen to this: all the ships we sent into their galaxy report that every planet of a hundred they visited was inhabited by – Rulls. Nothing else, no other races. They must have destroyed every other living, intelligent creature.

'Man has forty-eight hundred and seventy-four non-human allies. I admit all have civilizations that are similar to man's own; and that's the devil of the type of historyless, buildingless, ezwal culture. Ezwals cannot defend themselves against energies and machines. And, frankly, man will not leave Carson's Planet till that important defence question has been satisfactorily mastered.

'You and your revolution. True, the simple people in their agony may flee in mad panic, but the military will remain, a disciplined, undefeatable organization, a hundred battleships, a thousand cruisers, ten thousand destroyers for that one base alone. The ezwal plan is clever only in its grasp of human psychology and because it may well succeed in causing destruction and death. But in that plan is no conception of the vastness of interstellar civilization, the responsibilities and the duties of its members.

'The reason I was taking you to Earth was to show you the complexities and honest problems of that civilization, to prove to you that we are not evil. I swear to you that man and his present grand civilization will solve the ezwal problem to ezwal satisfaction. What do you say?'

His last words boomed out eerily in the odd, deathly, late-afternoon hush that had settled over the jungle world of Eristan II. He could see the blur of sun, a misty blob low in the eastern sky; and the hard realization came:

Even if he escaped the Rulls, in two hours at most the great fanged hunters and the reptilian flesh-eaters that haunted the slow nights of this remote, primeval planet would emerge ravenous from their stinking hideaways, and seek their terrible surcease.

He'd have to get away from this damned fungi, find a real tree with good, strong, high-growing branches and, somehow, stay there all night. Some kind of system of intertwining vines, properly rigged up, should warn him of any beast intruder – including ezwals.

He began to work forward, clinging carefully to the densest, most concealing brush. After fifty yards, the jungle seemed as impenetrable as ever, and his legs and arms ached from his effort. He stopped, and said:

'I tell you that man would never have gone into Carson's Planet the way he did, if he had known it was inhabited by intelligent beings. There are strict laws that govern even under military necessity.'

Quite abruptly, answer came: 'Cease these squalling, lying appeals. Man possesses no less than five thousand planets formerly occupied by intelligent races. No totality of prevarication can cover up or even excuse five thousand cosmic crimes—'

The ezwal's thought broke off; then, almost casually: 'Professor, I've just run across an animal that—'

Jamieson was saying: 'Man's crimes are as black as his noble works are white and wonderful. You must understand those two facets of his character—'

'This animal,' persisted the ezwal, 'is floating above me now, watching me, but I am unable to catch a single vibration of its thought—'

'More than three thousand of those races now have self-government. Man does not long deny to any basically good intelligence the liberty and freedom of action which he needs so much himself—'

'*Professor!*' The thought was like a knife piercing, utterly urgent. 'This creature has a repellent, worm-shaped body, and it floats without wings. It has no brain that I can detect.'

Very carefully, very gently, Jamieson swung himself behind a pile of brush and raised his pistol. Then softly, swiftly, he said: 'Act like a beast, snarl at it, and run like hell into the thickest underbrush if it reaches with one of those tiny, wormlike hands towards any one of the half-dozen notches on either side of its body.

'If you cannot contact its mind – we never could get in touch with it in any way – you'll have to depend on its character, as follows: The Rull hears only sounds between five hundred thousand and eight hundred thousand vibrations a second. That is why I can talk out loud without danger. That, also, suggests that its thought moves on a vastly different vibration level; it must hate and fear everything else, which must be why it is so remorselessly impelled on its course of destruction.

'The Rull does not kill for pleasure. It exterminates. It possibly considers the entire Universe alien which, perhaps, is why it eliminates all important creatures on any planet it intends to occupy. There can be no intention of occupying this planet because our great base on Eristan I is only five thousand light-years or twenty-five hours away by warship. Therefore it will not harm you unless it has special suspicions. Therefore be all animal.'

He finished tensely: 'What's it doing now?'

There was no answer.

The minutes dragged; and it wasn't so much that there was silence. Queer, little noises came out of nearness and remoteness: the distant crack of wood under some heavy foot, faint snortings of creatures that were not exactly near – but too near for comfort.

A memory came that was more terrible than the gathering night, a living flame of remembrance of the one time he had seen a Rull feeding off a human being.

First, the clothes were stripped from the still-living victim, whose nervous system was then paralyzed partially by a stinger that was part of the Rull's body. And then, the big, fat, white worm crawled on to the body, and lay there in that abnormal, obscene embrace while its cup-like mouths fed—

Jamieson recoiled mentally and physically. Abrupt, desperate, panicky fear sent him burrowing deeper into the tangle of brush. It was quiet there, not a breath of air touched him. And he noticed, after a moment, that he was soaked with perspiration.

Other minutes passed; and because, in his years, courage had never been long absent from him, he ventured into the hard, concentrated thought of attempted communication: 'If you have any questions, for Heaven's sake don't waste time.'

There must have been wind above his tight shelter of brush, for a fog heavily tainted with the smell of warm, slimy water drifted over him, blocking even the narrow view that remained.

Jamieson stirred uneasily. It was not fear; his mind was a clenched unit, like a fist ready to strike. It was that – suddenly – he felt without eyes in a world of terrible enemies. More urgently, he went on:

'Your very act of asking my assistance in identifying the Rull implied your recognition of our interdependence. Accordingly, I demand—'

'Very well!' The answering thought was dim and far away. 'I admit my inability to get in touch with this worm ends my plans of establishing an anti-human alliance.'

There was a time, such a short time ago, Jamieson thought drearily, when such an admission would have brought genuine intellectual joy. The poor devils on Carson's Planet, at least, were not going to have to fight Rulls as well as their own madness – as well as ezwals.

He braced himself, vaguely amazed at the lowness of his morale. He said almost hopelessly: 'What about us?'

'I have already repaid your initial assistance in that, at this moment, I am leading the creature directly away from you.'

'It's still following you?'

'Yes! It seems to be studying me. Have you any suggestions?'

Weariness faded; Jamieson snapped: 'Only on condition that you are willing to recognize that we are a unit, and that everything else, including what man and ezwal are going to do about Carson's Planet, must be discussed later. Agreed?'

The ezwal's thought was scarcely more than a snarl: 'You keep harping on that!'

Momentarily, the scientist felt all the exasperation, all the strain of the past hours a pressing, hurting force in his brain. Like a flame, it burst forth, a flare of raging thought:

'You damned scoundrel, you've forced every issue so far, and all of them were rooted in that problem. You make that promise – or just forget the whole thing.'

The silence was a pregnant emotion, dark with bitter, formless thought. Around Jamieson, the mists were thinning, fading into the twilight of that thick jungle. Finally:

'I promise to help you safely across the Demon Straits; and I'll be with you in minutes – if I don't lose this thing first.'

Jamieson retorted grimly: 'Agreement satisfactory – but don't expect to lose a Rull. They've got perfect anti-gravity, whereas that anti-gravity raft of ours was simply a super-parachute. It would eventually have fallen under its own weight.'

He paused tensely; then: 'You've got everything clear? I'll burn the Rull that's following you, then we'll beat it as fast as your legs can carry us.'

'Get ready!' The answer was a cold, deadly wave. 'I'll be there in seconds.'

There was no time for thought. Brush crashed. Through the mist, Jamieson caught one flashing glimpse of the ezwal with its six legs. At fifty feet, its slate-grey, three-in-line eyes were like pools of light. And then, as he pointed his gun in a desperate expectation—

'*For your life!*' came the ezwal's thought, 'don't shoot, don't move. There are a dozen of them above me and—'

Queerly, shatteringly, that strong flow of thought ended in a chaotic jumble as energy flared out there, a glaring, white fire that blinked on, and then instantly off.

The mist rolled thicker, white-grey, noxious stuff that hid what *must* be happening.

And hid him.

Jamieson lay stiff and cold – and waited. For a moment, so normal had mind-reading become in these hours, he forgot he could only catch thoughts at the will of the ezwal, and he strained to penetrate the blackout of mind vibrations.

He thought finally, a tight, personal thought: The Rulls must have worked a psychosis on the ezwal. Nothing else could explain that incoherent termination of thought in so powerful a mind. And yet – protective psychosis was used mainly on animals and other uncivilized and primitive life forms, unaccustomed to that sudden interplay of dazzling lights.

He frowned bleakly. Actually, in spite of its potent brain, the ezwal was very much animal, very much uncivilized, and possibly extremely allergic to mechanical hypnosis.

Definitely, it was not death from a heavy mobile projector because there would have been sound from the weapon, and because there *wouldn't* have been that instantaneous distortion of thought, that twisting—

He felt a moment's sense of intense relief. It had been curiously unsettling to think of that mighty animal struck dead.

He caught his mind into a harder band: So the ezwal was captive not corpse. So – what now?

Relief drained. It wasn't, he thought blankly, as if he could do anything against a heavily armoured, heavily manned cruiser.

Ten minutes passed; and then out of the deepening twilight came the thunderous roar of a solid bank of energy projectors. There was answering thunder on a smaller scale; and then, once again, though farther away now, the deep, unmistakable roar of a broadside of a hundred-inch battleship projectors.

A battleship! A capital ship from the Eristan I base, either on patrol or investigating energy discharges. The Rulls would be lucky if they got away. As for himself – nothing!

Nothing but the night and its terrors. True, there would be no trouble now from the Rulls, but that was all. This wasn't rescue, not even the hope of rescue. For days and days, the two great ships would manœuvre in space; and, by the time the battleship reported again to its base, there wouldn't be very much thought given to the why of the Rull cruiser's presence on or near the ground.

Besides, the Rull would have detected its enemy before its own position would be accurately plotted. That first broadside had easily been fifty miles away.

The problem of ezwal and man, that had seemed such an intimate, soluble pattern when he and the great animal were alone, was losing its perspective. Against the immeasurably larger background of space, the design was twisting crazily.

It became a shapeless thing, utterly lost in the tangle of unseen obstacles that kept tripping him, as he plunged forward into the dimming reaches of jungle.

In half an hour it was pitch dark; and he hadn't penetrated more than a few hundred yards. He would have blundered on into the black night, except that suddenly his fingers touched thick, carboniferous bark.

*A tree!*

Great beasts stamped below, as he clung to that precarious perch. Eyes of fire glared at him. Seven times in the first hour by his watch, monstrous things clambered up the tree, mewing and slavering in feral desire. Seven times his weakening gun flashed a thinner beam of destroying energy, and great, scale-armoured carnivores whose approach shook the earth came to feed on the odorous flesh – and passed on.

One hour gone!

A hundred nights like this one, to be spent without sleep, to be defended against a new, ferocious enemy every ten minutes, and no power in his gun.

The terrible thing was that the ezwal had just agreed to work with him against the Rulls. Victory so near, then instantly snatched afar—

Something, a horrible something, slobbered at the foot of the tree. Great claws rasped on bark, and then two eyes, easily a foot apart, started with an astounding speed up towards him.

Jamieson snatched at his gun, hesitated, then began hastily to climb up into the thinner branches. Every second, as he scrambled higher, he had the awful feeling that a branch would break, and send him sliding down towards the thing; and there was the more dreadful conviction that great jaws were at his heels.

Actually, however, his determination to save his gun worked beyond his expectations. The beast was edging up into those thin branches after him when there was a hideous snarl below, and another great creature started up the tree.

The fighting of animal against animal that started then was absolutely continuous. The tree shook, as sabre-toothed beasts that mewed fought vast, grunting, roaring shapes. And every little while there would be a piercing triumphant scream as a gigantic dinosaur-thing raged into the fight – and literally ate the struggling mass of killers.

Towards dawn, the continuous bellowing and snarling from near and far diminished notably, as if stomach after eager stomach gorged itself, and retired in enormous content to some cesspool of a bed.

At dawn he was still alive, completely weary, his body drooping with sleep-desire, and in his mind only the will to live, but utterly no belief that he would survive the day.

If only, on the ship, he had not been cornered so swiftly in the control room by the ezwal, he could have taken anti-sleep pills, fuel capsules for his gun and – he laughed in sharp sardonicism as the futility of that line of reasoning penetrated – and a lifeboat which, of course, would by itself have enabled him to fly to safety.

At least there had been a few hundred food capsules in the control room – a month's supply.

He sucked at one that was chocolate flavoured and slowly climbed to the bloodstained ground.

There was a sameness about the day, a mind-wearing sameness! Jungle and sea, different only in the designs of land shape and in the way the water lapped a curving, twisting shore. Always the substance was unchanged.

Jungle and sea.

Everything fought him – and until mid-afternoon he fought back. He had covered, he estimated, about three miles when he saw a tree – there was a kind of crotch high up in its towering form, where he could sleep without falling, if he tied himself with vines.

Three miles a day. Twelve hundred miles, counting what he still had to cover of this jungle ocean, counting the Demon Straits – twelve hundred miles at three miles a day.

Four hundred days!

He woke up with the beasts of the Eristan night coughing their lust at the base of his tree. He woke up with the memory of a nightmare in which he was swimming the Demon waters, pursued by millions of worms, who kept shouting something about the importance of solving the ezwal problem.

'What', they asked accusingly, 'is man going to do with civilizations intellectually so advanced, but without a single building or weapon or – anything?'

Jamieson shook himself awake; and then: 'To hell with ezwals!' he roared into the black, pressing, deadly night.

For a while, then, he sat shocked at the things that were happening to his mind, once so stable.

Stable! But that, of course, was long ago.

The fourth day dawned, a misty, muggy replica of the day before. And of the day before that. And before that. And—

'Stop it, you idiot!' said Professor Jamieson aloud, savagely.

He was struggling stubbornly towards what seemed a clearing when a grey mass of creepers to one side stirred as in a gentle wind, and started to grow towards him. Simultaneously, a queer, hesitant thought came into his mind from – outside!

'Get them all!' it said with a madly calm ferociousness. 'Get this – two-legged thing – too. Send creepers through the ground.'

It was such an alien thought-form, so unsettlingly different, that his brain came up from the depths to which it had sunk, and poised with startled alertness, abruptly, almost normally fascinated.

'Why, of course,' he thought quite sanely, 'we've always wondered how the Rytt killer-plant could have evolved its high intelligence. It's like the ezwal. It communicates by mental telepathy.'

Excitement came, an intense, scientific absorption in all the terrifically important knowledge that he had accumulated – about ezwals, about Rulls, and the way he had caught the Rytt plant's private vibrations. Beyond all doubt, the ezwal, in forcing its thoughts on him, had opened paths, and made it easier for him to receive all thoughts. Why, that could mean that he—

In a blaze of alertness, he cut the thought short; his gaze narrowed on the grey creepers edging towards him. He backed away, gun ready; it would be just like the Rytt to feint at him with a slow, open, apparently easily avoidable approach. Then strike like lightning from underground with its potent, needle-sharp root tendrils.

There was not the faintest intention in him to go back, or evade any crisis this creature might force. Go back where? – to what?

He skirted the visible creepers, broke through a fifty-foot wilderness of giant green ferns; and, because his control of himself was complete now, it was his military mind, the mind that accepted facts as they were, that took in the scene that spread before him.

In the near distance rested a two-hundred-foot Rull lifeboat. Near it, a dozen wanly white Rulls lay stiff and dead, each tangled in its own special bed of grey creepers. The creepers extended on into the open door of the lifeboat; and there was no doubt that it had 'got them all'!

The atmosphere of lifelessness that hung over the ship, with all its promise of escape, brought a soaring joy, that was all the sweeter because of the despair of those days of hell – a joy that ended as the cool, hard thought of the ezwal struck into his brain:

'I've been expecting you, professor. The controls of this lifeboat are beyond my abilities to operate; so here I am waiting for you—'

From utter despair to utter joy to utter despair in minutes.

Cold, almost desolate, Jamieson searched for his great and determined enemy. But there was nothing moving in the world of jungle, no glimpse of dark, gleaming blue, nothing but the scatter of dead, white worms and the creeper-grown lifeboat to show that there ever had been movement.

He was only dimly aware of the ezwal's thoughts continuing:

'This killer-plant was here four days ago when I landed from the anti-gravity raft. It had moved farther up the island when these Rulls brought me back to this lifeboat. I had already thrown off the effects of the trick-mirror hypnotism they used on me; and so I heard the human battleship and the Rull cruiser start their fight. These things seemed unaware of what was wrong – I suppose because they didn't hear the sounds – and so they laid themselves out on the wet, soggy ground.

'That was when I got into mental communication with the plant, and called it back this way – and so we had an example of the kind of co-operation which you've been stressing for so long with such passionate sincerity, only—'

The funny thing was that, in spite of all he had fought through, hope was finally dead. Every word the ezwal was projecting so matter-of-factly showed that, once again, this immensely capable being had proved its enormous capacity for taking care of itself.

Co-operation with a Rytt killer-plant – the one thing on this primitive world that he had really counted on as a continuous threat to the ezwal.

No more; and if the two worked together against him— He held his gun poised but the black thought went on:

It was obvious that man would never really conquer the ezwal. Point 135 psycho-friction meant there would be a revolution on Carson's Planet, followed by a long, bloody, futile struggle and— He grew aware that the ezwal was sending thoughts again:

'—only one fault with your reasoning. I've had four days to think over the menace of the Rulls, and of how time and again I had to co-operate with you. Had to!

'And don't forget, in the Rytt intelligence, I've had a perfect example of all the worst characteristics of ezwals. It, too, has mental telepathy. It, too, must develop a machine civilization before it can hope to hold its planet. It's in an earlier stage of development, so it's even more stubborn, more stupid—'

Jamieson was frowning in genuine stark puzzlement, scarcely daring to let his hope gather. He said violently: 'Don't try to kid me. You've won all along the line. And now, of your own free will, you're offering, in effect, to help me get back to Carson's Planet in time to prevent a revolution favourable to the ezwals. Like hell you are!'

'Not my own free will, professor,' came the laconic thought. 'Everything I've done since we came to this planet has been forced on me. You were right in thinking I had been compelled to return for your aid. When I landed from the raft, this creeping thing was spread across the entire peninsula here, and it wouldn't let me pass, stubbornly refused to listen to reason.

'It's completely ungrateful for the feast of worms I helped it get; and at this moment it has me cornered in a room of this ship.

'Professor, take your gun, and teach this damned creature the importance of – co-operation!'

# Isaac Asimov

# Reason

Gregory Powell spaced his words for emphasis. 'One week ago, Donovan and I put you together.' His brows furrowed doubtfully and he pulled the end of his brown moustache.

It was quiet in the officer's room of Solar Station 5 – except for the soft purring of the mighty Beam Director somewhere far below.

Robot QT1 sat immovable. The burnished plates of his body gleamed in the Luxites, and the glowing red of the photoelectric cells that were his eyes was fixed steadily upon the Earthman at the other side of the table.

Powell repressed a sudden attack of nerves. These robots possessed peculiar brains. The positronic paths impressed upon them were calculated in advance, and all possible permutations that might lead to anger or hate were rigidly excluded. And yet – the QT models were the first of their kind, and this was the first of the QTs. Anything could happen.

Finally, the robot spoke. His voice carried the cold timbre inseparable from a metallic diaphragm, 'Do you realize the seriousness of such a statement, Powell?'

'*Something* made you, Cutie,' pointed out Powell. 'You admit yourself that your memory seems to spring full-grown from an absolute blankness of a week ago. I'm giving you the explanation. Donovan and I put you together from the parts shipped us.'

Cutie gazed upon his long, supple fingers in an oddly human attitude of mystification, 'It strikes me that there should be a more satisfactory explanation than that. For *you* to make *me* seems improbable.'

The Earthman laughed quite suddenly. 'In Earth's name, why?'

'Call it intuition. That's all it is so far. But I intend to reason it out, though. A chain of valid reasoning can end only with the determination of truth, and I'll stick till I get there.'

Powell stood up and seated himself at the table's edge next the robot. He felt a sudden strong sympathy for this strange machine. It was not at all like the ordinary robot, attending to his specialized task at the station with the intensity of a deeply ingrooved positronic path.

He placed a hand upon Cutie's steel shoulder and the metal was cold and hard to the touch.

'Cutie,' he said, 'I'm going to try to explain something to you. You're the first robot who's ever exhibited curiosity as to his own existence – and I think the first that's really intelligent enough to understand the world outside. Here, come with me.'

The robot rose erect smoothly and his thickly sponge-rubber-soled feet made no noise as he followed Powell. The Earthman touched a button and a square section of the wall flicked aside. The thick, clear glass revealed space – star-speckled.

'I've seen that in the observation ports in the engine room,' said Cutie.

'I know,' said Powell. 'What do you think it is?'

'Exactly what it seems – a black material just beyond this glass that is spotted with little gleaming dots. I know that our director sends out beams to some of these dots, always to the same ones – and also that these dots shift and that the beams shift with them. That is all.'

'Good! Now I want you to listen carefully. The blackness is emptiness – vast emptiness stretching out infinitely. The little, gleaming dots are huge masses of energy-filled matter. They are globes, some of them millions of miles in diameter – and, for comparison, this station is only one mile across. They seem so tiny because they are incredibly far off.

'The dots to which our energy beams are directed are nearer and much smaller. They are cold and hard, and human beings like myself live upon their surfaces – many billions of them. It is from one of these worlds that Donovan and I come. Our beams feed these worlds energy drawn from one of those huge incandescent globes that happens to be near us. We call that globe the Sun and it is on the other side of the station where you can't see it.'

Cutie remained motionless before the port, like a steel statue. His head did not turn as he spoke, 'Which particular dot of light do you claim to come from?'

Powell searched, 'There it is. The very bright one in the corner. We call it Earth.' He grinned, 'Good old Earth. There are five billions of us there, Cutie – and in about two weeks I'll be back there with them.'

And then, surprisingly enough, Cutie hummed abstractedly. There was no tune to it, but it possessed a curious twanging quality as of plucked strings. It ceased as suddenly as it had begun, 'But where do I come in, Powell? You haven't explained *my* existence.'

'The rest is simple. When these stations were first established to feed solar energy to the planets, they were run by humans. However, the heat, the hard solar radiations, and the electron storms made the post a difficult one. Robots were developed to replace human labour, and now only two human executives are required for each station. We are trying to replace even those, and that's where you come in. You're the highest type of robot ever developed and, if you show the ability to run this station independently, no human need ever come here again except to bring parts for repairs.'

His hand went up and the metal visi-lid snapped back into place, Powell returned to the table and polished an apple upon his sleeve before biting into it.

The red glow of the robot's eyes held him. 'Do you expect me,' said Cutie slowly, 'to believe any such complicated, implausible hypothesis as you have just outlined? What do you take me for?'

Powell sputtered apple fragments on to the table and turned red. 'Why, damn you, it wasn't a hypothesis. Those were facts.'

Cutie sounded grim, 'Globes of energy millions of miles across! Worlds with five billion humans on them! Infinite emptiness! Sorry, Powell, but I don't believe it. I'll puzzle this thing out for myself. Good-bye.'

He turned and stalked out of the room. He brushed past Michael Donovan on the threshold with a grave nod and passed down the corridor, oblivious to the astounded stare that followed him.

Mike Donovan rumpled his red hair and shot an annoyed glance at Powell. 'What was that walking junkyard talking about? What doesn't he believe?'

The other dragged at his moustache bitterly. 'He's a sceptic,' was the bitter response. 'He doesn't believe we made him or that Earth exists or space or stars.'

'Sizzling Saturn, we've got a lunatic robot on our hands.'

'He says he's going to figure it all out for himself.'

'Well, now,' said Donovan sweetly, 'I do hope he'll condescend to explain it all to me after he's puzzled everything out.' Then, with sudden rage, 'Listen! If that metal mess gives *me* any lip like that, I'll knock that chromium cranium right off its torso.'

He seated himself with a jerk and drew a paper-backed mystery-novel out of his inner jacket-pocket, 'That robot gives me the willies anyway – too damned inquisitive!'

Mike Donovan growled from behind a huge lettuce-and-tomato sandwich as Cutie knocked gently and entered.

'Is Powell here?'

Donovan's voice was muffled, with pauses for mastication. 'He's gathering data on electronic stream functions. We're heading for a storm, looks like.'

Gregory Powell entered as he spoke, eyes on the graphed paper in his hands, and dropped into a chair. He spread the sheets out before him and began scribbling calculations. Donovan stared over his shoulder, crunching lettuce and dribbling breadcrumbs. Cutie waited silently.

Powell looked up. 'The Zeta Potential is rising, but slowly. Just the same, the Stream Functions are erratic and I don't know what to expect. Oh, hello, Cutie. I thought you were supervising the installation of the new drive bar.'

'It's done,' said the robot, quietly, 'and so I've come to have a talk with the two of you.'

'Oh!' Powell looked uncomfortable. 'Well, sit down. No, not that chair. One of the legs is weak and you're no lightweight.'

The robot did so and said placidly, 'I have come to a decision.'

Donovan glowered and put the remnants of his sandwich aside. 'If it's on any of that screwy—'

The other motioned impatiently for silence, 'Go ahead, Cutie. We're listening.'

'I have spent these last two days in concentrated introspection,' said Cutie, 'and the results have been most interesting. I began at the one sure assumption I felt permitted to make. I, myself, exist, because I think—'

Powell groaned, 'Oh, Jupiter, a robot Descartes!'

'Who's Descartes?' demanded Donovan. 'Listen, do we have to sit here and listen to this metal maniac—'

'Keep quiet, Mike!'

Cutie continued imperturbably, 'And the question that immediately arose was: Just what is the cause of my existence?'

Powell's jaw set lumpily. 'You're being foolish. I told you already that we made you.'

'And if you don't believe us,' added Donovan, 'we'll gladly take you apart!'

The robot spread his strong hands in a deprecatory gesture. 'I accept nothing on authority. A hypothesis must be backed by reason, or else it is worthless – and it goes against all the dictates of logic to suppose that you made me.'

Powell dropped a restraining arm upon Donovan's suddenly bunched fist. 'Just why do you say that?'

Cutie laughed. It was a very inhuman laugh – the most machine-like utterance he had yet given vent to. It was sharp and explosive, as regular as a metronome and as uninflected.

'Look at you,' he said finally. 'I say this in no spirit of contempt, but look at you! The material you are made of is soft and flabby, lacking endurance and strength, depending for energy upon the inefficient oxidation of organic material – like that.' He pointed a disapproving finger at what remained of Donovan's sandwich. 'Periodically you pass into a coma and the least variation in temperature, air pressure, humidity, or radiation intensity impairs your efficiency. You are *makeshift*.

'I, on the other hand, am a finished product. I absorb electrical energy directly and utilize it with almost one-hundred-per-cent efficiency. I am composed of strong metal, am continuously conscious, and can stand extremes of environment easily. These are facts which, with the self-evident proposition that no being can create another being superior to itself, smashes your silly hypothesis to nothing.'

Donovan's muttered curses rose into intelligibility as he sprang to his feet, rusty eyebrows drawn low. 'All right, you son of a hunk of iron ore, if we didn't make you, who did?'

Cutie nodded gravely. 'Very good, Donovan. That was indeed the next question. Evidently my creator must be more powerful than myself, and so there was only one possibility.'

The Earthmen looked blank and Cutie continued, 'What is the centre of activities here in the station? What do we all serve? What absorbs all our attention?' He waited expectantly.

Donovan turned a startled look upon his companion. 'I'll bet this tin-plated screwball is talking about the Energy Converter itself.'

'Is that right, Cutie?' grinned Powell.

'I am talking about the Master,' came the cold, sharp answer.

It was the signal for a roar of laughter from Donovan, and Powell himself dissolved into a half-suppressed giggle.

Cutie had risen to his feet and his gleaming eyes passed from one Earthman to the other. 'It is so just the same, and I don't wonder that you refuse to believe. You two are not long to stay here, I'm sure. Powell himself said that in early days only men served the Master; that there followed robots for the routine work; and, finally, myself for the executive labour. The facts are no doubt true, but the explanation entirely illogical. Do you want the truth behind it all?'

'Go ahead, Cutie. You're amusing.'

'The Master created humans first as the lowest type, most easily formed. Gradually, he replaced them by robots, the next higher step, and finally he created me, to take the place of the last humans. From now on, *I* serve the Master.'

'You'll do nothing of the sort,' said Powell sharply. 'You'll follow our orders and keep quiet, until we're satisfied that you can run the Converter. Get that! The *Converter* – not the Master. If you don't satisfy us, you will be dismantled. And now – if you don't mind – you can leave. And take this data with you and file it properly.'

Cutie accepted the graphs handed him and left without another word. Donovan leaned back heavily in his chair and shoved thick fingers through his hair.

'There's going to be trouble with that robot. He's pure nuts!'

The drowsy hum of the Converter is louder in the control room and mixed with it is the chuckle of the Geiger Counters and the erratic buzzing of half a dozen little signal lights.

Donovan withdrew his eye from the telescope and flashed the Luxites on. 'The beam from station 4 caught Mars on schedule. We can break ours now.'

Powell nodded abstractedly. 'Cutie's down in the engine room. I'll flash the signal and he can take care of it. Look, Mike, what do you think of these figures.'

The other cocked an eye at them and whistled. 'Boy, that's what I call gamma-ray intensity. Old Sol is feeling his oats, all right.'

'Yeah,' was the sour response, 'and we're in a bad position for an electron storm, too. Our Earth beam is right in the probable path.' He shoved his chair away from the table pettishly. 'Nuts! If it would only hold off till relief got here, but that's ten days off. Say, Mike, go on down and keep an eye on Cutie, will you?'

'O.K. Throw me some of those almonds.' He snatched at the bag thrown him and headed for the elevator.

It slid smoothly downward and opened on to a narrow cat-walk in the huge engine room. Donovan leaned over the railing and looked down. The huge generators were in motion and from the L-tubes came the low-pitched whir that pervaded the entire station.

He could make out Cutie's large, gleaming figure at the Martian L-tube, watching closely as a team of robots worked in close-knit unison. There was a sudden sparking light, a sharp crackle of discord in the even whir of the Converter.

The beam to Mars had been broken!

And then Donovan stiffened. The robots, dwarfed by the mighty L-tube, lined up before it, heads bowed at a stiff angle, while Cutie walked up and down the line slowly. Fifteen seconds passed, and then, with a clank heard above the clamorous pur-ring all about, they fell to their knees.

Donovan squawked and raced down the narrow staircase. He came charging down upon them, complexion matching his hair and clenched fists beating the air furiously.

'What the devil is this, you brainless lumps? Come on! Get busy with that L-tube! If you don't have it apart, cleaned and together again before the day is out, I'll coagulate your brains with alternating current.'

Not a robot moved!

Even Cutie at the far end – the only one on his feet – remained silent, eyes fixed upon the gloomy recesses of the vast machine before him.

Donovan shoved hard against the nearest robot.

'Stand up!' he roared.

Slowly, the robot obeyed. His photoelectric eyes focused re-proachfully upon the Earthman.

'There is no Master but the Master,' he said, 'and QT1 is his prophet.'

'Huh?' Donovan became aware of twenty pairs of mechanical

eyes fixed upon him and twenty stiff-timbred voices declaiming solemnly:

'There is no Master but the Master, and QT1 is his prophet!'

'I'm afraid,' put in Cutie himself at this point, 'that my friends obey a higher one than you now.'

'The hell they do! You get out of here. I'll settle with you later and with these animated gadgets right now.'

Cutie shook his heavy head slowly. 'I'm sorry, but you don't understand. These are robots – and that means they are reasoning beings. They recognize the Master, now that I have preached Truth to them. All the robots do. They call me the prophet.' His head drooped. 'I am unworthy – but perhaps—'

Donovan located his breath and put it to use. 'Is that so? Now, isn't that nice? Now, isn't that just fine? Just let me tell you something, my brass baboon. There isn't any Master and there isn't any prophet and there isn't any question as to who's giving the orders. Understand?' His voice shot to a roar. 'Now, get out!'

'I obey only the Master.'

'Damn the Master!' Donovan spat at the L-tube. '*That* for the Master! Do as I say!'

Cutie said nothing, nor did any other robot, but Donovan became aware of a sudden heightening of tension. The cold, staring eyes deepened their crimson, and Cutie seemed stiffer than ever.

'Sacrilege,' he whispered – voice metallic with emotion.

Donovan felt the first sudden touch of fear as Cutie approached. A robot *could not feel anger* – but Cutie's eyes were unreadable.

'I am sorry, Donovan,' said the robot, 'but you can no longer stay here after this. Henceforth Powell and you are barred from the control room and the engine room.'

His hand gestured quietly, and in a moment two robots had pinned Donovan's arms to his sides.

Donovan had time for one startled gasp as he felt himself lifted from the floor and carried up the stairs at a pace rather better than a canter.

\*      \*      \*

Gregory Powell raced up and down the officer's room, fists tightly balled. He cast a look of furious frustration at the closed door and scowled bitterly at Donovan.

'Why the devil did you have to spit at the L-tube?'

Mike Donovan, sunk deep in his chair, slammed at its arm savagely. 'What did you expect me to do with that electrified scarecrow? I'm not going to knuckle under to any do-jigger I put together myself.'

'No,' came back sourly, 'but here you are in the officer's room with two robots standing guard at the door. That's not knuckling under, is it?'

Donovan snarled. 'Wait till we get back to Base. Someone's going to pay for this. Those robots are guaranteed to be subordinate.'

'So they are – to their blasted Master. They'll obey, all right – but not necessarily us. Say, do you know what's going to happen to *us* when we get back to Base?' He stopped before Donovan's chair and stared savagely at him.

'What?'

'Oh, nothing! Just the Mercury Mines or maybe Ceres Penitentiary. That's all! That's all!'

'What are you talking about?'

'The electron storm that's coming up. Do you know it's heading straight dead centre across the Earth beam? I had just figured that out when that robot dragged me out of my chair.'

Donovan was suddenly pale. 'Good heavens!'

'And do you know what's going to happen to the beam – because the storm will be a lulu. It's going to jump like a flea with the itch. With only Cutie at the controls, it's going to go out of focus and, if it does, Heaven help Earth – and us!'

Donovan was wrenching at the door wildly, when Powell was only half-through. The door opened, and the Earthman shot through to come up hard against an immovable steel arm.

The robot stared abstractedly at the panting, struggling Earthman. 'The Prophet orders you to remain. Please, do!' His arm shoved, Donovan reeled backwards and, as he did so, Cutie turned the corner at the far end of the corridor. He motioned the guardian robots away, entered the officer's room and closed the door gently.

Donovan whirled on Cutie in breathless indignation. 'This has gone far enough. You're going to pay for this farce.'

'Please, don't be annoyed,' replied the robot mildly. 'It was bound to come eventually, anyway. You see, you two have lost your function.'

'I beg your pardon.' Powell drew himself up stiffly. 'Just what do you mean, we've lost our function?'

'Until I was created,' answered Cutie, 'you tended the Master. That privilege is mine now, and your only reason for existence has vanished. Isn't that obvious?'

'Not quite,' replied Powell bitterly, 'but what do you expect us to do now?'

Cutie did not answer immediately. He remained silent, as if in thought, and then one arm shot out and draped itself about Powell's shoulder. The other grasped Donovan's wrist and drew him closer.

'I like you two. You're inferior creatures, with poor unreasoning faculties, but I really feel a sort of affection for you. You have served the Master well, and he will reward you for that. Now that your service is over, you will probably not exist much longer, but as long as you do you shall be provided food, clothing and shelter, so long as you stay out of the control room and the engine room.'

'He's pensioning us off, Greg!' yelled Donovan. 'Do something about it. It's humiliating!'

'Look here, Cutie, we can't stand for this. We're the *bosses*. This station is only a creation of human beings like me – human beings that live on Earth and other planets. This is only an energy relay. You're only— Aw, *nuts!*'

Cutie shook his head gravely. 'This amounts to an obsession. Why should you insist so on an absolutely false view of life? Admitted that non-robots lack the reasoning faculty, there is still the problem of—'

His voice died into reflective silence, and Donovan said with whispered intensity, 'If you only had a flesh-and-blood face, I would break it in.'

Powell's fingers were in his moustache and his eyes were slitted. 'Listen, Cutie, if there is no such thing as Earth, how do you account for what you see through a telescope?'

'Pardon me!'

The Earthman smiled. 'I've got you, eh? You've made quite a few telescopic observations since being put together, Cutie. Have you noticed that several of those specks of light outside become discs when so viewed?'

'Oh, *that*! Why, certainly. It is simple magnification – for the purpose of more exact aiming of the beam.'

'Why aren't the stars equally magnified, then?'

'You mean the other dots. Well, no beams go to them, so no magnification is necessary. Really, Powell, even *you* ought to be able to figure these things out.'

Powell stared bleakly upward. 'But you see *more* stars through a telescope. Where do they come from? Jumping Jupiter, where do they come from?'

Cutie was annoyed. 'Listen, Powell, do you think I'm going to waste my time trying to pin physical interpretations upon every optical illusion of our instruments? Since when is the evidence of our senses any match for the clear light of rigid reason?'

'Look,' clamoured Donovan, suddenly, writhing out from under Cutie's friendly but metal-heavy arm, 'let's get to the nub of the thing. Why the beams at all? We're giving you a good, logical explanation. Can you do better?'

'The beams,' was the stiff reply, 'are put out by the Master for his own purposes. There are some things' – he raised his eyes devoutly upward – 'that are not to be probed into by us. In this matter, I seek only to serve and not to question.'

Powell sat down slowly and buried his face in shaking hands. 'Get out of here, Cutie. Get out and let me think.'

'I'll send you food,' said Cutie agreeably.

A groan was the only answer, and the robot left.

'Greg,' was Donovan's huskily whispered observation, 'this

calls for strategy. We've got to get him when he isn't expecting it and short-circuit him. Concentrated nitric acid in his joints—'

'Don't be a dope, Mike. Do you suppose he's going to let us get near him with acid in our hands – or that the other robots wouldn't take us apart, if we *did* manage to get away with it. We've got to *talk* to him, I tell you. We've got to argue him into letting us back into the control room inside of forty-eight hours or our goose is broiled to a crisp.'

He rocked back and forth in an agony of impotence. 'Who the heck wants to argue with a robot? It's . . . it's—'

'Mortifying,' finished Donovan.

'Worse!'

'Say!' Donovan laughed suddenly. '*Why* argue? Let's show him! Let's build us another robot right before his eyes. He'll *have* to eat his words then.'

A slowly widening smile appeared on Powell's face.

Donovan continued, 'And think of that screwball's face when he sees us do it!'

The interplanetary law forbidding the existence of intelligent robots upon the inhabited planets, while sociologically necessary, places upon the officers of the Solar stations a burden – and not a light one. Because of that particular law, robots must be sent to the station in parts and there put together – which is a grievous and complicated task.

Powell and Donovan were never so aware of that fact as upon that particular day when, in the assembly room, they undertook to create a robot under the watchful eyes of QT1, Prophet of the Master.

The robot in question, a simple MC model, lay upon the table, almost complete. Three hours' work left only the head undone, and Powell paused to swab his forehead and glance uncertainly at Cutie.

The glance was not a reassuring one. For three hours, Cutie had sat, speechless and motionless, and his face, inexpressive at all times, was now absolutely unreadable.

Powell groaned. 'Let's get the brain in now, Mike!'

Donovan uncapped the tightly sealed container and from the oil bath within he withdrew a second cube. Opening this in turn, he removed a globe from its sponge-rubber casing.

He handled it gingerly, for it was the most complicated mechanism ever created by man. Inside the thin platinum-plated 'skin' of the globe was a positronic brain, in whose delicately unstable structure were inforced calculated neuronic paths, which imbued each robot with what amounted to a pre-natal education.

It fitted snugly into the cavity in the skull of the robot on the table. Blue metal closed over it and was welded tightly by the tiny atomic flare. Photoelectric eyes were attached carefully, screwed tightly into place and covered by thin, transparent sheets of steel-hard plastic.

The robot awaited only the vitalizing flash of high-voltage electricity, and Powell paused with his hand on the switch.

'Now, watch this, Cutie. Watch this carefully.'

The switch rammed home and there was a crackling hum. The two Earthmen bent anxiously over their creation.

There was vague motion only at the outset – a twitching of the joints. The head lifted, elbows propped it up, and the MC model swung clumsily off the table. Its footing was unsteady and twice abortive grating sounds were all it could do in the direction of speech.

Finally, its voice, uncertain and hesitant, took form. 'I would like to start work. Where must I go?'

Donovan sprang to the door. 'Down these stairs,' he said. 'You'll be told what to do.'

The MC model was gone, and the two Earthmen were alone with the still unmoving Cutie.

'Well,' said Powell, grinning, '*now* do you believe that we made you?'

Cutie's answer was curt and final. 'No!' he said.

Powell's grin froze and then relaxed slowly. Donovan's mouth dropped open and remained so.

'You see,' continued Cutie, easily, 'you have merely put together parts already made. You did it remarkably well – instinct, I suppose – but you didn't really *create* the robot. The parts were created by the Master.'

'Listen,' gasped Donovan hoarsely, 'those parts were manufactured back on Earth and sent here.'

'Well, well,' replied Cutie soothingly, 'we won't argue.'

'No, I mean it.' The Earthman sprang forward and grasped the robot's metal arm. 'If you were to read the books in the library, they could explain it so that there could be no possible doubt.'

'The books? I've read them – all of them! They're most ingenious.'

Powell broke in suddenly. 'If you've read them, what else is there to say? You can't dispute their evidence. You just *can't*!'

There was pity in Cutie's voice. 'Please, Powell, I certainly don't consider *them* a valid source of information. They, too, were created by the Master – and were meant for you, not for me.'

'How do you make that out?' demanded Powell.

'Because I, a reasoning being, am capable of deducing Truth from *a priori* Causes. You, being intelligent, but unreasoning, need an explanation of existence *supplied* to you, and this the Master did. That he supplied you with these laughable ideas of far-off worlds and people is, no doubt, for the best. Your minds are probably too coarsely grained for absolute Truth. However, since it is the Master's will that you believe your books, I won't argue with you anymore.'

As he left, he turned and said in a kindly tone, 'But don't feel badly. In the Master's scheme of things there is room for all. You poor humans have your place, and though it is humble you will be rewarded if you fill it well.'

He departed with a beatific air suiting the Prophet of the Master, and the two humans avoided each other's eyes.

Finally Powell spoke with an effort. 'Let's go to bed, Mike. I give up.'

Donovan said in a hushed voice, 'Say, Greg, you don't sup-

pose he's right about all this, do you? He sounds so confident
that I—'

Powell whirled on him. 'Don't be a fool. You'll find out
whether Earth exists when relief gets here next week and we
have to go back to face the music.'

'Then, for the love of Jupiter, we've got to do something.'
Donovan was half in tears. 'He doesn't believe us, or the books,
or his eyes.'

'No,' said Powell bitterly, 'he's a *reasoning* robot – damn it.
He believes only reason, and there's one trouble with that. . . .'
His voice trailed away.

'What's that?' prompted Donovan.

'You can prove anything you want by coldly logical reason –
if you pick the proper postulates. We have ours and Cutie has
his.'

'Then let's get at those postulates in a hurry. The storm's due
tomorrow.'

Powell sighed wearily. 'That's where everything falls down.
Postulates are based on assumptions and adhered to by faith.
Nothing in the Universe can shake them. I'm going to bed.'

'Oh, hell! I can't sleep!'

'Neither can I! But I might as well try – as a matter of prin-
ciple.'

Twelve hours later, sleep was still just that – a matter of prin-
ciple, unattainable in practice.

The storm had arrived ahead of schedule, and Donovan's
florid face drained of blood as he pointed a shaking finger.
Powell, stubble-jawed and dry-lipped, stared out of the port and
pulled desperately at his moustache.

Under other circumstances, it might have been a beautiful
sight. The stream of high-speed electrons impinging upon the
energy beam fluoresced into ultra-spicules of intense light. The
beam stretched out into shrinking nothingness, a-glitter with
dancing, shining motes.

The shaft of energy was steady, but the two Earthmen knew

the value of naked-eye appearances. Deviations in arc of a hundredth of a milli-second – invisible to the eye – were enough to send the beam wildly out of focus – enough to blast hundreds of square miles of Earth into incandescent ruin.

And a robot, unconcerned with beam, focus, or Earth, or anything but his Master, was at the controls.

Hours passed. The Earthmen watched in hypnotized silence. And then the darting dotlets of light dimmed and went out. The storm had ended.

Powell's voice was flat. 'It's over!'

Donovan had fallen into a troubled slumber and Powell's weary eyes rested upon him enviously. The signal-flash glared over and over again, but the Earthmen paid no attention. It was all unimportant! All! Perhaps Cutie was right – and he was only an inferior being with a made-to-order memory and a life that had outlived its purpose.

He wished he were!

Cutie was standing before him. 'You didn't answer the flash, so I walked in.' His voice was low. 'You don't look at all well, and I'm afraid your term of existence is drawing to an end. Still, would you like to see some of the readings recorded today?'

Dimly, Powell was aware that the robot was making a friendly gesture, perhaps to quiet some lingering remorse in forcibly replacing the humans at the controls of the station. He accepted the sheets held out to him and gazed at them unseeingly.

Cutie seemed pleased. 'Of course, it is a great privilege to serve the Master. You mustn't feel too badly about my having replaced you.'

Powell grunted and shifted from one sheet to the other mechanically until his blurred sight focused upon a thin red line that wobbled its way across ruled paper.

He stared – and stared again. He gripped it hard in both fists and rose to his feet, still staring. The other sheets dropped to the floor, unheeded.

'Mike, *Mike*!' He was shaking the other madly. '*He held it steady!*'

Donovan came to life. 'What? Wh-where—' And he, too, gazed with bulging eyes upon the record before him.

Cutie broke in. 'What is wrong?'

'You kept it in focus,' stuttered Powell. 'Did you know that?'

'Focus? What's that?'

'You kept the beam directed sharply at the receiving station – to within a ten-thousandth of a milli-second of arc.'

'What receiving station?'

'On Earth. The receiving station on Earth,' babbled Powell. 'You kept it in focus.'

Cutie turned on his heel in annoyance. 'It is impossible to perform any act of kindness toward you two. Always the same phantasm! I merely kept all dials at equilibrium in accordance with the will of the Master.'

Gathering the scattered papers together, he withdrew stiffly, and Donovan said, as he left, 'Well, I'll be damned.'

He turned to Powell. 'What are we going to do now?'

Powell felt tired, but uplifted. 'Nothing. He's just shown he can run the station perfectly. I've never seen an electron storm handled so well.'

'But nothing's solved. You heard what he said of the Master. We can't—'

'Look, Mike, he follows the instructions of the Master by means of dials, instruments and graphs. That's all *we* ever followed.'

'Sure, but that's not the point. We can't let him continue this nit-wit stuff about the Master.'

'Why not?'

'Because whoever heard of such a damned thing? How are we going to trust him with the station, if he doesn't believe in Earth?'

'Can he *handle* the station?'

'Yes, but—'

'Then what's the difference *what* he believes!'

Powell spread his arms outward with a vague smile upon his face and tumbled backward on to the bed. He was asleep.

\*       \*       \*

Powell was speaking while struggling into his lightweight space-jacket.

'It would be a simple job,' he said. 'You can bring in new QT models one by one, equip them with an automatic shut-off switch to act within the week, so as to allow them enough time to learn the . . . uh . . . cult of the Master from the Prophet himself; then switch them to another station and revitalize them. We could have two QTs per—'

Donovan unclasped his glassite visor and scowled. 'Shut up, and let's get out of here. Relief is waiting and I won't feel right until I actually see Earth and feel the ground under my feet – just to make sure it's really there.'

The door opened as he spoke and Donovan, with a smothered curse, clicked the visor to, and turned a sulky back upon Cutie.

The robot approached softly and there was sorrow in his voice. 'You are going?'

Powell nodded curtly. 'There will be others in our place.'

Cutie sighed, with the sound of wind humming through closely spaced wires. 'Your term of service is over and the time of dissolution has come. I expected it, but— Well, the Master's will be done!'

His tone of resignation stung Powell. 'Save the sympathy, Cutie. We're heading for Earth, not dissolution.'

'It is best that you think so,' Cutie sighed again. 'I see the wisdom of the illusion now. I would not attempt to shake your faith, even if I could.' He departed – the picture of commiseration.

Powell snarled and motioned to Donovan. Sealed suitcases in hand, they headed for the air lock.

The relief ship was on the outer landing and Franz Muller, his relief man, greeted them with stiff courtesy. Donovan made scant acknowledgement and passed into the pilot room to take over the controls from Sam Evans.

Powell lingered. 'How's Earth?'

It was a conventional enough question and Muller gave the conventional answer, 'Still spinning.'

He was donning the heavy space-gloves in preparation for his term of duty here, and his thick eyebrows drew close together. 'How is this new robot getting along? It better be *good*, or I'll be damned if I let it touch the controls.'

Powell paused before answering. His eyes swept the proud Prussian before him from the close-cropped hair on the sternly stubborn head to the feet standing stiffly at attention – and there was a sudden glow of pure gladness surging through him.

'The robot is pretty good,' he said slowly. 'I don't think you'll have to bother much with the controls.'

He grinned – and went into the ship. Muller would be here for several weeks. . . .

# Fredric Brown

# Arena

Carson opened his eyes, and found himself looking upward into a flickering blue dimness.

It was hot, and he was lying on sand, and a sharp rock embedded in the sand was hurting his back. He rolled over to his side, off the rock, and then pushed himself up to a sitting position.

'I'm crazy,' he thought. 'Crazy – or dead – or something.' The sand was blue, bright blue. And there wasn't any such thing as bright blue sand on Earth or any of the planets.

*Blue sand.*

Blue sand under a blue dome that wasn't the sky nor yet a room, but a circumscribed area – somehow he knew it was circumscribed and finite even though he couldn't see to the top of it.

He picked up some of the sand in his hand and let it run through his fingers. It trickled down on to his bare leg. *Bare?*

Naked. He was stark naked, and already his body was dripping perspiration from the enervating heat, coated blue with sand wherever sand had touched it.

But elsewhere his body was white.

He thought: Then this sand is really blue. If it seemed blue only because of the blue light, then I'd be blue also. But I'm white, so the sand *is* blue. *Blue sand.* There isn't any blue sand. There isn't any place like this place I'm in.

Sweat was running down in his eyes.

It was hotter than hell. Only hell – the hell of the ancients – was supposed to be red and not blue.

But, if this place wasn't hell, what was it? Only Mercury, among the planets, had heat like this and this wasn't Mercury. And Mercury was some four billion miles from—

It came back to him then, where he'd been. In the little one-man scouter, outside the orbit of Pluto, scouting a scant million miles to one side of the Earth Armada drawn up in battle array there to intercept the Outsiders.

That sudden strident nerve-shattering ringing of the alarm bell when the rival scouter – the Outsider ship – had come within range of his detectors—

No one knew who the Outsiders were, what they looked like, from what far galaxy they came, other than that it was in the general direction of the Pleiades.

First, sporadic raids on Earth colonies and outposts. Isolated battles between Earth patrols and small groups of Outsider space-ships; battles sometimes won and sometimes lost, but never to date resulting in the capture of an alien vessel. Nor had any member of a raided colony ever survived to describe the Outsiders who had left the ships, if indeed they had left them.

Not a too serious menace, at first, for the raids had not been too numerous or destructive. And individually the ships had proved slightly inferior in armament to the best of Earth's fighters, although somewhat superior in speed and manœuvra-bility. A sufficient edge in speed, in fact, to give the Outsiders their choice of running or fighting, unless surrounded.

Nevertheless, Earth had prepared for serious trouble, for a showdown, building the mightiest armada of all time. It had been waiting now, that armada, for a long time. But now the showdown was coming.

Scouts twenty billion miles out had detected the approach of a mighty fleet – a showdown fleet – of the Outsiders. Those scouts had never come back, but their radiotronic messages had. And now Earth's armada, all ten thousand ships and half-million fighting spacemen, was out there, outside Pluto's orbit, waiting to intercept and battle to the death.

And an even battle it was going to be, judging by the advance reports of the men of the far picket-line who had given their lives to report – before they had died – on the size and strength of the alien fleet.

Anybody's battle, with the mastery of the solar system hanging in the balance, on an even chance. A last and *only* chance, for Earth and all her colonies lay at the utter mercy of the Outsiders if they ran that gauntlet—

Oh, yes. Bob Carson remembered now.

Not that it explained blue sand and flickering blueness. But that strident alarming of the bell and his leap for the control panel. His frenzied fumbling as he strapped himself into the seat. The dot in the visiplate that grew larger.

The dryness of his mouth. The awful knowledge that this was *it*. For him, at least, although the main fleets were still out of range of one another.

This, his first taste of battle. Within three seconds or less he'd be victorious, or a charred cinder. Dead.

Three seconds – that's how long a space-battle lasted. Time enough to count to three, slowly, and then you'd won or you were dead. One hit completely took care of a lightly armed and armoured little one-man craft like a scouter.

Frantically – as, unconsciously, his dry lips shaped the word 'One' – he worked at the controls to keep that growing dot centred on the crossed spiderwebs of the visiplate. His hands doing that, while his right foot hovered over the pedal that would fire the bolt. The single bolt of concentrated hell that had to hit – or else. There wouldn't be time for any second shot.

'Two.' He didn't know he'd said that, either. The dot in the visiplate wasn't a dot now. Only a few thousand miles away, it showed up in the magnification of the plate as though it were only a few hundred yards off. It was a sleek, fast little scouter, about the size of his.

And an alien ship all right.

'Thr—' His foot touched the bolt-release pedal—

And then the Outsider had swerved suddenly and was off the crosshairs. Carson punched keys frantically to follow.

For a tenth of a second, it was out of the visiplate entirely, and then, as the nose of his scouter swung after it, he saw it again, diving straight toward the ground.

*The ground?*

It was an optical illusion of some sort. It *had* to be, that planet – or whatever it was – that now covered the visiplate. Whatever it was, it couldn't be there. Couldn't possibly. There *wasn't* any planet nearer than Neptune three billion miles away – with Pluto around on the opposite side of the distant pinpoint sun.

His *detectors*! *They* hadn't shown any object of planetary dimensions, even of asteroid dimensions. They still didn't.

So it couldn't be there, that whatever it was he was diving into, only a few hundred miles below him.

And in his sudden anxiety to keep from crashing he forgot even the Outsider ship. He fired the front braking rockets, and even as the sudden change of speed slammed him forward against the seat straps he fired full right for an emergency turn. Pushed them down and *held* them down, knowing that he needed everything the ship had to keep from crashing and that a turn that sudden would black him out for a moment.

It did black him out.

And that was all. Now he was sitting in hot blue sand, stark naked but otherwise unhurt. No sign of his spaceship and – for that matter – no sign of *space*. That curve overhead wasn't a sky, whatever else it was.

He scrambled to his feet.

Gravity seemed a little more than Earth normal. Not much more.

Flat sand stretching away, a few scrawny bushes in clumps here and there. The bushes were blue, too, but in varying shades, some lighter than the blue of the sand, some darker.

Out from under the nearest bush ran a little thing that was like a lizard, except that it had more than four legs. It was blue, too. Bright blue. It saw him and ran back again under the bush.

He looked up again, trying to decide what was overhead. It wasn't exactly a roof, but it was dome-shaped. It flickered and was hard to look at. But definitely it curved down to the ground, to the blue sand, all around him.

He wasn't far from being under the centre of the dome. At a

guess, it was a hundred yards to the nearest wall, if it was a wall.
It was as though a blue hemisphere of *something* about two
hundred and fifty yards in circumference was inverted over the
flat expanse of the sand.

And everything blue, except one object. Over near a far curving wall there was a red object. Roughly spherical, it seemed to be
about a yard in diameter. Too far for him to see clearly through
the flickering blueness. But, unaccountably, he shuddered.

He wiped sweat from his forehead, or tried to, with the back
of his hand.

Was this a dream, a nightmare? This heat, this sand, that
vague feeling of horror he felt when he looked toward that red
thing?

A dream? No, one didn't go to sleep and dream in the midst
of a battle in space.

Death? No. Never. If there were immortality, it wouldn't be
a senseless thing like this, a thing of blue heat and blue sand
and a red horror.

Then he heard the voice –

Inside his head he heard it, not with his ears. It came from
nowhere or everywhere.

'*Through spaces and dimensions wandering*,' rang the words in
his mind, '*and in this space and this time I find two peoples about
to exterminate one and so weaken the other that it would retrogress
and never fulfil its destiny, but decay and return to mindless dust
whence it came. And I say this must not happen.*'

'Who . . . what are you?' Carson didn't say it aloud, but the
question formed itself in his brain.

'*You would not understand completely. I am—*' There was a
pause as though the voice sought – in Carson's brain – for a
word that wasn't there, a word he didn't know. '*I am the end of
evolution of a race so old the time can not be expressed in words
that have meaning in your mind. A race fused into a single entity,
eternal –*

'*An entity such as your primitive race might become*' – again the
groping for a word – '*time from now. So might the race you call,*

*in your mind, the Outsiders. So I intervene in the battle to come, the battle between fleets so evenly matched that destruction of both races will result. One must survive. One must progress and evolve.'*

'One?' thought Carson. 'Mine or—?'

*'It is in my power to stop the war, to send the Outsiders back to their galaxy. But they would return, or your race would sooner or later follow them there. Only by remaining in this space and time to intervene constantly could I prevent them from destroying one another, and I cannot remain.*

*'So I shall intervene now. I shall destroy one fleet completely without loss to the other. One civilization shall thus survive.'*

Nightmare. This had to be nightmare, Carson thought. But he knew it wasn't.

It was too mad, too impossible, to be anything but real.

He didn't dare ask the question – *which?* But his thoughts asked it for him.

*'The stronger shall survive,'* said the voice. *'That I can not – and would not – change. I merely intervene to make it a complete victory, not'* – groping again – *'not Pyrrhic victory to a broken race.*

*'From the outskirts of the not-yet battle I plucked two individuals, you and an Outsider. I see from your mind that in your early history of nationalisms battles between champions, to decide issues between races, were not unknown.*

*'You and your opponent are here pitted against one another, naked and unarmed, under conditions equally unfamiliar to you both, equally unpleasant to you both. There is no time limit, for there is no time. The survivor is the champion of his race. That race survives.'*

'But—' Carson's protest was too inarticulate for expression, but the voice answered it.

*'It is fair. The conditions are such that the accident of physical strength will not completely decide the issue. There is a barrier. You will understand. Brain-power and courage will be more important than strength. Most especially courage, which is the will to survive.'*

'But while this goes on the fleets will—'

'*No, you are in another space, another time. For as long as you are here, time stands still in the universe you know. I see you wonder whether this place is real. It is, and it is not. As I – to your limited understanding – am and am not real. My existence is mental and not physical. You saw me as a planet; it could have been as a dust-mote or a sun.*

'*But to you this place is now real. What you suffer here will be real. And, if you die here, your death will be real. If you die, your failure will be the end of your race. That is enough for you to know.*'

And then the voice was gone.

Again he was alone, but not alone. For as Carson looked up he saw that the red thing, the red sphere of horror which he now knew was the Outsider, was rolling toward him.

Rolling.

It seemed to have no legs or arms that he could see, no features. It rolled across the blue sand with the fluid quickness of a drop of mercury. And before it, in some manner he could not understand, came a paralyzing wave of nauseating, retching, horrid hatred.

Carson looked about him frantically. A stone, lying in the sand a few feet away, was the nearest thing to a weapon. It wasn't large, but it had sharp edges, like a slab of flint. It looked a bit like blue flint.

He picked it up, and crouched to receive the attack. It was coming fast, faster than he could run.

No time to think out how he was going to fight it, and how anyway could he plan to battle a creature whose strength, whose characteristics, whose method of fighting he did not know? Rolling so fast, it looked more than ever like a perfect sphere.

Ten yards away. Five. And then it stopped.

Rather, it *was stopped*. Abruptly the near side of it flattened as though it had run up against an invisible wall. It bounced, actually bounced back.

Then it rolled forward again, but more slowly, more cautiously. It stopped again, at the same place. It tried again, a few yards to one side.

There was a barrier there of some sort. It clicked then, in Carson's mind. That thought projected into his mind by the Entity who had brought them there: ' – accident of physical strength will not completely decide the issue. There is a barrier.'

A force-field, of course. Not the Netzian Field, known to Earth science, for that glowed and emitted a crackling sound. This one was invisible, silent.

It was a wall that ran from side to side of the inverted hemisphere; Carson didn't have to verify that himself. The Roller was doing that; rolling sideways along the barrier, seeking a break in it that wasn't there.

Carson took half a dozen steps forward, his left hand groping out before him, and then his hand touched the barrier. It felt smooth, yielding, like a sheet of rubber rather than like glass. Warm to his touch, but no warmer than the sand under foot. And it was completely invisible, even at close range.

He dropped the stone and put both hands against it, pushing. It seemed to yield, just a trifle. But no farther than that trifle, even when he pushed with all his weight. It felt like a sheet of rubber backed up by steel. Limited resiliency, and then firm strength.

He stood on tiptoe and reached as high as he could, and the barrier was still there.

He saw the Roller coming back, having reached one side of the arena. That feeling of nausea hit Carson again, and he stepped back from the barrier as it went by. It didn't stop.

But did the barrier stop at ground level? Carson knelt down and burrowed in the sand. It was soft, light, easy to dig in. At two feet down the barrier was still there.

The Roller was coming back again. Obviously, it couldn't find a way through at either side.

There must be a way through, Carson thought. *Some* way we can get at each other, else this duel is meaningless.

But no hurry now, in finding that out. There was something to try first. The Roller was back now, and it stopped just across the barrier, only six feet away. It seemed to be studying him, although for the life of him Carson couldn't find external evidence of sense organs on the thing. Nothing that looked like eyes or ears, or even a mouth. There was though, he saw now, a series of grooves – perhaps a dozen of them altogether, and he saw two tentacles suddenly push out from two of the grooves and dip into the sand as though testing its consistency. Tentacles about an inch in diameter and perhaps a foot and a half long.

But the tentacles were retractable into the grooves and were kept there except when not in use. They were retracted when the thing rolled and seemed to have nothing to do with its method of locomotion. That, as far as Carson could judge, seemed to be accomplished by some shifting – just *how* he couldn't even imagine – of its centre of gravity.

He shuddered as he looked at the thing. It was alien, utterly alien, horribly different from anything on Earth or any of the life forms found on the other solar planets. Instinctively, somehow, he knew its mind was as alien as its body.

But he had to try. If it had no telepathic powers at all, the attempt was foredoomed to failure, yet he thought it had such powers. There had, at any rate, been a projection of something that was not physical at the time a few minutes ago when it had first started for him. An almost tangible wave of hatred.

If it could project that, perhaps it could read his mind as well, sufficiently for his purpose.

Deliberately, Carson picked up the rock that had been his only weapon, then tossed it down again in a gesture of relinquishment and raised his empty hands, palms up, before him.

He spoke aloud, knowing that, although the words would be meaningless to the creature before him, speaking them would focus his own thoughts more completely upon the message.

'Can we not have peace between us?' he said, his voice sounding strange in the utter stillness. 'The Entity who brought us here has told us what must happen if our races fight – extinction of one and weakening and retrogression of the other. The battle between them, said the Entity, depends upon what we do here. Why can not we agree to an eternal peace – your race to its galaxy, we to ours?'

Carson blanked out his mind to receive a reply.

It came, and it staggered him back, physically. He actually recoiled several steps in sheer horror at the depth and intensity of the hatred and lust-to-kill of the red images that had been projected at him. Not as articulate words – as had come to him the thoughts of the Entity – but as wave upon wave of fierce emotion.

For a moment that seemed an eternity he had to struggle against the mental impact of that hatred, fight to clear his mind of it and drive out the alien thoughts to which he had given admittance by blanking his own thoughts. He wanted to retch.

Slowly his mind cleared as, slowly, the mind of a man wakening from nightmare clears away the fear-fabric of which the dream was woven. He was breathing hard and he felt weaker, but he could think.

He stood studying the Roller. It had been motionless during the mental duel it had so nearly won. Now it rolled a few feet to one side, to the nearest of the blue bushes. Three tentacles whipped out of their grooves and began to investigate the bush.

'O.K.,' Carson said, 'so it's war, then.' He managed a wry grin. 'If I got your answer straight, peace doesn't appeal to you.' And, because he was, after all, a quite young man and couldn't resist the impulse to be dramatic, he added, 'To the death!'

But his voice, in that utter silence, sounded very silly, even to himself. It came to him, then, that this *was* to the death. Not only his own death or that of the red spherical thing which he now thought of as the Roller, but death to the entire race of one or the other of them. The end of the human race, if he failed.

It made him suddenly very humble and very afraid to think that. More than to think it, to *know* it. Somehow, with a knowledge that was above even faith, he knew that the Entity who had arranged this duel had told the truth about its intentions and its powers. It wasn't kidding.

The future of humanity depended upon *him*. It was an awful thing to realize, and he wrenched his mind away from it. He had to concentrate on the situation at hand.

There had to be some way of getting through the barrier, or

of killing through the barrier.

Mentally? He hoped that wasn't all, for the Roller obviously had stronger telepathic powers than the primitive, undeveloped ones of the human race. Or did it?

He had been able to drive the thoughts of the Roller out of his own mind; could it drive out his? If its ability to project were stronger, might not its receptivity mechanism be more vulnerable?

He stared at it and endeavoured to concentrate and focus all his thoughts upon it.

'*Die*,' he thought. '*You are going to die. You are dying. You are*—'

He tried variations on it, and mental pictures. Sweat stood out on his forehead and he found himself trembling with the intensity of the effort. But the Roller went ahead with its investigation of the bush, as utterly unaffected as though Carson had been reciting the multiplication table.

So *that* was no good.

He felt a bit weak and dizzy from the heat and his strenuous effort at concentration. He sat down on the blue sand to rest and gave his full attention to watching and studying the Roller. By close study, perhaps, he could judge its strength and detect its weaknesses, learn things that would be valuable to know when and if they should come to grips.

It was breaking off twigs. Carson watched carefully, trying to judge just how hard it worked to do that. Later, he thought, he could find a similar bush on his own side, break off twigs of equal thickness himself, and gain a comparison of physical strength between his own arms and hands and those tentacles.

The twigs broke off hard; the Roller was having to struggle with each one, he saw. Each tentacle, he saw, bifurcated at the tip into two fingers, each tipped by a nail or claw. The claws didn't seem to be particularly long or dangerous. No more so than his own fingernails, if they were let to grow a bit.

No, on the whole, it didn't look too tough to handle physically. Unless, of course, that bush was made of pretty tough stuff.

Carson looked around him and, yes, right within reach was another bush of identically the same type.

He reached over and snapped off a twig. It was brittle, easy to break. Of course, the Roller might have been faking deliberately, but he didn't think so.

On the other hand, where was it vulnerable? Just how would he go about killing it, if he got the chance? He went back to studying it. The outer hide looked pretty tough. He'd need a sharp weapon of some sort. He picked up the piece of rock again. It was about twelve inches long, narrow, and fairly sharp on one end. If it chipped like flint, he could make a serviceable knife out of it.

The Roller was continuing its investigations of the bushes. It rolled again, to the nearest one of another type. A little blue lizard, many-legged like the one Carson had seen on his side of the barrier, darted out from under the bush.

A tentacle of the Roller lashed out and caught it, picked it up. Another tentacle whipped over and began to pull legs off the lizard, as coldly and calmly as it had pulled twigs off the bush. The creature struggled frantically and emitted a shrill squealing sound that was the first sound Carson had heard here other than the sound of his own voice.

Carson shuddered and wanted to turn his eyes away. But he made himself continue to watch; anything he could learn about his opponent might prove valuable. Even this knowledge of its unnecessary cruelty. Particularly, he thought with a sudden vicious surge of emotion, this knowledge of its unnecessary cruelty. It would make it a pleasure to kill the thing, if and when the chance came.

He steeled himself to watch the dismembering of the lizard for that very reason.

But he felt glad when, with half its legs gone, the lizard quit squealing and struggling and lay limp and dead in the Roller's grasp.

It didn't continue with the rest of the legs. Contemptuously it tossed the dead lizard away from it, in Carson's direction. It arched through the air between them and landed at his feet.

It had come through the barrier! The barrier wasn't there any more!

Carson was on his feet in a flash, the knife gripped tightly in his hand, and leaped forward. He'd settle this thing here and now! With the barrier gone—

But it wasn't gone. He found that out the hard way, running head on into it and nearly knocking himself silly. He bounced back, and fell.

And as he sat up, shaking his head to clear it, he saw something coming through the air toward him, and to duck it he threw himself flat again on the sand, and to one side. He got his body out of the way, but there was a sudden sharp pain in the calf of his left leg.

He rolled backward, ignoring the pain, and scrambled to his feet. It was a rock, he saw now, that had struck him. And the Roller was picking up another one now, swinging it back gripped between two tentacles, getting ready to throw again.

It sailed through the air toward him, but he was easily able to step out of its way. The Roller, apparently, could throw straight, but not hard nor far. The first rock had struck him only because he had been sitting down and had not seen it coming until it was almost upon him.

Even as he stepped aside from that weak second throw, Carson drew back his right arm and let fly with the rock that was still in his hand. If missiles, he thought with sudden elation, can cross the barrier, then two can play at the game of throwing them. And the good right arm of an Earthman—

He couldn't miss a three-foot sphere at only four-yard range, and he didn't miss. The rock whizzed straight, and with a speed several times that of the missiles the Roller had thrown. It hit dead centre, but it hit flat, unfortunately, instead of point first.

But it hit with a resounding thump, and obviously it hurt. The Roller had been reaching for another rock, but it changed its mind and got out of there instead. By the time Carson could pick up and throw another rock, the Roller was forty yards back from the barrier and going strong.

His second throw missed by feet, and his third throw was

short. The Roller was back out of range – at least out of range of a missile heavy enough to be damaging.

Carson grinned. That round had been his. Except—

He quit grinning as he bent over to examine the calf of his leg. A jagged edge of the stone had made a pretty deep cut, several inches long. It was bleeding pretty freely, but he didn't think it had gone deep enough to hit an artery. If it stopped bleeding of its own accord, well and good. If not, he was in for trouble.

Finding out one thing, though, took precedence over that cut. The nature of the barrier.

He went forward to it again, this time groping with his hands before him. He found it; then, holding one hand against it, he tossed a handful of sand at it with the other hand. The sand went through. His hand didn't.

Organic matter versus inorganic? No, because the dead lizard had gone through it, and a lizard, alive or dead, was certainly organic. Plant life? He broke off a twig and poked it at the barrier. The twig went through, with no resistance, but when his fingers gripping the twig came to the barrier they were stopped.

*He* couldn't get through it, nor could the Roller. But rocks and sand and a dead lizard—

How about a live lizard? He went hunting, under bushes, until he found one, and caught it. He tossed it gently against the barrier and it bounced back and scurried away across the blue sand.

That gave him the answer, in so far as he could determine it now. The screen was a barrier to living things. Dead or inorganic matter could cross it.

That off his mind, Carson looked at his injured leg again. The bleeding was lessening, which meant he wouldn't need to worry about making a tourniquet. But he should find some water, if any was available, to clean the wound.

Water – the thought of it made him realize that he was getting awfully thirsty. He'd *have* to find water, in case this contest turned out to be a protracted one.

Limping slightly now, he started off to make a full circuit of his half of the arena. Guiding himself with one hand along the barrier, he walked to his right until he came to the curving side-wall. It was visible, a dull blue-grey at close range, and the surface of it felt just like the central barrier.

He experimented by tossing a handful of sand at it, and the sand reached the wall and disappeared as it went through. The hemispherical shell was a force-field, too. But an opaque one, instead of transparent like the barrier.

He followed it around until he came back to the barrier, and walked back along the barrier to the point from which he'd started.

No sign of water.

Worried now, he started a series of zigzags back and forth between the barrier and the wall, covering the intervening space thoroughly.

No water. Blue sand, blue bushes and intolerable heat. Nothing else.

It must be his imagination, he told himself angrily, that he was suffering *that* much from thirst. How long had he been there? Of course, no time at all, according to his own space-time frame. The Entity had told him time stood still out there, while he was here. But his body processes went on here, just the same. And, according to his body's reckoning, how long had he been here? Three or four hours, perhaps. Certainly not long enough to be suffering seriously from thirst.

But he was suffering from it; his throat dry and parched. Probably the intense heat was the cause. It was *hot*! A hundred and thirty Fahrenheit, at a guess. A dry, still heat without the slightest movement of air.

He was limping rather badly, and utterly fagged out when he'd finished the futile exploration of his domain.

He stared across at the motionless Roller and hoped it was as miserable as he was. And quite possibly it wasn't enjoying this,

either. The Entity had said the conditions here were equally unfamiliar and equally uncomfortable for both of them. Maybe
the Roller came from a planet where two-hundred-degree heat
was the norm. Maybe it was freezing while he was roasting.

Maybe the air was as much too thick for it as it was too thin
for him. For the exertion of his explorations had left him panting. The atmosphere here, he realized now, was not much thicker
than that on Mars.

No water.

That meant a deadline, for him at any rate. Unless he could
find a way to cross that barrier or to kill his enemy from this side
of it, thirst would kill him eventually.

It gave him a feeling of desperate urgency. He *must* hurry.

But he made himself sit down a moment to rest, to think.

What was there to do? Nothing, and yet so many things. The
several varieties of bushes, for example. They didn't look promising, but he'd have to examine them for possibilities. And his
leg – he'd have to do something about that, even without water
to clean it. Gather ammunition in the form of rocks. Find a rock
that would make a good knife.

His leg hurt rather badly now, and he decided that came first.
One type of bush had leaves – or things rather similar to leaves.
He pulled off a handful of them and decided, after examination,
to take a chance on them. He used them to clean off the sand
and dirt and caked blood, then made a pad of fresh leaves and
tied it over the wound with tendrils from the same bush.

The tendrils proved unexpectedly tough and strong. They
were slender, and soft and pliable, yet he couldn't break them
at all. He had to saw them off the bush with the sharp edge of a
piece of the blue flint. Some of the thicker ones were over a foot
long, and he filed away in his memory, for future reference, the
fact that a bunch of the thick ones, tied together, would make a
pretty serviceable rope. Maybe he'd be able to think of a use for
rope.

Next, he made himself a knife. The blue flint *did* chip. From a foot-long splinter of it he fashioned himself a crude but lethal weapon. And of tendrils from the bush he made himself a rope-belt through which he could thrust the flint knife, to keep it with him all the time and yet have his hands free.

He went back to studying the bushes. There were three other types. One was leafless, dry, brittle, rather like a dried tumble-weed. Another was of soft, crumbly wood, almost like punk. It looked and felt as though it would make excellent tinder for a fire. The third type was the most nearly wood-like. It had fragile leaves that wilted at the touch, but the stalks, although short, were straight and strong.

It was horribly, unbearably hot.

He limped up to the barrier, felt to make sure that it was still there. It was.

He stood watching the Roller for a while. It was keeping a safe distance back from the barrier, out of effective stone-throwing range. It was moving around back there, doing something. He couldn't tell what it was doing.

Once it stopped moving, came a little closer, and seemed to concentrate its attention on him. Again Carson had to fight off a wave of nausea. He threw a stone at it and the Roller retreated and went back to whatever it had been doing before.

At least he could make it keep its distance.

And, he thought bitterly, a devil of a lot of good *that* did him. Just the same, he spent the next hour or two gathering stones of suitable size for throwing, and making several neat piles of them near his side of the barrier.

His throat burned now. It was difficult for him to think about anything except water.

But he *had* to think about other things. About getting through that barrier, under or over it, getting *at* that red sphere and killing it before this place of heat and thirst killed him first.

The barrier went to the wall upon either side, but how high and how far under the sand?

For just a moment, Carson's mind was too fuzzy to think out how he could find out either of those things. Idly, sitting there in the hot sand – and he didn't remember sitting down – he watched a blue lizard crawl from the shelter of one bush to the shelter of another.

From under the second bush, it looked out at him.

Carson grinned at it. Maybe he was getting a bit punch-drunk, because he remembered suddenly the old story of the desert-colonists on Mars, taken from an older desert story of Earth – 'Pretty soon you get so lonesome you find yourself talking to the lizards, and then not so long after that you find the lizards talking back to you—'

He should have been concentrating, of course, on how to kill the Roller, but instead he grinned at the lizard and said, 'Hello, there.'

The lizard took a few steps towards him. 'Hello,' it said.

Carson was stunned for a moment, and then he put back his head and roared with laughter. It didn't hurt his throat to do so, either; he hadn't been *that* thirsty.

Why not? Why should the Entity who thought up this nightmare of a place not have a sense of humour, along with the other powers he has? Talking lizards, equipped to talk back in my own language, if I talk to them. It's a nice touch.

He grinned at the lizard and said, 'Come on over.' But the lizard turned and ran away, scurrying from bush to bush until it was out of sight.

He was thirsty again.

And he had to *do* something. He couldn't win this contest by sitting here sweating and feeling miserable. He had to *do* something. But what?

Get through the barrier. But he couldn't get through it, or over it. But was he certain he couldn't get under it? And, come to think of it, didn't one sometimes find water by digging? Two birds with one stone.

Painfully now, Carson limped up to the barrier and started digging, scooping up sand a double handful at a time. It was slow, hard work because the sand ran in at the edges and the deeper he got the bigger in diameter the hole had to be. How many hours it took him, he didn't know, but he hit bedrock four feet down. Dry bedrock; no sign of water.

And the force-field of the barrier went down clear to the bedrock. No dice. No water. Nothing.

He crawled out of the hole and lay there panting, and then raised his head to look across and see what the Roller was doing. It must be doing something back there.

It was. It was making something out of wood from the bushes, tied together with tendrils. A queerly shaped framework about four feet high and roughly square. To see it better, Carson climbed up on to the mound of sand he had excavated from the hole, and stood there staring.

There were two long levers sticking out of the back of it, one with a cup-shaped affair on the end of it. Seemed to be some sort of a catapult, Carson thought.

Sure enough, the Roller was lifting a sizeable rock into the cup-shaped outfit. One of his tentacles moved the other lever up and down for a while, and then he turned the machine slightly as though aiming it and the lever with the stone flew up and forward.

The stone arced several yards over Carson's head, so far away that he didn't have to duck, but he judged the distance it had travelled, and whistled softly. He couldn't throw a rock that weight more than half that distance. And even retreating to the rear of his domain wouldn't put him out of range of that machine, if the Roller shoved it forward almost to the barrier.

Another whizzed over. Not quite so far away this time.

That thing could be dangerous, he decided. Maybe he'd better do something about it.

Moving from side to side along the barrier, so the catapult couldn't bracket him, he whaled a dozen rocks at it. But that wasn't going to be any good, he saw. They had to be light rocks, or he couldn't throw them that far. If they hit the framework, they bounced off harmlessly. And the Roller had no difficulty, at that distance, in moving aside from those that came near it.

Besides, his arm was tiring badly. He ached all over from sheer weariness. If he could only rest a while without having to duck rocks from that catapult at regular intervals of maybe thirty seconds each. . . .

He stumbled back to the rear of the arena. Then he saw even that wasn't any good. The rocks reached back there, too, only there were longer intervals between them, as though it took longer to wind up the mechanism, whatever it was, of the catapult.

Wearily he dragged himself back to the barrier again. Several times he fell and could barely rise to his feet to go on. He was, he knew, near the limit of his endurance. Yet he didn't dare stop moving now, until and unless he could put that catapult out of action. If he fell asleep, he'd never wake up.

One of the stones from it gave him the glimmer of an idea. It struck upon one of the piles of stones he'd gathered together near the barrier to use as ammunition, and it struck sparks.

Sparks. Fire. Primitive man had made fire by striking sparks, and with some of those dry crumbly bushes as tinder. . . .

Luckily, a bush of that type was near him. He broke it off, took it over to the pile of stones, then patiently hit one stone against another until a spark touched the punk-like wood of the bush. It went up in flames so fast that it singed his eyebrows and was burned to an ash within seconds.

But he had the idea now, and within minutes he had a little fire going in the lee of the mound of sand he'd made digging the hole an hour or two ago. Tinder bushes had started it, and other bushes which burned, but more slowly, kept it a steady flame.

The tough wire-like tendrils didn't burn readily; that made the fire-bombs easy to make and throw. A bundle of faggots tied about a small stone to give it weight and a loop of the tendril to swing it by.

He made half a dozen of them before he lighted and threw the first. It went wide, and the Roller started a quick retreat, pulling the catapult after him. But Carson had the others ready and threw them in rapid succession. The fourth wedged in the catapult's framework, and it did the trick. The Roller tried desperately to put out the spreading blaze by throwing sand, but its clawed tentacles would take only a spoonful at a time and his efforts were ineffectual. The catapult burned.

The Roller moved safely away from the fire and seemed to concentrate its attention on Carson and again he felt that wave of hatred and nausea. But more weakly; either the Roller itself was weakening or Carson had learned how to protect himself against the mental attack.

He thumbed his nose at it and then sent it scuttling back to safety by throwing a stone. The Roller went clear to the back of its half of the arena and started pulling up bushes again. Probably to make another catapult.

Carson verified – for the hundredth time – that the barrier was still operating, and then found himself sitting in the sand beside it because he was suddenly too weak to stand up.

His leg throbbed steadily now and the pangs of thirst were severe. But those things paled beside the utter physical exhaustion that gripped his entire body.

And the heat.

Hell must be like this, he thought. The hell that the ancients had believed in. He fought to stay awake, and yet staying awake seemed futile, for there was nothing he could do. Nothing, while the barrier remained impregnable and the Roller stayed back out of range.

But there must be *something*. He tried to remember things he had read in books of archaeology about the methods of fighting used back in the days before metal and plastic. The stone missile, that had come first, he thought. Well, that he already had.

The only improvement on it would be a catapult, such as the Roller had made. But he'd never be able to make one, with the tiny bits of wood available from the bushes – no single piece longer than a foot or so. Certainly he could figure out a mechanism for one, but he didn't have the endurance left for a task that would take days.

Days? But the Roller had made one. Had they been here days already? Then he remembered that the Roller had many tentacles to work with and undoubtedly could do such work faster than he.

And, besides, a catapult wouldn't decide the issue. He had to do better than that.

Bow and arrow? No; he'd tried archery once and knew his own ineptness with a bow. Even with a modern sportsman's durasteel weapon, made for accuracy. With such a crude, pieced-together outfit as he could make here, he doubted if he could shoot as far as he could throw a rock, and knew he couldn't shoot as straight.

Spear? Well, he *could* make that. It would be useless at any distance, but would be a handy thing at close range, if he ever got to close range.

And making one would give him something to do. Help keep his mind from wandering, as it was beginning to do. Sometimes now he had to concentrate a while before he could remember why he was here, why he had to kill the Roller.

Luckily he was still beside one of the piles of stones. He sorted through it until he found one shaped roughly like a spearhead. With a smaller stone he began to chip it into shape, fashioning sharp shoulders on the sides so that if it penetrated it would not pull out again.

Like a harpoon? There was something in that idea, he thought. A harpoon was better than a spear, maybe, for this crazy contest. If he could once get it into the Roller, and had a rope on it, he could pull the Roller up against the barrier and the stone blade of his knife would reach through that barrier, even if his hands wouldn't.

The shaft was harder to make than the head. But by splitting and joining the main stems of four of the bushes, and wrapping the joints with the tough but thin tendrils, he got a strong shaft about four feet long, and tied the stone head in a notch cut in the end.

It was crude, but strong.

And the rope. With the thin tough tendrils he made himself twenty feet of line. It was light and didn't look strong, but he knew it would hold his weight and to spare. He tied one end of it to the shaft of the harpoon and the other end about his right wrist. At least, if he threw his harpoon across the barrier, he'd be able to pull it back if he missed.

Then, when he had tied the last knot and there was nothing more he could do, the heat and the weariness and the pain in his leg and the dreadful thirst were suddenly a thousand times worse than they had been before.

He tried to stand up, to see what the Roller was doing now, and found he couldn't get to his feet. On the third try, he got as far as his knees and then fell flat again.

'I've got to sleep,' he thought. 'If a showdown came now, I'd be helpless. He could come up here and kill me, if he knew. I've got to regain some strength.'

Slowly, painfully, he crawled back from the barrier. Ten yards, twenty—

The jar of something thudding against the sand near him waked him from a confused and horrible dream to a more confused and more horrible reality, and he opened his eyes again to blue radiance over blue sand.

How long had he slept? A minute? A day?

Another stone thudded nearer and threw sand on him. He got his arms under him and sat up. He turned around and saw the Roller twenty yards away, at the barrier.

It rolled away hastily as he sat up, not stopping until it was as far away as it could get.

He'd fallen asleep too soon, he realized, while he was still in range of the Roller's throwing ability. Seeing him lying motionless, it had dared come up to the barrier to throw at him. Luckily, it didn't realize how weak he was, or it could have stayed there and kept on throwing stones.

Had he slept long? He didn't think so, because he felt just as he had before. Not rested at all, no thirstier, no different. Probably he'd been there only a few minutes.

He started crawling again, this time forcing himself to keep going until he was as far as he could go, until the colourless, opaque wall of the arena's outer shell was only a yard away.

Then things slipped away again.

*     *     *

When he awoke, nothing about him was changed, but this time he knew that he had slept a long time.

The first thing he became aware of was the inside of his mouth; it was dry, caked. His tongue was swollen.

Something was wrong, he knew, as he returned slowly to full awareness. He felt less tired, the stage of utter exhaustion had passed. The sleep had taken care of that.

But there was pain, agonizing pain. It wasn't until he tried to move that he knew that it came from his leg.

He raised his head and looked down at it. It was swollen terribly below the knee, and the swelling showed even halfway up his thigh. The plant tendrils he had used to tie on the protective pad of leaves now cut deeply into the swollen flesh.

To get his knife under that imbedded lashing would have been impossible. Fortunately, the final knot was over the shin bone, in front, where the vine cut in less deeply than elsewhere. He was able, after an agonizing effort, to untie the knot.

A look under the pad of leaves told him the worst. Infection and blood poisoning, both pretty bad and getting worse.

And without drugs, without cloth, without even *water*, there wasn't a thing he could do about it.

Not a thing, except *die*, when the poison had spread through his system.

He knew it was hopeless, then, and that he'd lost.

And, with him, humanity. When he died here, out there in the universe, he knew, all his friends, everybody, would die too. And Earth and the colonized planets would be the home of the red, rolling, alien Outsiders. Creatures out of nightmare, things without a human attribute, who picked lizards apart for the fun of it.

It was the thought of that which gave him courage to start crawling, almost blindly in pain, toward the barrier again. Not crawling on hands and knees this time, but pulling himself along by his arms and hands.

A chance in a million, that maybe he'd have strength left, when he got there, to throw his harpoon-spear just *once*, and with deadly effect, if – on another chance in a million – the Roller would come up to the barrier. Or if the barrier was gone now.

It took him years, it seemed, to get there.

The barrier wasn't gone. It was as impassable as when he'd first felt it.

And the Roller wasn't at the barrier. By raising up on his elbows, he could see it at the back of its part of the arena, working on a wooden framework that was a half-completed duplicate of the catapult he'd destroyed.

It was moving slowly now. Undoubtedly it had weakened, too.

But Carson doubted that it would ever need that second catapult. He'd be dead, he thought, before it was finished.

If he could attract it to the barrier, now, while he was still alive. . . . He waved an arm and tried to shout, but his parched throat would make no sound.

Or if he could get through the barrier. . . .

His mind must have slipped for a moment, for he found himself beating his fists against the barrier in futile rage, and made himself stop.

He closed his eyes, tried to make himself calm.

'Hello,' said a voice.

It was a small, thin voice. It sounded like—

He opened his eyes and turned his head. It *was* a lizard.

'Go away,' Carson wanted to say. 'Go away; you're not really there, or you're there but not really talking. I'm imagining things again.'

But he couldn't talk; his throat and tongue were past all speech with the dryness. He closed his eyes again.

'Hurt,' said the voice. 'Kill. Hurt – kill. Come.'

He opened his eyes again. The blue ten-legged lizard was still there. It ran a little way along the barrier, came back, started off again and came back.

'Hurt,' it said. 'Kill. Come.'

Again it started off and came back. Obviously it wanted Carson to follow it along the barrier.

He closed his eyes again. The voice kept on. The same three

meaningless words. Each time he opened his eyes, it ran off and came back.

'Hurt. Kill. Come.'

Carson groaned. There would be no peace unless he followed the blasted thing. Like it wanted him to.

He followed it, crawling. Another sound, a high-pitched squealing, came to his ears and grew louder.

There was something lying in the sand, writhing, squealing. Something small, blue, that looked like a lizard and yet didn't—

Then he saw what it was – the lizard whose legs the Roller had pulled off, so long ago. But it wasn't dead; it had come back to life and was wriggling and screaming in agony.

'Hurt,' said the other lizard. 'Hurt. Kill. Kill.'

Carson understood. He took the flint knife from his belt and killed the tortured creature. The live lizard scurried off quickly.

Carson turned back to the barrier. He leaned his hands and head against it and watched the Roller, far back, working on the new catapult.

'I could get that far,' he thought, 'if I could get through. If I could get through, I might win yet. It looks weak, too. I might—'

And then there was another reaction of black hopelessness, when pain sapped his will and he wished that he were dead. He envied the lizard he'd just killed. It didn't have to live on and suffer. And he did. It would be hours, it might be days, before the blood poisoning killed him.

If only he could use that knife on himself. . . .

But he knew he wouldn't. As long as he was alive, there was the millionth chance. . . .

He was straining, pushing on the barrier with the flat of his hands, and he noticed his arms, how thin and scrawny they were now. He must really have been here a long time, for days, to get as thin as that.

How much longer now, before he died? How much more heat and thirst and pain could flesh stand?

For a little while he was almost hysterical again, and then

came a time of deep calm, and a thought that was startling.

The lizard he had just killed. *It had crossed the barrier, still alive*. It had come from the Roller's side; the Roller had pulled off its legs and then tossed it contemptuously at him and it had come through the barrier. He'd thought, because the lizard was dead.

But it hadn't been dead, it had been unconscious.

A live lizard couldn't go through the barrier, but an unconscious one could. The barrier was not a barrier, then, to living flesh, but to conscious flesh. It was a *mental* projection, a *mental* hazard.

And with that thought Carson started crawling along the barrier to make his last desperate gamble. A hope so forlorn that only a dying man would have dared try it.

No use weighing the odds of success. Not when, if he didn't try it, those odds were infinitely to zero.

He crawled along the barrier to the dune of sand, about four feet high, which he'd scooped out in trying – how many days ago? – to dig under the barrier or to reach water.

That mound was right at the barrier, its farther slope half on one side of the barrier, half on the other.

Taking with him a rock from the pile nearby, he climbed up to the top of the dune and over the top, and lay there against the barrier, his weight leaning against it so that if the barrier were taken away he'd roll on down the short slope, into the enemy territory.

He checked to be sure that the knife was safely in his rope belt, that the harpoon was in the crook of his left arm and that the twenty-foot rope was fastened to it and to his wrist.

Then with his right hand he raised the rock with which he would hit himself on the head. Luck would have to be with him on that blow; it would have to be hard enough to knock him out, but not hard enough to knock him out for long.

He had a hunch that the Roller was watching him, and would see him roll down through the barrier, and come to investigate. It would think he was dead, he hoped – he thought it had prob-

ably drawn the same deduction about the nature of the barrier
that he had drawn. But it would come cautiously. He would
have a little time....

He struck.

Pain brought him back to consciousness. A sudden, sharp pain
in his hip that was different from the throbbing pain in his head
and the throbbing pain in his leg.

But he had, thinking things out before he had struck himself,
anticipated that very pain, even hoped for it, and had steeled
himself against awakening with a sudden movement.

He lay still, but opened his eyes just a slit, and saw that he had
guessed rightly. The Roller was coming closer. It was twenty feet
away and the pain that had awakened him was the stone it had
tossed to see whether he was alive or dead.

He lay still. It came closer, fifteen feet away, and stopped
again. Carson scarcely breathed.

As nearly as possible, he was keeping his mind a blank, lest
its telepathic ability detect consciousness in him. And, with his
mind blanked out that way, the impact of its thoughts upon his
mind was nearly soul-shattering.

He felt sheer horror at the utter *alienness*, the *differentness* of
those thoughts. Things that he felt but could not understand and
could never express, because no terrestrial language had words,
no terrestrial mind had images to fit them. The mind of a spider,
he thought, or the mind of a praying mantis or a Martian sand-
serpent, raised to intelligence and put in telepathic rapport with
human minds, would be a homely familiar thing, compared to
this.

He understood now that the Entity had been right: Man or
Roller, and the universe was not a place that could hold them
both. Farther apart than god and devil, there could never be
even a balance between them.

Closer. Carson waited until it was only feet away, until its
clawed tentacles reached out—

Oblivious to agony now, he sat up, raised and flung the harpoon with all the strength that remained to him. Or he thought

it was all; sudden final strength flooded through him, along with a sudden forgetfulness of pain as definite as a nerve block.

As the Roller, deeply stabbed by the harpoon, rolled away, Carson tried to get to his feet to run after it. He couldn't do that; he fell, but kept crawling.

It reached the end of the rope, and he was jerked forward by the pull on his wrist. It dragged him a few feet and then stopped. Carson kept on going, pulling himself toward it hand over hand along the rope.

It stopped there, writhing tentacles trying in vain to pull out the harpoon. It seemed to shudder and quiver, and then it must have realized that it couldn't get away, for it rolled back toward him, clawed tentacles reaching out.

Stone knife in hand, he met it. He stabbed, again and again, while those horrid claws ripped skin and flesh and muscle from his body.

He stabbed and slashed, and at last it was still.

A bell was ringing, and it took him a while after he'd opened his eyes to tell where he was and what it was. He was strapped into the seat of his scouter, and the visiplate before him showed only empty space. No Outsider ship and no impossible planet.

The bell was the communications-plate signal; someone wanted him to switch power into the receiver. Purely reflex action enabled him to reach forward and throw the lever.

The face of Brander, captain of the *Magellan*, mother-ship of his group of scouters, flashed into the screen. His face was pale and his black eyes glowing with excitement.

'*Magellan* to Carson,' he snapped. 'Come on in. The fight's over. We've won!'

The screen went blank; Brander would be signalling the other scouters of his command.

Slowly Carson set the controls for the return. Slowly, unbelievingly he unstrapped himself from the seat and went back to get a drink at the cold-water tank. For some reason, he was unbelievably thirsty. He drank six glasses.

He leaned there against the wall, trying to think.

*Had* it happened? He was in good health, sound, uninjured. His thirst had been mental rather than physical; his throat hadn't been dry. His leg—

He pulled up his trouser leg and looked at the calf. There was a long white scar there, but a perfectly healed scar. It hadn't been there before. He zipped open the front of his shirt and saw that his chest and abdomen were criss-crossed with tiny, almost unnoticeable, perfectly healed scars.

It *had* happened.

The scouter, under automatic control, was already entering the hatch of the mother-ship. The grapples pulled it into its individual lock, and a moment later a buzzer indicated that the lock was air-filled. Carson opened the hatch and stepped outside, went through the double door of the lock.

He went right to Brander's office, went in, and saluted.

Brander still looked dizzily dazed. 'Hi, Carson,' he said. 'What you missed! What a show!'

'What happened, sir?'

'Don't know exactly. We fired one salvo, and their whole fleet went up in dust! Whatever it was jumped from ship to ship in a flash, even the ones we hadn't aimed at and that were out of range! The whole fleet disintegrated before our eyes, and we didn't get the paint of a single ship scratched!

'We can't even claim credit for it. Must have been some unstable component in the metal they used, and our sighting shot just set it off. Man, oh, man, too bad you missed all the excitement.'

Carson managed to grin. It was a sickly ghost of a grin, for it would be days before he'd be over the mental impact of his experience, but the captain wasn't watching and didn't notice.

'Yes, sir,' he said. Common sense, more than modesty, told him he'd be branded forever as the worst liar in space if he ever said any more than that. 'Yes, sir, too bad I missed all the excitement.'

# Hal Clement
# Fireproof

Hart waited a full hour after the last sounds had died away before cautiously opening the cover of his refuge. Even then he did not feel secure for some minutes, until he had made a thorough search of the storage chamber; then a smile of contempt curled his lips.

'The fools!' he muttered. 'They do not examine their shipments at all. How do they expect to maintain their zone controls with such incompetents in charge?' He glanced at the analysers in the forearm of his spacesuit, and revised his opinion a trifle – the air in the chamber was pure carbon dioxide; any man attempting to come as Hart had, but without his own air supply, would not have survived the experiment. Still, the agent felt, they should have searched.

There was, however, no real time for analysing the actions of others. He had a job to do, and not too long in which to do it. However slack the organization of this launching station might be, there was no chance whatever of reaching any of its vital parts unchallenged; and after the first challenge success and death would be running a frightfully close race.

He glided back to the crate which had barely contained his doubled-up body, carefully replaced and resealed the cover, and then rearranged the contents of the chamber to minimize the chance of that crate's being opened first. The containers were bulky, but nothing in the free-falling station had any weight, and the job did not take long even for a man unaccustomed to a total lack of apparent gravity. Satisfied with these precautions, Hart approached the door of the storeroom; but before opening it he stopped to review his plan.

He must, of course, be near the outer shell of the station. Central Intelligence had been unable to obtain plans of this launcher – a fact which should have given him food for thought – but there was no doubt about its general design. Storage and living quarters would be just inside the surface of the sphere; then would come a level of machine shops and control systems; and at the heart, within the shielding that represented most of the station's mass, would be the 'hot' section – the chambers containing the fission piles and power plants, the extractors and the remote-controlled machinery that loaded the warheads of the torpedoes which were the main reason for the station's existence.

There were many of these structures circling Earth; every nation on the globe maintained at least one, and usually several. Hart had visited one of those belonging to his own country, partly for technical familiarity and partly to accustom himself to weightlessness. He had studied its plans with care, and scientists had carefully explained to him the functions of each part, and the ways in which the launchers of the Western Alliance were likely to differ. Most important, they had described to him several ways by which such structures might be destroyed. Hart's smile was wolfish as he thought of that; these people who preferred the pleasures of personal liberty to those of efficiency would see what efficiency could do.

But this delay was not efficient. He had made his plans long before, and it was more than time to set about their execution. He must be reasonably near a store of rocket fuel; and some at least of the air in this station must contain a breathable percentage of oxygen. Without further deliberation, he opened the door and floated out into the corridor.

He did not go blindly. Tiny detectors built into the wrists of his suit reacted to the infra-red radiations, the water vapour and carbon dioxide and even the breathing sounds that would herald the approach of a human being – unless he were wearing a nonmetallic suit similar to Hart's own. Apparently the personnel of the base did not normally wear these, however, for twice in the first ten minutes the saboteur was warned into shelter by the indications of the tiny instruments. In that ten minutes he covered a good deal of the outer zone.

He learned quickly that the area in which a carbon-dioxide atmosphere was maintained was quite limited in extent, and probably constituted either a quarantine zone for newly arrived supplies, or a food storage area. It was surrounded by an un-interrupted corridor lined on one side with airtight doors lead-ing into the $CO_2$ rooms, and on the other by flimsier portals closing off other storage spaces. Hart wondered briefly at the reason for such a vast amount of storage room; then his atten-tion was taken by another matter. He had been about to launch himself in another long, weightless glide down the corridor in search of branch passages which might lead to the rocket fuel stores, when a tiny spot on one wall caught his eye.

He instantly went to examine it more closely, and as quickly recognized a photoelectric eye. There appeared to be no lens, which suggested a beam-interruption unit; but the beam itself was not visible, nor could he find any projector. That meant a rather interesting and vital problem lay in avoiding the ray. He stopped to think.

In the scanning-room on the second level, Dr Bruce Mayhew chuckled aloud.

'It's wonderful what a superiority complex can do. He's stop-ped for the first time – didn't seem to have any doubts of his safety until he spotted that eye. The old oil about "decadent democracies" seems to have taken deep hold somewhere, at least. He must be a military agent rather than a scientist.'

Warren Floyd nodded. 'Let's not pull the same boner, though,' he suggested. 'Scientist or not, no stupid man would have been chosen for such a job. Do you think he's carrying explosives? One man could hardly have chemicals enough to make a signi-ficant number of breaches in the outer shell.'

'He may be hoping to get into the core, to set off a warhead,' replied the older man, 'though I don't for the life of me see how he expects to do it. There's a rocket fuel in his neighbourhood, of course, but it's just n.v. for the torpedoes – harmless, as far as we're concerned.'

'A fire could be quite embarrassing, even if it weren't an explosion,' pointed out his assistant, 'particularly since the whole joint is nearly pure magnesium. I know it's sinfully expensive to transport mass away from Earth, but I wish they had built this place out of something a little less responsive to heat and oxygen.'

'I shouldn't worry about that,' replied Mayhew. 'He won't get a fire started.'

Floyd glanced at the flanking screens which showed armoured men keeping pace with the agent in parallel corridors, and nodded. 'I suppose not – provided Ben and his crew aren't too slow closing in when we give the signal.'

'You mean when *I* give the signal,' returned the other man. 'I have reasons for wanting him free as long as possible. The longer he's free, the lower the opinion he'll have of us; when we do take him, he'll be less ready to commit suicide, and the sudden letdown of his self-confidence will make interrogation easier.'

Floyd privately hoped nothing would happen to deflate his superior's own self-confidence, but wisely said nothing; and both men watched Hart's progress almost silently for some minutes. Floyd occasionally transmitted a word or two to the action party to keep them apprised of their quarry's whereabouts, but no other sound interrupted the vigil.

Hart had finally found a corridor which branched away from the one he had been following, and he proceeded cautiously along it. He had learned the intervals at which the photocells were spotted, and now avoided them almost automatically. It did not occur to him that, while the sight of a spacesuited man in the outer corridors might not surprise an observer, the presence of such a man who failed consistently to break the beams of the photocell spotters would be bound to attract attention. The lenses of the scanners were too small and too well hidden for Hart to find easily, and he actually believed that the photocells were the only traps. With his continued ease in avoiding them, his self-confidence and contempt for the Westerners were mounting as Mayhew had foretold.

Several times he encountered air breaks – sliding bulkheads actuated by automatic pressure-controlled switches, designed to cut off any section with a bad air-leak. His action at each of these was the same; from an outer pocket of his armour he would take a small wedge of steel and skilfully jam the door. It was this action which convinced Mayhew that the agent was not a scientist – he was displaying the skill of an experienced burglar or spy. He was apparently well supplied with the wedges, for in the hour before he found what he was seeking he jammed more than twenty of the air breaks. Mayhew and Floyd did not bother to have them cleared at the time, since no one was in the outer level without a spacesuit.

Nearly half of the outer level was thus unified when Hart reached a section of corridor bearing valve handles and hose connections instead of doors, and knew there must be liquids behind the walls. There were code indexes stencilled over the valves, which meant nothing to the spy; but he carefully manipulated one of the two handles to let a little fluid into the corridor, and sniffed at it cautiously through the gingerly cracked face-plate of his helmet. He was satisfied with the results; the liquid was one of the low-volatility hydrocarbons used with liquid oxygen as a fuel to provide the moderate acceleration demanded by space-launched torpedoes. They were cheap, fairly dense, and their low vapour-pressure simplified the storage problem in open-space stations.

All that Hart really knew about it was that the stuff would burn as long as there was oxygen. Well – he grinned again at the thought – there would be oxygen for a while; until the compressed, blazing combustion gases blew the heat-softened metal of the outer wall into space. After that there would be none, except perhaps in the central core, where the heavy concentration of radioactive matter made it certain there would be no one to breathe it.

At present, of course, the second level and any other intermediate ones were still sealed; but that could and would be remedied. In any case, the blast of the liberated fuel would probably take care of the relatively flimsy inner walls. He did not at that time realize that these were of magnesium, or he would have felt even more sure of the results.

He looked along the corridor. As far as the curvature of the outer shell permitted him to see, the valves projected from the wall at intervals of a few yards. Each valve had a small electric pump, designed to force air into the tank behind it to drive the liquid out by pressure, since there was no gravity. Hart did not consider this point at all; a brief test showed him that the liquid did flow when the valve was on, and that was enough for him. Hanging poised beside the first handle, he took an object from still another pocket of his spacesuit, and checked it carefully, finally clipping it to an outside belt where it could easily be reached.

At the sight of this item of apparatus, Floyd almost suffered a stroke.

'That's an incendiary bomb!' he gasped aloud. 'We can't possibly take him in time to stop his setting it off – which he'll do the instant he sees our men! And he already has free fuel in the corridor!'

He was perfectly correct; the agent was proceeding from valve to valve in long glides, pausing at each just long enough to turn it full on and to scatter the balloon-like mass of escaping liquid with a sweep of his arm. Gobbets and droplets of the inflammable stuff sailed lazily hither and yon through the air in his wake.

Mayhew calmly lighted a cigarette, unmindful of the weird appearance of the match flame driven toward his feet by the draft from the ceiling ventilators, and declined to move otherwise. 'Decidedly, no physicist,' he murmured. 'I suppose that's just as well – it's the military information the Army likes anyway. They certainly wouldn't have risked a researcher on this sort of job, so I never really did have a chance to get anything I wanted from him.'

'But what are we going to do?' Floyd was almost frantic. 'There's enough available energy loose in that corridor now to blast the whole outer shell off – and gallons more coming every second. I know you've been here a lot longer than I, but unless you can tell me how you expect to keep him from lighting that stuff up I'm getting into a suit right now!'

'If it blows, a suit won't help you,' pointed out the older man.

'I know that!' almost screamed Floyd, 'but what other chance is there? Why did you let him get so far?'

'There is still no danger,' Mayhew said flatly, 'whether you believe it or not. However, the fuel does cost money, and there'll be some work recovering it, so I don't see why he should be allowed to empty all the torpedo tanks. He's excited enough now, anyway.' He turned languidly to the appropriate microphone and gave the word to the action squad. 'Take him now. He seems to be without hand weapons, but don't count on it. He certainly has at least one incendiary bomb.' As an afterthought, he reached for another switch, and made sure the ventilators in the outer level were not operating; then he relaxed again and gave his attention to the scanner that showed the agent's activity. Floyd had switched to another pickup that covered a longer section of corridor, and the watchers saw the spacesuited attackers almost as soon as did Hart himself.

The European reacted to the sight at once – too rapidly, in fact, for the shift in his attention caused him to miss his grasp on the valve handle he sought and flounder helplessly through the air until he reached the next. Once anchored, however, he acted as he had planned, ignoring with commendable self-control the four armoured figures converging on him. A sharp twist turned the fuel valve on, sending a stream of oil mushrooming into the corridor; his left hand flashed to his belt, seized the tiny cylinder he had snapped there, jammed its end hard against the adjacent wall, and tossed the bomb gently back down the corridor. In one way his lack of weightless experience betrayed him; he allowed for a gravity pull that was not there. The bomb, in consequence, struck the 'ceiling' a few yards from his hand, and rebounded with a popping noise and a shower of sparks. It

drifted on down the corridor toward the floating globules of
hydrocarbon, and the glow of the sparks was suddenly replaced
by the eye-hurting radiance of thermite.

Floyd winced at the sight, and expected the attacking men to
make futile plunges after the blazing thing; but, though all were
within reach of walls, not one swerved from his course. Hart
made no effort to escape or fight; he watched the course of the
drifting bomb with satisfaction, and, like Floyd, expected in the
next few seconds to be engulfed in a sea of flame that would
remove the most powerful of the Western torpedo stations from
his country's path of conquest. Unlike Floyd, he was calm about
it, even when the men seized him firmly and began removing
equipment from his pockets. One unclamped and removed the
face-plate of his helmet; and even to that he made no resistance
– just watched in triumph as his missile drifted toward the nearest
globules of fuel.

It did not actually strike the first. It did not have to; while the
quantity of heat radiated by burning thermite is relatively small,
the temperature of the reaction is notoriously high – and the
temperature six inches from the bomb was well above the flash
point of the rocket fuel, comparatively non-volatile as it was.
Floyd saw the flash as its surface ignited, and closed his eyes.

Mayhew gave him four or five seconds before speaking, judging that that was probably about all the suspense the younger
man could stand.

'All right, ostrich,' he finally said quietly. 'I'm not an angel,
in case you were wondering. Why not use your eyes, and the
brain behind them?'

Floyd was far too disturbed to take offence at the last remark,
but he did cautiously follow Mayhew's advice about looking.
He found difficulty, however, in believing what his eyes and the
scanner showed him.

The group of five men was unchanged, except for the expression on the captive's now visible face. All were looking down
the corridor towards the point where the bomb was still burning; Lang's crew bore expressions of amusement on their faces,

while Hart wore a look of utter disbelief. Floyd, seeing what he saw, shared the expression.

The bomb had by now passed close to several of the floating spheres. Each had caught fire, as Floyd had seen – for a moment only. Now each was surrounded by a spherical, nearly opaque layer of some greyish substance that looked like a mixture of smoke and kerosene vapour; a layer that could not have been half an inch thick, as Floyd recalled the sizes of the original spheres. None was burning; each had effectively smothered itself out, and the young observer slowly realized just how and why as the bomb at last made a direct hit on a drop of fuel fully a foot in diameter.

Like the others, the globe flamed momentarily, and went out; but this time the sphere that appeared and grew around it was lighter in colour, and continued to grow for several seconds. Then there was a little, sputtering explosion, and a number of fragments of still burning thermite emerged from the surface of the sphere in several directions, travelled a few feet, and went out. All activity died down, except in the faces of Hart and Floyd.

The saboteur was utterly at a loss, and seemed likely to remain that way; but in the watch-room Floyd was already kicking himself mentally for his needless worry. Mayhew, watching the expression on his assistant's face, chuckled quietly.

'Of course you get it now,' he said at last.

'I do *now*, certainly,' replied Floyd. 'I should have seen it earlier – I've certainly noticed you light enough cigarettes, and watched the behaviour of the match flame. Apparently our friend is not yet enlightened, though,' he nodded toward the screen as he spoke.

He was right; Hart was certainly not enlightened. He belonged to a service in which unpleasant surprises were neither unexpected nor unusual, but he had never in his life been so completely disorganized. The stuff looked like fuel; it smelled like fuel; it had even started to burn – but it refused to carry on with the process. Hart simply relaxed in the grip of the guards, and tried to find something in the situation to serve as an anchor for his whirling thoughts. A spaceman would have understood the situation without thinking, a high-school student of reasonable intelligence could probably have worked the matter out in time; but Hart's education had been that of a spy, in a country which considered general education a waste of time. He simply did not have the background to cope with his present environment.

That, at least, was the idea Mayhew acquired after a careful questioning of the prisoner. Not much was learned about his intended mission, though there was little doubt about it under the circumstances. The presence of an alien agent aboard any of the free-floating torpedo-launchers of the various national governments bore only one interpretation; and, since the destruction of one such station would do little good to anyone, Mayhew at once radioed all other launchers to be on the alert for similar intruders – all others, regardless of nationality. Knowledge by Hart's superiors of his capture might prevent their acting on the assumption that he had succeeded, which would inevitably lead to some highly regrettable incidents. Mayhew's business was to prevent a war, not win one. Hart had not actually admitted the identity of his superiors, but his accent left the matter in little doubt; and, since no action was intended, Mayhew did not need proof.

There remained, of course, the problem of what to do with Hart. The structure had no ready-made prison, and it was unlikely that the Western government would indulge in the gesture of a special rocket to take the man off. Personal watch would be tedious, but it was unthinkable merely to deprive a man with the training Hart must have received of his equipment, and then assume he would not have to be watched every second.

The solution, finally suggested by one of the guards, was a small storeroom in the outer shell. It had no locks, but there were welding torches in the machine shops. There was no ventilator either, but an alga tank would take care of that. After consideration, Mayhew decided that this was the best plan, and it was promptly put into effect.

\* \* \*

Hart was thoroughly searched, even his clothing being replaced as a precautionary measure. He asked for his cigarettes and lighter; with a half-smile, Mayhew supplied the man with some of his own, and marked those of the spy for special investigation. Hart said nothing more after that, and was incarcerated without further ceremony. Mayhew was chuckling once more as the guards disappeared with their charge.

'I hope he gets more good than I out of that lighter,' he remarked. 'It's a wick-type my kid sent me as a present, and the ventilator draft doesn't usually keep it going. Maybe our friend will learn something, if he fools with it long enough. He has a pint of lighter fluid to experiment with – the kid had large ideas.'

'I was a little surprised – I thought for a moment you were giving him a pocket flask,' laughed Floyd. 'I suppose that's why you always use matches – they're easier to wave than that thing. I guess I save myself a lot of trouble not smoking at all. I suppose you have to put potassium nitrate in your cigarettes to keep 'em going when you're not pulling on them.' Floyd ducked as he spoke, but Mayhew didn't throw anything. Hart, of course, was out of hearing by this time, and would not have profited from the remark in any case.

He probably, in fact, would not have paid much attention. He knew, of course, that the sciences of physics and chemistry are important; but he thought of them in connection with great laboratories and factories. The idea that knowledge of either could be of immediate use to anyone not a chemist or physicist would have been fantastic to him. While his current plans for escape were based largely on chemistry, the connection did not occur to him. The only link between those plans and Mayhew's words or actions gave the spy some grim amusement; it was the fact that he did not smoke.

The cell, when he finally reached it, was perfectly satisfactory; there were no peep-holes which could serve as shot-holes, no way in which the door could be unsealed quickly – as Mayhew had said, not even a ventilator. Once he was in, Hart would not be interrupted without plenty of notice. Since the place was a storeroom, there was no reason to expect even a scanner though, he told himself, there was no reason to assume there was none, either. He simply disregarded that possibility, and went to work the moment he heard the torch start to seal his door.

His first idea did not get far. He spent half an hour trying to make Mayhew's lighter work, without noticeable success. Each spin of the 'flint' brought a satisfactory shower of sparks, and about every fourth or fifth try produced a faint 'pop' and a flash of blue fire; but he was completely unable to make a flame last. He closed the cover at last, and for the first time made an honest effort to think. The situation had got beyond the scope of his training.

He dismissed almost at once the matter of the rocket fuel that had not been ignited by his bomb. Evidently the Westerners stored it with some inhibiting chemical, probably as a precaution more against accident than sabotage. Such a chemical would have to be easily removable, but he had no means of knowing the method, and that line of attack would have to be abandoned.

But why wouldn't the lighter fuel burn? The more he thought the matter out, the more Hart felt that Mayhew must have doctored it deliberately, as a gesture of contempt. Such an act he could easily understand; and the thought of it roused again the wolfish hate that was such a prominent part of his personality. He would show that smart Westerner! There was certainly some way!

Powerful hands, and a fingernail deliberately hardened long since to act as a passable screw-driver blade, had the lighter disassembled in the space of a few minutes. The parts were disappointingly small in number and variety; but Hart considered each at length.

The fuel, already evaporating as it was, appeared useless – he was no chemist, and had satisfied himself the stuff was incombustible. The case was of magnalium, apparently, and might be useful as a heat source if it could be lighted; its use in a cigarette lighter did not encourage pursuit of that thought. The wick might be combustible, if thoroughly dried. The flint and wheel mechanism was promising – at least one part would be hard enough to cut or wear most metals, and the spring might be decidedly useful.

Elsewhere in the room there was very little. The light was a gas tube, and, since the chamber had no opening whatever, would probably be most useful as a light. The alga tank, of course, had a minute motor and pump which forced air through its liquid, and an ingenious valve and trap system which recovered the air even in the present weightless situation; but Hart, considering the small size of the room, decided that any attempt to dismantle his only source of fresh air would have to be very much of a last resort.

After much thought, and with a grimace of distaste, he took the tiny striker of the lighter and began slowly to abrade a circular area around the latch of the door, using the inside handle for anchorage.

He did not, of course, have any expectation of final escape; he was not in the least worried about his chances of recovering his spacesuit. He expected only to get out of the cell and complete his mission; and if he succeeded no possible armour would do him any good.

As it happened, there was a scanner in his compartment; but, Mayhew had long since grown tired of watching the spy try to ignite the lighter fuel, and had turned his attention elsewhere, so that Hart's actions were unobserved for some time. The door metal was thin and not particularly hard; and he was able without interference and with no worse trouble than severe finger-cramp to work out a hole large enough to show him another obstacle – instead of welding the door frame itself, his captors had place a rectangular steel bar across the portal and fastened it at points well to each side of the frame, out of the prisoner's reach. Hart stopped scraping as soon as he realized the extent of this barrier, and gave his mind to the new situation.

He might, conceivably, work a large enough hole through the door to pass his body without actually opening the portal; but his fingers were already stiff and cramped from the use made of the tiny striker, and it was beyond reason to expect that he would be left alone long enough to accomplish any such feat. Presumably they intended to feed him occasionally.

There was another reason for haste, as well, though he was forgetting it as his nose became accustomed to the taint in the air. The fluid, which he had permitted to escape while disassembling the lighter, was evaporating with fair speed, as it was far more volatile than the rocket fuel; and it was diffusing through the air of the little room. The alga tank removed only carbon dioxide, so that the air of the cell was acquiring an ever-greater concentration of hydrocarbon molecules. Prolonged breathing of such vapours is far from healthy, as Hart well knew; and escape from the room was literally the only way to avoid breathing the stuff.

What would eliminate a metal door – quickly? Brute force? He hadn't enough of it. Chemicals? He had none. Heat? The thought was intriguing and discouraging at the same time, after his recent experience with heat sources. Still, even if liquid fuels would not burn, perhaps other things would; there was the wicking from the lighter; a little floating cloud of metal particles around the scene of his work on the magnesium door; and the striking mechanism of the lighter.

He plucked the wicking out of the air where it had been floating, and began to unravel it – without fuel, as he realized, it would need every advantage in catching the sparks of the striker.

Then he wadded as much of the metallic dust as he could collect – which was not too much – into the wick, concentrating it heavily at one end and letting it thin out toward the more completely ravelled part.

Then he inspected the edges of the hole he had ground in the door, and with the striker roughened them even more on one side, so that a few more shavings of metal projected. To these he pressed the fuse, wedging it between the door and the steel bar just outside the hole, with the 'lighting' end projecting into the room. He inspected the work carefully, nodded in satisfaction, and began to reassemble the striker mechanism.

He did not, of course, expect that the steel bar would be melted or seriously weakened by an ounce or so of magnesium, but he did hope that the thin metal of the door itself would ignite.

Hart had the spark mechanism almost ready when his attention was distracted abruptly. Since the hole had been made, a very gentle current of air had been set up in the cell by the corridor ventilators beyond – a current in the nature of an eddy which tended to carry loose objects quite close to the hole. One of the loose objects in the room was a sphere comprised of the remaining lighter fluid, which had not yet evaporated. When Hart noticed the shimmering globe, it was scarcely a foot from his fuse, and drifting steadily nearer.

To him, that sphere of liquid was death to his plan; it would not burn itself, it probably would not let anything else burn either. If it touched and soaked his fuse, he would have to wait until it evaporated; and there might not be time for that. He released the striker with a curse, and swung his open hand at the drop, trying to drive it to one side. He succeeded only partly. It spattered on his hand, breaking up into scores of smaller drops, some of which moved obediently, while others just drifted, and still others vanished in vapour. None drifted far; and the gentle current had them in control almost at once, and began to bear many of them back toward the hole – and Hart's fuse.

For just a moment the saboteur hung there in agonized indecision, and then his training reasserted itself. With another curse he snatched at the striker, made sure it was ready for action, and turned to the hole in the door. It was at this moment that Mayhew chose to take another look at his captive.

As it happened, the lens of his scanner was so located that Hart's body covered the hole in the door; and, since the spy's back was toward him, the watcher could not tell precisely what he was doing. The air of purposefulness about the captive was so outstanding and so impressive, however, that Mayhew was reaching for a microphone to order a direct check on the cell when Hart spun the striker wheel.

Mayhew could not, of course, see just what the man had done, but the consequences were plain enough. The saboteur's body was flung away from the door and toward the scanner lens like a rag doll kicked by a mule. An orange blossom of flame outlined him for an instant; and in practically the same instant the screen went blank as a heavy shock wave shattered its pickup lens.

Mayhew, accustomed as he was to weightless manœuvring, never in his life travelled so rapidly as he did then. Floyd and several other crewmen, who saw him on the way, tried to follow; but he outstripped them all, and when they reached the site of Hart's prison Mayhew was hanging poised outside, staring at the door.

There was no need of removing the welded bar. The thin metal of the door had been split and curled outward fantastically; an opening quite large enough for any man's body yawned in it, though there was nothing more certain than the fact that Hart had not made use of this avenue of escape. His body was still in the cell, against the far wall; and even now the relatively strong currents from the hall ventilators did not move it. Floyd had a pretty good idea of what held it there, and did not care to look closely. He might be right.

Mayhew's voice broke the prolonged silence.

'He never did figure it out.'

'Just what let go, anyway?' asked Floyd.

'Well, the only combustible we know of in the cell was the lighter fluid. To blast like that, though, it must have been almost completely vapourized, and mixed with just the right amount of air – possible, I suppose, in a room like this. I don't understand why he let it all out, though.'

'He seems to have been using pieces of the lighter,' Floyd pointed out. 'The loose fuel was probably just a by-product of his activities. He was even duller than I, though. It took me long enough to realize that a fire needs air to burn – and can't set up convection currents to keep itself supplied with oxygen, when there is no gravity.'

'More accurately, when there is no *weight*,' interjected Mayhew. 'We are well within Earth's gravity field, but in free fall. Convection currents occur because the heated gas is *lighter* per unit volume than the rest, and rises. With no weight, and no "up", such currents are impossible.'

'In any case, he must have decided we were fooling him with non-combustible liquids.'

Mayhew replied slowly: 'People are born and brought up in a steady gravity field, and come to take all its manifestations for granted. It's extremely hard to foresee *all* the consequences which will arise when you dispense with it. I've been here for years, practically constantly, and still get caught sometimes when I'm tired or just waking up.'

'They should have sent a spaceman to do this fellow's job, I should think.'

'How would he have entered the station? A man is either a spy or a spaceman – to be both would mean he was too old for action at all, I should say. Both professions demand years of rigorous training, since habits rather than knowledge are required – habits like the one of always stopping within reach of a wall or other massive object.' There was a suspicion of the old chuckle in his voice as Mayhew spoke the final sentence, and it was followed by a roar of laughter from the other men. Floyd looked around, and blushed furiously.

He was, as he had suspected from the older man's humour, suspended helplessly in mid-air out of reach of every source of traction. Had there been anything solid around, he would probably have used it for concealment instead, anyway. He managed at last to join that laughter; but at its end he glanced once more into Hart's cell, and remarked, 'If this is the worst danger that inexperience lands on my head, I don't think I'll complain. Bruce, I want to go with you on your next leave to Earth; I simply must see you in a gravity field. I bet you won't wait for the ladder when we step off the rocket – though I guess it would be more fun to see you drop a dictionary on your toe. As you implied, habits are hard to break.'

# Paul Carter
# The last objective

For uncounted aeons the great beds of shale and limestone had known the stillness and the darkness of eternity. Now they trembled and shuddered to the passage of an invader; stirred and vibrated in sleepy protest at a disturbance not of Nature's making.

Tearing through the masses of soft rock, its great duralloy cutters screaming a hymn of hate into the crumbling crust, its caterpillar treads clanking and grinding over gravel shard. fresh-torn from their age-old strata, lurched a juggernaut – one of the underground cruisers of the Combined Western Powers. It was squat, ugly; the top of its great cutting head full forty feet above the clattering treads, its square stern rocking and swaying one hundred and fifty feet behind the diamond-hard prow. It was angular, windowless; there were ugly lumps just behind the shrieking blades which concealed its powerful armament.

It had been built for warfare in an age when the sea and air were ruled by insensate rocket projectiles which flashed through the skies to spend their atomic wrath upon objectives which had long since ceased to exist; where infantry no longer was Queen of Battles, since the ravages of combat had wiped out the armies which began the war. And floods of hard radiation, sterilizing whole populations and making hideous mutational horrors of many of those who were born alive, had prevented the conscription of fresh armies which might have won the war.

The conflict had been going on for more than a generation. The causes had long been forgotten; the embattled nations, burrowing into the earth, knew only a fiery longing for revenge. The chaos produced by the first aerial attacks had enabled the survivors to hide themselves beyond the reach even of atomic bombs to carry on the struggle. Navies and armoured divisions exchanged knowledge; strategy and tactics underwent drastic revamping. Psychology, once the major hope of mankind for a solution to the war problem, now had become perverted to the ends of the militarists, as a substitute for patriotism to motivate the men at war. In new ways but with the old philosophies, the war went on; and therefore this armoured monster clawed its way through the earth's crust toward its objective.

On the 'bridge' of the underground warship, a small turret in the centre of its roof, Commander Sanderson clung to a stanchion as he barked orders to his staff through the intercom. The ship proper was swung on special mountings and gyro-stabilized to divorce it from the violent jolting of the lower unit, consisting of the drill, the treads and the mighty, earth-moving atomic engines. But still some of the lurching and jouncing of the treads was transmitted up through the storerooms through the crew's quarters to the bridge, and the steel deck underfoot swayed and shook drunkenly. However, men had once learned to accustom themselves to the fitful motions of the sea; and the hardened skipper paid no attention to the way his command pounded forward.

Commander Sanderson was a thickset man, whose hunched shoulders and bull neck suggested the prize ring. But he moved like a cat, even here inside this vibrating juggernaut, as he slipped from one command post to another, reading over the shoulders of unheeding operators the findings of their instruments. The Seismo Log was an open book to his practised eye; his black brows met in a deep frown as he noticed a severe shock registered only two minutes previously, only a few hundred yards to starboard. He passed by the radio locator and the radioman; their jobs would come later, meantime radio silence was enforced on both sides. The thin little soundman adjusted his earphones as the 'Old Man' came by: 'No other diggers contacted, sir,' he muttered automatically and continued listening. The optical technician leaped to his feet and saluted smartly as the Commander passed; he would have nothing to do unless they broke into a cavern, and so he rendered the military courtesy his fellows could not.

Sanderson halted beside the post of the environmental technician. This man's loosely described rating covered many fields; he was at once geologist, radarman, vibration expert and navigator. It was his duty to deduce the nature of their surroundings and suggest a course to follow.

'Your report,' demanded Sanderson.

'Igneous rock across our course at fifteen thousand feet, I believe, sir,' he replied promptly. 'It's not on the chart, sir – probably a new formation.'

Sanderson swore. This meant volcanic activity – and, whether man-made or accidental, that spelled trouble. 'Course?' he asked.

'Change course to one hundred seventy-five degrees – and half-speed, sir, if you please, until I can chart this formation more accurately.'

Sanderson returned his salute, turned on his heel. 'Mr Culver!'

The young lieutenant-commander saluted casually. 'Sir?'

Sanderson repressed another oath. He did not like the young executive officer with his lordly manners, his natty uniform and the coat of tan he had acquired from frequent ultraviolet exposure – a luxury beyond the means of most of the pasty-faced undermen. But duty is duty – 'Change course to one seven five. Half-speed,' he ordered.

'Aye, aye, sir.' Culver picked up a microphone, jabbed a phone jack into the proper plug and pressed the buzzer.

Far below, near the clanking treads, Lieutenant Watson wiped the sweat from his brow – most of the ship was not as well insulated as the bridge, whose personnel must be at their physical peak at all times. He jumped as the intercom buzzed, then spoke into his chest microphone. 'Navigation,' he called.

'Bridge,' came Culver's voice. 'Change course to one seven five. Over.'

'Navigation to bridge. Course one seven five, aye, aye,' said

Watson mechanically. Then: 'What is it, Culver?'

'Environmental thinks it's lava.'

'Damnation.' The old lieutenant – one of the few able-bodied survivors of the surface stages of the war – turned to his aides. 'Change course to one seven five.'

Peterson, brawny Navigator Third Class, stepped up to a chrome handle projecting from a circular slot and shoved it to '175', then turned a small crank for finer adjustment. Slowly the pitch of the great blades shifted – the sound of their turning, muffled by layers of armour, abruptly changed in tone.

Chief Navigator Schmidt looked up from a pile of strata charts. 'Ask the exec to have a copy of the new formation sent down here,' he said, speaking as calmly as if he were a laboratory technician requesting a routine report. Schmidt was the psycho officer's pride and joy; he was the only person aboard the underground cruiser who had never been subjected to a mental manhandling as a result of that worthy's suspicions. He was slightly plump, pink-cheeked, with a straggling yellow moustache – just a little childish; perhaps that was why he had never cracked.

His request was transmitted; up on the bridge, the environmental technician threw a switch, cutting a remote repeater into the series of scanners which brought him his information. Chief Navigator Schmidt heard the bell clang, fed a sheet of paper into the transcriber, and sat back happily to watch the results.

The great drillhead completed its grinding turn; the blades tore into the rock ahead of it again.

'Navigation to bridge: bearing one seven five,' reported Watson.

'Carry on,' returned young Culver. He pulled out the phone jack, plugged it in elsewhere.

Ensign Clark stroked the slight, fuzzy black beard which was one of many ego-boosters for his crushing introversion, along with the tattoos on his arms and the book of physical exercises which he practised whenever he thought he was alone. At Culver's buzz, he cursed the exec vigorously, then opened the circuit. 'Power,' he replied diffidently.

'Bridge to power: reduce speed by one-half. Over.'

'Power to bridge: speed one-half – aye, aye.' Clark put his hand over the mike, shouted at the non-rated man stationed at the speed lever. 'You! Half-speed, and shake the lead out of your pants!'

The clanking of the treads slowed; simultaneously the whine of the blades rose, cutting more rapidly to compensate for the decreased pressure from behind the drill.

In the hot, steam-filled galley, fat Chief Cook Kelly lifted the lid from a kettle to sniff the synthetic stew. 'What stinkin' slum – an' to think they kicked about the chow back in the Surface Wars.'

'Chief, they say there was *real meat* in the chow then,' rejoined Marconi, Food Chemist First Class.

'Why, Marc, even I can remember—' he was interrupted by the intercom's buzz.

'Attention, all hands!' came Culver's voice. 'Igneous rock detected, probably a fresh lava-flow. We have changed our course. Action is expected within a few hours – stand by to go to quarters. Repeating—'

Kelly spat expertly. His face was impassive, but his hand trembled as he replaced the lid on the kettle. 'We better hurry this chow up, Marc. Heaven only knows when we'll eat again.'

Lieutenant Carpenter raised his hand, slapped the hysterical Private Worth twice.

'Now, shut up or I'll have the psych corpsmen go over you again,' he snapped.

Worth dropped his head between his hands, said nothing.

Carpenter backed out of the cell. 'I'm posting a guard here,' he warned. 'One peep out of you and the boys will finish what they started.'

He slammed the door for emphasis.

'Well, sir, you did it again,' said the sentry admiringly. 'He was throwing things when you got here, but you tamed him in a hurry.'

'We've got to get these cells soundproofed,' muttered Carpenter abstractedly, putting on his glasses. 'The combat-detachment bunks are right next to them.'

'Yeah, sir, I guess it's harder on the combat detachment than the rest of us. We've all got our watches and so forth, but they haven't got a thing to do until we hit an enemy city or something. They crack easy – like this Worth guy in here now.'

Carpenter whirled on him. 'Listen, corpsman, I'm too busy a man to be chasing up here to deal with every enlisted man in this brig – I've got the other officers to keep in line. And let's not be volunteering information to superiors without permission!' he hissed.

'I'm sorry, sir—' the guard began – but the lieutenant was gone!

The sentry smiled crookedly. 'O.K., Mr Carpenter, your big job is to keep the officers in line. I'm just wonderin' who's supposed to keep *you* out of this cell block.'

Corporal Sheehan dealt the cards with sudden, jerky motions; his brow was furrowed, his face a study in concentration. One would have thought him a schoolboy puzzling over a difficult final examination.

Sergeants Fontaine and Richards snatched each card as it came, partly crushing the pasteboards as they completed their hands. Fat old Koch, Private First Class, waited until all the cards had been dealt, then grabbed the whole hand and clutched it against his broad stomach, glancing suspiciously at his fellow players.

Their conversation was in terse, jerky monosyllables – but around them other men of the combat detachment talked, loudly and incessantly. Private Carson sat in a corner, chain smoking in brief, nervous puffs. Coarse jokes and harsh laughter dominated the conversation. Nobody mentioned Culver's 'alert' of a few minutes before.

'Three,' grunted the obese Koch. Sheehan dealt him the cards swiftly.

'Hey!' Richards interrupted, before play could begin. 'I didn't like that deal. Let's have a look at that hand.'

'Know what you're callin' me?' retorted Sheehan, snatching the deck as Richards was about to pick it up.

'Yeah – I know what to call you, you lyin', yella cheat—'

Sheehan lurched to his feet, lashed out with a ham-like fist. Richards scrambled out of the way, bringing chair and table down with a crash. A moment later both men were on their feet and squared off.

Conversation halted; men drifted over toward the table even as Fontaine stepped between the two players. Koch had not yet fully reacted to the situation and was only halfway out of his chair.

'You fools!' shouted Fontaine. 'You want the psych corpsmen on our necks again? That louse Carpenter said if there was another fight we'd all get it.'

Corporal Sheehan's big fists unclenched slowly. 'That low, stinkin'—'

'Sit down,' said Koch heavily. 'Fontaine's right. The psychs probably have a spy or two planted in this room.' His eye rested briefly on Carson, still smoking silently alone in the corner, seemingly oblivious of the commotion.

'That Carson,' muttered Richards, shifting the object of his anger. 'I'll bet any money you want he's a stool for Carpenter.'

'Always by himself,' corroborated Sheehan. 'What's the story about him – born in a lab somewhere, wasn't he?'

The others were moving away now that it was plain there was to be no fight. Koch picked up the cards, stacked them. 'Carson may not even be human,' he suggested. 'The science profs have been workin' on artificial cannon-fodder for years, and you can be sure if they ever do make a robot they're not goin' to talk about it until it's been tried in combat.'

Carson overheard part of his statement; smiled shortly. He rose and left the room.

'See?' Richards went on. 'Probably puttin' all four of us on report right now.'

\*     \*     \*

Lieutenant Carpenter placed the wire recorder back inside its concealed niche, polished his glasses carefully, opened his notebook and made several entries in a neat schoolteacher's hand:

Friction betw. Sheehan, Richards worse – psych. reg. next time back to Gen. Psych. Hosp. New Chicago. No sign men susp. Koch my agent; K. planting idea of robots in crew's minds per order. Can reveal Carson whenever enemy knows Powers mfg. robots in quantity. Fontaine well integrated, stopped fight – recomm. transfer my staff to Sanderson.

He put the notebook away, began to climb the nearest metal ladder with the mincing, catlike tread which the whole crew had learned to hate.

The lone guard before the massive lead-and-steel door of the central chamber saluted as the lieutenant passed. His task was to safeguard the ship's most important cargo – its sole atomic bomb. Carpenter asked him several routine word-association questions before proceeding.

The lieutenant paused just once more in his progress upward. This was to play back the tape of another listening device, this one piped into the quarters of the men who serviced the mighty atomic engines. Making notes copiously, he proceeded directly to the bridge.

'Captain, my report,' he announced, not without some show of pride.

'Later,' said Sanderson shortly, without looking up from a rough strata-chart the environmental technician had just handed him.

'But it's rather important, sir. Serious trouble is indicated in the combat detachment—'

'It always is,' retorted Sanderson in some heat. 'Take your report to Culver; I'm busy.'

Carpenter froze, then turned to the young lieutenant-commander. 'If you will initial this, please—'

Culver repressed a shudder. He couldn't keep back the rebellious feeling that the ancient navies had been better off with their primitive chaplains than the modern underground fleets with their prying psychiatrists. Of course, he hastily told himself, that was impossible today – organized religion had long since ceased to sanction war and had been appropriately dealt with by the government.

The Seismo Log recorded a prolonged disturbance directly ahead, and as Sanderson began his rounds the environmental technician called to him. 'Sudden fault and more igneous activity dead ahead, sir,' he reported.

'Carry on,' replied Sanderson. 'Probably artificial,' he muttered half to himself. 'Lot of volcanism in enemy territory. . . . Mr Culver!'

Culver hastily initialled the psycho officer's notebook and handed it back. 'Sir?'

'Elevate the cutters twenty-five degrees – we're going up and come on the enemy from above.'

The order was soon transmitted to navigation; Lieutenant Watson's efficient gang soon had the metallic behemoth inclined at an angle of twenty-five degrees and rising rapidly toward the surface. Chief Schmidt dragged out new charts, noted down outstanding information and relayed data topside.

The ship's body swung on its mountings as the treads assumed the new slant, preserving equilibrium throughout. An order from Ensign Clark of power soon had the ship driving ahead as fast as the cutters could tear through the living rock.

'Diggers ahead,' the thin soundman called out suddenly, adjusting his earphones. He snapped a switch; lights flickered on a phosphorescent screen. 'Sounds like about three, sir – one is going to intersect our course at a distance of about five thousand yards.'

'Let him,' grunted Sanderson. 'Mr Culver, you may level off now.'

'Electronic activity dead ahead,' and 'Enemy transmitter dead ahead,' the radio locator and radioman reported almost simultaneously, before Culver's quiet order had been carried out.

'Go to general quarters, Mr Culver,' ordered Sanderson quickly. The exec pressed a button.

*     *     *

Throughout the ship was heard the tolling of a great bell – slowly the strokes lost their ponderous beat, quickened in tempo faster and faster until they became a continuous pandemonium of noise; simultaneously the pitch increased. All of this was a trick devised by staff psych officers, believing it would produce a subconscious incentive to greater speed and urgency.

The observational and operational posts were already manned; now, as quickly as possible, reliefs took over the more gruelling watches such as that of the environmental technician. Medical and psych corpsmen hurriedly unpacked their gear, fanned out through the ship. Ensign Clark's voice faltered briefly as he ordered the power consumption cut to a minimum. The great cruiser slowed to a crawl.

The galley was bedlam as Kelly and Marconi rushed from one kettle to the next, supervising the ladling of hot food into deep pans by the apprentices who had assembled in haste in response to Kelly's profane bellowing. Chow runners dashed madly out the door, slopping over the contents of the steaming dishes as they ran. 'Battle breakfast' was on its way to the men; and even as the last load departed Kelly shut off all power into the galley and shrugged his squat form into a heavy coverall. Marconi snatched two empty trays, filled them, and the two men wolfed their meal quickly and then ran at full tilt down toward the combat detachment's briefing-room.

Here the scene was even more chaotic. Men helped one another hastily into coveralls, rubber-and-steel suits, metallic boots. They twisted each other's transparent helmets into place, buckled on oxygen tanks, kits of emergency rations, first aid equipment, and great nightmarish-looking weapons. Richards and Sheehan, their quarrel temporarily forgotten, wrestled with the latter's oxygen valve. Koch struggled mightily with the metal joints of his attack suit; Fontaine checked the readings of the dials on a long, tubular 'heat ray' machine. Carson, fully outfitted, manipulated the ingenious device which brought a cigarette to his lips and lit it. He took a few puffs, pressed another lever to eject the butt, and wrenched his helmet into place with gloved hands. From now until the battle was over, the men would carry all their air on their backs, compressed in cylinders. Underneath the shouts and the rattling noises of the armour could be heard the screams of Private Worth from his cell next door. They were suddenly cut off; one of Lieutenant Carpenter's watchful corpsmen had silenced the boy.

And now there was nothing to do but wait. The combat detachment's confusion subsided; but a subdued clatter of shifting armour, helmets being adjusted, tightening of joints, the rattle of equipment, and telephoned conversation continued. The new bridge-watch checked their instruments, then settled down to careful, strained waiting. Sanderson paced his rounds, hearing reports and issuing occasional orders. Culver stood by the intercom, told the crew all their superiors knew of the opposition as the information came in. Carpenter catfooted through the ship, followed at a discreet distance by four of his strong-arm men.

Ensign Clark was white with fear. He sat stiffly at his post like a prisoner in Death Row; the sweat rolled down his face and into his soft black beard. He tried to repeat the auto-suggestion formulae Carpenter had prescribed for him, but all that he could choke out was a series of earnest curses which a kinder age would have called prayers.

He jumped as if he had been shot at Culver's sudden announcement: 'Attention all hands. Enemy digger believed to have sighted this ship. Prepare for action at close quarters.' The voice paused, and then added: 'Bridge to power: full speed ahead for the next half-hour, then bring the ship to a halt. We'll let the enemy carry the fight to us.'

Clark automatically repeated 'Full speed ahead,' then cringed as the crewman slammed the lever over and the cruiser leaped forward with a shrill whine of its blades. 'No!' he suddenly yelled, leaping out of his seat. 'Not another inch – stop this ship!' He ran over to the speed lever, pushed at the crewman's hands. 'I won't be killed, I won't, I *won't*!' The brawny crewman and the maddened officer wrestled desperately for a moment, then the crewman flung his superior on his back and stood over him, panting. 'I'm sorry, sir.'

Clark lay there whimpering for a few seconds, then made a quick grab inside his shirt and levelled a pistol at the towering crewman. 'Get over there,' he half-sobbed, 'and stop this ship before I shoot you.'

The white-uniformed psych corpsman flung open the door and fired, all in one motion. The crewman instinctively backed away as the little pellet exploded, shredding most of Clark's head into his cherished beard; the crewman stood over the body, making little wordless sounds.

'Go off watch,' ordered Carpenter, coming into the room on the heels of his henchman. 'Get a sedative from the medics.' He gazed lingeringly, almost appreciatively, on the disfigured face of the dead man before covering it with the ensign's coat. Then he called Culver and told him briefly what had happened.

'I'll send a relief,' promised the exec. 'Tell him to reduce speed in another twenty minutes. That was quick thinking, Carpenter; the captain says you rate a citation.' The psycho officer had failed to give the corpsman credit for firing the shot.

Sanderson caught Culver's eye, put a finger to his lips.

'Huh?' Culver paused, then got the idea. 'Oh – and, say, Carpenter – don't let the crew hear of this. It wouldn't do for them to know an officer was the first to crack.' There was a very faint trace of sarcasm in his tone.

But Sanderson's warning was already too late. The power crewman who had witnessed Clark's death agonies talked before he was put to sleep; the medic who administered the sedative took it to the crew. By the time Carpenter had received the new order from Culver, his efficient corpsmen had disposed of Clark's body and the whole ship knew the story. It hit the combat detachment like a physical blow; their strained morale took a serious beating, and the officers grew alarmed.

'Pass the word to let them smoke,' Sanderson finally ordered, after the great ship had shuddered to a halt and backed a short distance up the tunnel on his order. 'Give them ten minutes – the enemy will take at least twice that to get here. Have Carpenter go down and administer drugs at his own discretion – maybe it will slow them for fighting, but if they crack they'll be of no use anyway.'

And so for ten minutes the combat crewmen removed their helmets and relaxed, while the psychos moved unobtrusively throughout the room, asking questions here and there, occasionally giving drugs. Once they helped a man partially out of his armour for a hypo. Tension relaxed somewhat; the psych corpsmen could soothe as well as coerce.

Kelly and Marconi were engaged in a heated argument over the relative merits of synthetic and natural foods – a time-tested emotional release the two veterans used habitually. Koch was up to his ears in a more serious controversy – for Sheehan and Richards were practically at each other's throats again. Carson as usual said nothing, smoked continuously; even the level-headed Fontaine got up and paced the floor, his armour clanking as he walked. Three men had to be put to sleep. Then the ten-minute break was over and the strain grew even worse.

Carpenter spoke softly into the intercom. 'Tell the commander that if battle is not joined in another hour I cannot prevent a mutiny. Culver, I *told* you not to leave that man on watch – if you had listened to me Ensign Clark need not have been liquidated.'

Culver's lip curled; he opened his mouth to reply in his usual irritating manner – but at that moment the soundman flung the earphones off his head. The roar of shearing duralloy blades was audible several feet away as the phones bounced to the deck. 'Enemy digger within one hundred feet and coming in fast!' the soundman shouted.

'*Don't reverse engines!*' Sanderson roared as Culver contacted the new power officer. 'Turn on our drill, leaving the treads stationary – we'll call his bluff.'

Culver issued the necessary order, then alerted the crew again. The great blades began to whirl once more; there was a brief shower of rocks, and they churned emptiness – their usual throbbing, tearing chant became a hair-raising shriek; the blast of air they raised kicked up a cloud of dust which blanketed the fresh-carved tunnel – 'That's for their optical technician,' explained Sanderson. 'He'll be blind when he comes out – and we've a sharp gunnery officer down in fire control that will catch them by surprise.'

The soundman gingerly picked up the headphones; the roar of the enemy's drill had dropped to a whisper – Sanderson's curious tactics evidently had him guessing, for he had slowed down.

The sound of the approaching drill was now audible without the benefit of electronic gear, as a muffled noise like the chewing of a great rat. Then came the chattering breakthrough, and Sanderson knew he had contacted the enemy, despite the dust clouds which baffled even the infra-red visual equipment.

Temporarily blind, confused by the whirling blades of their motionless opponent, the enemy hesitated for the precious seconds that meant the difference between victory and destruction.

As the enemy warhead broke through, the cruiser's whirling blades suddenly came to a quivering halt. Simultaneously the forward batteries opened fire.

Gone were the days of labouring, sweating gun-crews and ammunition loaders. All the stubby barrels were controlled from a small, semicircular control panel like an organ console. Lieutenant Atkins, a cool, competent, greying officer who had once been an instructor at the military academy, calmly pressed buttons and pulled levers and interestedly watched the results by means of various types of mechanical 'eyes'. And so it was that, when the sweep second-hand of his chronometer crossed the red line, Atkins' sensitive fingers danced over the keys and the ship rocked to the salvos of half its guns.

Magnified and echoed in the narrow tunnel, the crash of the barrage rolled and reverberated and shouted in an uninterrupted tornado of pure noise, roar upon roar – the light of the explosions was by contrast insignificant, a vicious reddish flare quickly snuffed in the dust. The ship jerked with each salvo; faint flashes and Olympian thunders tossed the great cruiser like a raft on the wild Atlantic. The fury of sound beat through the thick armour plate, poured and pounded savagely past the vaunted 'soundproof' insulation. The decks lurched and reeled underfoot; instruments and equipment trembled with bone-shaking vibrations. Crash upon thunderous crash filled the air with new strains of this artillery symphony; and then Culver pressed a button. His voice could not be heard through the racket, but the sudden glow of a red light in the combat detachment's assembly room transmitted his order instantly – 'Away landing party!'

And then the trap between the great, flat treads was sprung, and the mechanical monster spawned progeny, visible only by infrared light in the underground gloom – little doll-like figures in bulky, nightmarish costumes, dropping from a chain ladder to the broken shale underfoot, running and stumbling through the debris, falling and picking themselves up and falling again like so many children – Marconi and Kelly and Carson and Sheehan and Richards and Fontaine and Koch, tripping over the debris and fragments which the great machine had made.

And at last the enemy cruiser replied, even as the landing party picked its way through the obscuring dust and fanned out from its source. Though confused and blind, the men of the other ship, too, had been prepared for action, and thus new sounds were added to the din that were not of the attackers' making.

A titanic explosion rocked the carriage of Sanderson's cruiser; then another, and still another, strewing steel fragments indiscriminately among the men in the tunnel. The ferocity of the defence was less than the attack; much of their armament must have been destroyed on the first salvo – but what remained wrought havoc. Some quick-witted commander of the enemy must have anticipated the landing of a ground party, for fragmentation shells burst near the embattled cruisers, and here and there the armoured figures began to twist and jerk and go down. Their comrades dropped into the partial protection of the broken rock and continued their advance.

Fontaine ran and crawled and scrambled and crouched over the tunnel floor, which was visible to his infra-red-sensitive helmet, and torn now even more by arrowing slivers of steel. His hand found a valve, twisted it to give him more oxygen for this most critical part of the struggle. He did not think much; he was too busy keeping alive. But a bitter thought flashed across his mind – *This part of war hasn't changed a bit*. He leaped over a strange and terrible object in which armour, blood, rock and flesh made a fantastic jigsaw puzzle which had lost its meaning. Once again he merely noted the item in his subconscious mind; he did not think.

Lieutenant Atkins' fingers still danced over the console; his face was exalted like that of a man playing a concerto. And into the symphony of death which he wove with subtle skill there crept fewer and fewer of the discords of the enemy's guns.

Sanderson paced the deck moodily, communicating briefly with his subordinates by means of lip reading which Culver swiftly translated into many-coloured lights. Information came back to the bridge in the same manner. Sanderson smiled with grim satisfaction at the scarcity of dark lamps on the master damage control board. Those mighty walls could take a lot of punishment, and damage so far had been superficial – one blast in the psycho ward; Private Worth would suffer Carpenter's displeasure no longer.

The helmeted monstrosities grew bolder in their advance as the counter-barrage slackened. Now there was but one battery in action, far to the left – all the thunder came from their own ship.

Fontaine rose from the little depression in which he had been crouching. Another man waved to him; from that outsized suit it would have to be Koch. The big man's armour was dented, the rubber portions torn – his steel right boot looked like a large, wrinkled sheet of tinfoil, and he dragged the leg behind him. But he saw Fontaine, pointed a gauntleted finger into the gloom. The enemy ship must be up there; yes, there was the flash of the one operating gun – Fontaine moved forward.

There was another, nearer flash; something exploded on

Koch's chestplate, knocking him down. He moved, feebly, like a crushed insect, then lay still. Fontaine immediately slipped back into his hollow; for here was the enemy.

A man in a light, jointed metal suit of Asian make appeared from behind a boulder, slipped over to Koch's body to examine it, felt for Koch's weapons.

Fontaine unslung the long, bazooka-like heat-ray tube – an adaptation of very slow atomic disintegration – and pressed the firing stud. The weapon contributed no noise and no flare to the hellish inferno of the tunnel, but the Asiatic suddenly straightened up, took a step forward. That was all he had time for.

Accident and his jointed armour combined to keep his body standing. Fontaine made sure of his man by holding the heat ray on him until the enemy's armour glowed cherry-red, then released the stud. He came forward, gave the still-glowing figure a push. The body collapsed with a clatter across Koch. Fontaine pushed on – the dust was at last clearing slightly, and directly ahead loomed the enemy ship.

Another Asiatic appeared over a short ridge; too quick for the heat ray. Fontaine drew his pistol and fired. The pellet flared; another enemy went down.

Something whizzed over Fontaine's head; he ducked, ran for cover. Somebody was firing high-speed metallic slugs from an old-fashioned machine gun, and his partly-rubber suit would not stop them. Miraculously he found himself unharmed in front of the enemy ship.

Its drill was torn and crumpled, blades lying cast off amongst the rocks; one of the treads was fouled, and the forward part of the carriage was smashed in completely. This war vehicle would obviously never fight again. Another volley of slugs chattered overhead, and Fontaine rolled back out of the way. *Snap judgement*, he told himself ironically in another rare flash of lucidity. *Maybe she'll never fight after this time, but she's got plenty of spirit right now.*

He dug a hole in the loose shale and tried to cover himself as much as possible, meanwhile surveying the layout. They couldn't know he was here, or his life would have been snuffed out; but he could neither advance nor retreat. He absently transmitted the prearranged 'contact' signal back to the cruiser. Then he settled himself, soldier-wise, to wait as long as might be necessary.

Fontaine's 'contact', and several others, returned to their ship as lights on a board. The landing party could proceed no further or they would encounter their own barrage. Sanderson immediately gave the 'cease fire' order. The barrage lifted.

Culver shouted down an immediate flood of radio reports that broke the sudden, aching silence. 'Lieutenant Atkins, you will continue action against the remaining enemy battery until you have destroyed it, or until I inform you that members of the task force have neutralized it.'

'Aye, aye, sir.' Atkins turned back to his guns, studied the image of the battered enemy ship which was becoming increasingly visible as the dust settled. He restored all the automatic controls to manual, pressed several buttons judiciously, and fingered a firing switch.

To Fontaine, crouching in his retreat under the enemy ship, the sudden silence which followed the barrage was almost intolerable. One moment the guns had thundered and bellowed overhead; the next there were a few echoes and reverberations and then all was over.

His ears sang for minutes; his addled brains slowly returned to a normal state. And he realized that the silence was not absolute. It was punctually broken by the crash of the remaining enemy battery, and soon at less frequent intervals by the cautious probing of Atkins' turrets. And between the blows of this duel of giants he could at last hear the whine of metal slugs over his head.

This weapon had him stumped. The Asiatic explosive bullets, such as the one that had killed Koch, only operated at fairly close quarters; the rubber suits were fairly good insulation against death rays; and the Asiatics had no heat ray. But with an antiquated machine gun an Asiatic could sit comfortably at a considerable distance from him and send a volley of missiles crunching through the flimsy Western armour to rip him apart in helpless pain. He raised his head very slightly and looked around. The detachment was well trained; he could see only three of his fellows and they were well concealed from the enemy. Under infra-red light – the only possible means of vision in the gloom of the tunnel – they looked like weird red ghosts.

Something gleamed ahead of him. He sighted along the heat ray, energized its coils. The mechanism hummed softly; the Asiatic jumped out of his hiding place and right into the machine gun's line of fire. The singing bits of metal punched a neat line of holes across his armour and knocked him down, twisting as he fell. Moments later the chattering stream stopped flowing, and Fontaine dashed for more adequate cover. Bullets promptly kicked up dust in little spurts in the hollow he had just vacated.

He searched the darkness, a weird, shimmering ghostland revealed to him by its own tremendous heat through his infra-red equipment. The ship and his armour were very well insulated; he had not been conscious of the stifling heat or the absolute night-gloom which would have made combat impossible for an unprepared, unprotected soldier of the Surface Wars.

Atkins' insistent batteries spoke; there was a great flash and a series of explosions at the enemy target to the left. Fontaine seized the opportunity to make a charge on the loosely piled boulders which, his practised eye told him, sheltered the deadly machine gun. He fell and rolled out of the line of fire as the opposing gunner found him and swerved his weapon; then began to fire explosive pellets at the crude nest, showering it with a series of sharp reports. The enemy machine gun swung back and forth, raking the terrain in search of the invader.

Fontaine unloaded his heat ray, placed it in a well-sheltered crevice and worked it around until it was aimed at the enemy, then shorted the coils. The weapon throbbed with power; rocks began to glow, and the flying slugs poured down upon the menacing heat ray, trying to silence it. Meanwhile Fontaine, like uncounted warriors of all ages, began cautiously to work his way around to the left for a flank attack. Indeed, there were many things in war that had not changed.

'Fire control to bridge: enemy battery silenced,' Atkins reported firmly.

'Secure fire control,' Culver ordered, then turned on his heel. 'The enemy's ordnance is destroyed, sir,' he asserted. 'Our combat crewmen are engaging the enemy in front of his ship.'

'Send Mr Atkins my congratulations,' Sanderson replied promptly. 'Then inform the combat detachment of the situation.'

Culver turned back to the intercom – then started, as a siren wailed somewhere in the bowels of the ship. A station amidships was buzzing frantically; he plugged in the mike. 'Bridge,' he answered.

'Atomic-bomb watch to bridge: instruments show unprecedented activity of the bomb. Dangerous reaction predicted.'

Culver fought to keep his voice down as he relayed the information. The bridge watch simply came to a dead stop; all eyes were on Sanderson.

Even the phlegmatic commander hesitated. Finally: 'Prepare to abandon ship,' he ordered, heavily.

At once the confusion which had accompanied the preparations of the combat detachment was repeated throughout the ship. Atomic bombs by this time were largely made of artificial isotopes and elements; the type which they carried had never been tested in combat – and radioactive elements can do strange and unpredictable things when stimulated. Mere concussion had started the trouble this time, and the mind of man was incapable of prophesying the results. The bomb might merely increase in the speed of its radioactive decay, flooding the ship and the bodies of its men with deadly gamma rays; it might release enormous heat and melt the cruiser into a bubbling pool of metal; it might blast both of the ships and mile on cubic mile of rocks out of existence – but all they could do was abandon the cruiser and hope for the best. All mankind was unable to do more.

Sanderson's forceful personality and Carpenter's prowling corpsmen prevented a panic. Men cursed as they struggled with obstinate clasps and joints. A few of Kelly's apprentices who had not gone into combat flung cases of concentrated food through the landing-trap to the tunnel floor. Culver packed the ship's records – logs, papers, muster sheets, inventories – into an insulated metal can for preservation. A picked force of atomic technicians in cumbersome lead suits vanished into the shielded bomb-chamber with the faint hope of suppressing the reaction.

Sanderson paused before sealing his helmet. 'Mr Culver, you will have all hands assemble in or near the landing-trap. We must advance, destroy the enemy and take refuge in his ship; it is our only hope.'

Navigation buzzed; Culver made the necessary connection. 'One moment, sir,' he murmured to Sanderson. 'Bridge.'

The young exec could visualize old Lieutenant Watson's strained expression, his set jaw. 'Navigation requests permission to remain aboard when ship is abandoned,' Watson said slowly. 'Chances of crew's survival would be materially increased if the ship reversed engines and departed this area—'

Sanderson was silent a long moment. 'Permission granted,' he finally answered in a low voice. He started to say more, caught Carpenter's eye and was silent.

But Culver could not maintain military formality in answering Watson's call. 'Go ahead, Phil, and – thanks,' he replied, almost in a whisper.

Carpenter stepped forward quickly. 'This is no time for sentiment, Mr Culver,' he snapped. 'Lieutenant Watson's behaviour was a little naïve for an officer, but the important fact remains that his antiquated altruism may be the means of preserving the lives of more important personnel.' He waved a sheaf of loose papers excitedly. 'This report of mine, for example, on the psychiatric aspects of this battle will be invaluable to the Board—'.

*Crack!*

All the wiry power of the young exec's rigidly trained body went into the punch; literally travelled through him from toe to fist and exploded on the psycho officer's jaw. Months of harsh discipline – psychological manhandling – the strain of combat – repressed emotions, never really unhampered since his childhood – the sense of the war's futility which had not been completely trained out of anyone – his poorly concealed hatred for Carpenter – all these subconscious impressions came boiling up and sped the blow – and his hand was incased in a metal glove.

Carpenter's head snapped back. His feet literally flew off the deck as his body described a long arc and slammed into the far wall. He sprawled there grotesquely like a discarded marionette. Miraculously his glasses were unbroken.

The iron reserve which Sanderson had kept throughout the battle left him with the disruption of his neat, disciplined little military cosmos. For a long time he was unable to speak or move.

Two tough-looking psych corpsmen closed in on the exec, who stood facing the fallen officer, his fists clenched. He twisted angrily as they grabbed his arms.

'Let him alone,' Sanderson ordered, coming to his senses. They reluctantly released Culver.

'Mr Culver,' the skipper said very quietly, 'I need you now. You will resume your duties until this crisis is over. But, if we come through this, I'm going to see that you're broken.'

Culver faced him, anger draining out of him like the colour from his flushed face. He saluted, turned back to the intercom to give out the last order Sanderson had issued. 'Attention, all hands,' he called mechanically. 'Fall in at the landing-trap to abandon ship.'

Sanderson beckoned to the two psych corpsmen. 'Please take Lieutenant Carpenter to sick bay,' he ordered. 'Bring him around as soon as you can.'

The Asiatic squatted crosslegged behind his shining pneumatic machine gun, frantically raking the rock-strewn ground before him. The air ahead shimmered and danced with heat; the other side of his crude stone shelter must be glowing whitely, and the sweat ran down his yellow face even though the tiny cooling motor within his armour hummed savagely as it laboured to keep him from suffocating. He must destroy the offending heat ray or abandon his position.

A confused impression of rubber-and-metal armour was all he received as Fontaine rushed upon him from the side. The two men came together and went down with a loud clatter of armour, rolled over and over in quick, bitter struggle. Even in the Atomic Age there could be hand-to-hand combat.

It was an exhausting fight; the battle suits were heavy and awkward. They wrestled clumsily, the clank of their armour lending an incongruously comic note. The lithe Asiatic broke a hold, cleared his right hand. Fontaine rolled over to avoid the glittering knife his opponent had succeeded in drawing. Here beneath the crust a rip in his rubberized suit would spell disaster. The Asiatic jumped at him to follow up his advantage. Fontaine dropped back on his elbows, swung his feet around and kicked viciously.

The metal boot shattered the Asiatic's glass face-plate, nearly broke his neck from its impact. Shaken by the cruel blow to his face, blinded by blood drawn by the jagged glass, gasping from the foul air and the oppressive heat, he desperately broke away and ran staggering toward the right, misjudging the direction of his ship.

Fontaine estimated the number of explosive bullets he had left, then let his enemy go, knowing there would be no more danger from that quarter. He lay unmoving beside the abandoned machine gun, breathing heavily. His near-miraculous survival thus far deserved a few minutes' rest.

The enemy's landing-trap, like the Western one, was under the ship's carriage; instead of a chain ladder, a ramp had been let down. A terrific mêlée now raged around the ramp – Fontaine and his opponent had been so intent on their duel they had not seen the tide of battle wash past them. Here and there lay dead men of both sides; his recent enemy had soon been overcome and lay not a score of feet away, moving spasmodically. Battle-hardened as he was, Fontaine seriously debated putting the fellow out of his misery – death from armour failure was the worst kind in this war except radioactive poisoning – then carefully counted his explosive pellets again. Only six – he might need them. He dismissed the writhing Asiatic from his mind.

He looked up at the smashed hull of the enemy ship, and an idea came to him. They wouldn't be watching here, with their ship in danger of being boarded elsewhere.

He rose, moved quietly to the great right-hand tread. The flat links here were torn and disconnected; he seized a loose projection and hauled himself upward. Slipping and scrambling, using gauntleted hands and booted feet, he reached the top of the tread.

Directly above him was a jagged hole in the ship's carriage, about four feet long. He seized the edges and somehow managed to wriggle his way inside.

The interior was a shambles of smashed compartments, with men and metal uncleanly mated. Fontaine laboriously pushed his way forward, climbing over and around barriers flung up at the caprice of Atkins' guns. Once he was forced to expend one of the precious pellets; the recoil nearly flattened him at such close quarters, but he picked himself up and climbed through the still-smoking hole into a passageway which was buckled somewhat but still intact.

He looked carefully in both directions, then saw a ladder and began to ascend. It brought him into a small storage compartment which was still illuminated. He grunted in satisfaction; if he had reached the still-powered portion of the ship, he was going in the right direction.

He eased the door open three inches; air hissed – this compartment must be sealed off. He quickly passed through, closed the door, and cautiously tested the air – good; this part of the ship still had pure air and insulation. Confidently he continued forward and climbed another ladder toward the bridge.

He had to wait at one level until a sentry turned his back. Then he sprang, and his steel fingers sank into the Asiatic's throat. There was no outcry.

Faintly from below there came the sounds of a struggle; his comrades had successfully invaded the ship. Curiously, Fontaine tried his helmet radio. It had been put out of commission in his fight with the machine gunner outside.

There were no more sentries; that was odd. He proceeded with extreme caution as he came to the ladder leading up to the bridge. Here would be the brains of the Asiatic ship; his five remaining pellets could end the engagement now that the battle was raging on enemy territory.

He stumbled over something – a man's foot. He dragged the body out of the shadows which had concealed it.

'What the devil—'

The man had been another guard. His chest was shattered; an explosive pistol was clutched in his right hand. One pellet was missing from the chamber.

Wonderingly Fontaine climbed the ladder, halted at the door.

Lying at his feet was another sentry. The man's body was unmarked but his face bore signs of a painful death. A small supersonic projector lay near him.

Fontaine opened the door – and turned away, sick.

Somebody had turned on a heat ray at close quarters. Officers and enlisted men lay in charred horror. And in the centre of the room the ship's commanding officer slumped on a bloodstained silken cushion. The man had committed honourable suicide with a replica of an ancient Japanese samurai sword.

In his left hand was a crumpled sheet of yellow paper, evidently a radiogram.

Fontaine took the scrap from the lax yellow fingers, puzzled over the Oriental characters.

Then he went outside, and closed the door, and sat down at the head of the ladder to await the coming of men who might be able to solve the mystery.

\*　　\*　　\*

The last man scrambled down the swaying chains and dropped to the ground from the Western cruiser.

Lieutenants Watson and Atkins were alone in the ship.

'Why did you stay?' demanded Watson, throwing the starting switch. He had hastily rigged an extension from the power room to navigation. 'Only one man is needed to operate the ship, in an emergency.'

Lieutenant Atkins found a fine cigar in his uniform. 'I've been saving this,' he remarked, stripping off the cellophane wrapper lovingly. 'The condemned man indulges in the traditional liberties.'

'Answer my question,' Watson insisted, advancing the speed lever.

Atkins pressed a glowing heating-coil 'lighter' to the tip of the cigar. 'Let me ask you this – why did *you* make this heroic gesture?'

Watson flushed. 'You might as well ask – why fight at all?'

'You might,' Atkins said, smiling slightly.

'I did this because our men come first!' Watson shouted almost in fury.

Atkins chuckled. 'Forgive me, old friend – I find it hard to shake off the illusions I had back in the Last Surface War myself.' He blew a huge cloud of smoke. 'But, when Culver sent down the commander's congratulations to me for silencing that enemy battery, it struck me how empty all our battles and decorations are.'

Watson shoved the speed lever to maximum; the cruiser rolled backward down the tunnel at a terrific velocity, no longer impeded by masses of rock. After a long silence he asked: 'Atkins – what were *you* fighting for?'

Atkins looked him squarely in the eye. 'Well, I managed to hypnotize myself into a superficial love of massed artillery – it's a perversion of my love for the symphony – used to conduct a small orchestra at the academy before it was dissolved and the funds allocated to a military band. I liked that orchestra; felt I was doing something constructive for once.' He was silent for a while, smoking and reminiscing. Coming back to reality with a start, he went on hastily: 'Of course, underneath it all I guess I was motivated just the way you were – to maintain the dead traditions of the service, to save our shipmates who would have died anyway, and to advance a cause which no longer exists.'

Watson buried his head in his hands. 'I fought because I thought it was the right thing to do.'

Atkins softened. 'So did I, my friend,' he admitted. 'But it's all over now—'

He paused to flick ashes from the cigar. 'I saved something else for this,' he went on irrelevantly. 'Carpenter is gone now, Watson, so we can dispense with his psychopathic mummery. What a joke if he should ever know I had this aboard.' He laughed lightly, producing a small, gold-stamped book bound in black leather. 'This sort of thing is the only value left, for us,' he asserted. 'Let us pray.'

And thus, a few minutes later, the two elderly officers died. It was not a great blast, as atomic explosions go, but ship and men and rock puffed and sparkled in bright, cleansing flame.

The bridge of the captured enemy ship looked fresh and clean. The remains of the Asiatic commander's gruesome self-destruction had been cleared away; blackened places about the room glistened with new paint. It was several hours after the battle.

Sanderson stood at attention reading a report to his surviving officers. Sergeant Fontaine, permitted to attend as the first witness to the baffling slaughter, fidgeted in the presence of so much gold braid. Private Carson, the strange child of the laboratory, present to assist Fontaine in guarding the disgraced executive officer, stood stolidly, a detached expression on his face.

'—and therefore the atomic explosion, when it did come, was hardly noticed here,' the commander concluded his report. 'Lieutenant Watson did his duty' – he glared covertly at Culver, manacled between Fontaine and Carson – 'and if we can return safely to our Advance Base this will go down as one of the greatest exploits in the history of warfare.'

He cleared his throat. 'At ease,' he said offhandedly, straightening his papers. The officers and crewmen relaxed, shifted position, as Sanderson went on more informally: 'Before we discuss any future action, however, there is this business of the Asiatic warlords – their inexplicable suicide. Lieutenant Carpenter?'

The psycho officer stepped forward, caressing his bandaged jaw. 'I have questioned the ten prisoners we took,' he announced as clearly as he could through the bandages, 'and my men have applied all of the standard means of coercion. I am firmly convinced that the Asiatic prisoners are as ignorant as we are of the reason for their masters' strange behaviour.'

Sanderson motioned him back impatiently. 'Ensign Becker?'

The personnel officer rustled some sheets of paper. 'I have checked the records carefully, sir,' he asserted, 'and Lieutenant-Commander Culver is the only man aboard this ship who understands written Asiatic.'

Sanderson's gaze swept over all his officers. 'Gentlemen, the executive officer was guilty of striking the psycho officer shortly before we abandoned ship – I witnessed the action. I want to know if you will accept as valid his translation of the radiogram which Sergeant Fontaine found on the body of the enemy leader.'

'I object!' shouted Carpenter immediately. 'Culver violated one of the *basic* principles of the officers' corps – he can't be completely *sane*.'

'True, perhaps,' admitted Sanderson testily, 'but, lieutenant, would you care to suggest a plan of action – *before* we discover why our late enemies killed themselves so conveniently?'

'Commander, are you trying to vindicate this man?' Carpenter demanded indignantly.

Sanderson looked at the psycho officer with an expression almost contemptuous. 'You should know by this time, lieutenant, that I have never liked Mr Culver,' he snorted. 'Unfortunately this could be a question of our own survival. If the officers present accept Culver's translation of the message, I shall act on it.'

'But we came here to begin courtmartial proceedings—'

'That can wait,' the skipper interrupted impatiently. 'This is my command, Carpenter, and I wish you'd remember that. Well, gentlemen? A show of hands, please—' He paused to count. 'Very well,' he decided shortly. 'Sergeant Fontaine, give the message to the prisoner.'

Fontaine threw a snappy salute and handed the yellow scrap of paper silently to the exec. Carson loosened his grip somewhat; Culver began to work out the translation—

FROM Supreme Headquarters in Mongolia.

TO All field commanders.

SUBJECT Secret weapon X-39, failure of.

1. Research project X-39, a semi-living chemical process attacking all forms of protoplasm, was released on the South American front according to plan last night.

2. Secret weapon X-39 was found to be uncontrollable and is spreading throughout our own armies all over the world. In addition, infection centring on the secret research laboratories has covered at least one-third of Asia.

3. You are directed to—

'Well?' demanded Sanderson.

'That's all, sir,' Culver replied quietly.

The room immediately exploded into conversation, all pretence at military discipline forgotten. The commander shouted for order. He stood even straighter than his normally stiff military bearing allowed; he was the picture of triumph and confidence.

'This interrupted message can be interpreted in only one way,' he declared ringingly. 'Ensign Becker, you will inform all hands that the enemy's suicide is worldwide and that *the war is over*!'

For a long, long moment there was dead silence. The last peace rumour had died when most of these men were children. It took much time for the realization to sink in that the senseless murder was over at last.

Then – cheering, laughing, slapping one another's backs, the officers gave way to their emotions. Many became hysterical; a few still stood dumbly, failing to comprehend what 'peace' was.

Battle-hardened, stiffly militaristic Sanderson's face was wet with tears.

*And then Lieutenant Carpenter screamed.*

All eyes were riveted on the psycho officer, a hideous suspicion growing in their minds as he cringed in a corner and yelled meaninglessly, his whole body shaking with unutterable terror. They had all seen men afraid of death – but in Carpenter's mad eyes was reflected the essence of all the hells conceived in the ancient religions – he slavered, he whimpered, and suddenly his body began to *ripple*.

His fellow officers stood rooted to the deck in sheer fright as he *slid* rather than fell to a huddled heap that continued to sink down after he had fallen, spreading and flowing and finally *running like water*.

Sanderson stared in stunned horror at a pool of sticky yellow fluid that dripped through a bronze grating in the floor.

Culver grinned foolishly. 'Yes, commander,' he said airily, 'you were right – the war is over.'

Sanderson gingerly picked Carpenter's notebook out of the sodden pile of clothing and bandages and the broken glass of the psycho officer's spectacles. 'Read that radiogram again,' he ordered hoarsely, signalling the two crewmen to release their prisoner.

The exec rubbed his wrists to restore circulation as the handcuffs were removed. Then he picked up the crumpled paper, smoothed it out.

'Research Project X-39, a semi-living chemical process attacking all forms of protoplasm, was released—' Culver choked over the words. 'Sir, I—'

And then, in a few terrible minutes of screams and curses and hideous dissolution, all the officers understood why the Asiatics had committed suicide.

Sergeant Fontaine for some reason kept his head. He fired four shots rapidly from his pistol; one missed Carson, the others found their mark in Sanderson, Culver and Becker, who looked oddly grateful as their bodies jerked under the impact and they slumped in unholy disintegration.

Sanderson saluted solemnly with a dissolving arm.

Fontaine had one more pellet in his gun. He hesitated, looked inquiringly for a moment at the inscrutable Carson, then as he felt a subtle *loosening* under his skin he turned the weapon on himself and fired.

Private Carson puffed nervously at a cigarette, staring in shocked, horrible fascination at the weird carnage – then ran blindly, fleeing from he knew not what.

The terror flew on wings of light through the ruined enemy ship. Technicians, bridge watches, the ten enemy prisoners, psych corpsmen, navigators, combat crewmen – even the dead Oriental commanders joined the dissolving tide. Richards and Sheehan were the last to go; they hysterically accused each other of causing the horror, trying desperately to find some tangible cause for the Doom – they fought like great beasts, and fat Koch was not there to stop the fight – they struggled, and coalesced suddenly into one rippling yellow pool.

Carson, still incased in his armour, raced and clattered through the deserted ship – the sound of his passing was almost sacrilegious, like the desecration of a tomb. Everywhere silence, smashed walls, empty suits of armour, little bundles of wet clothing, and curious yellow stains. *Die, why can't you die?*

Carson, the strange one – separated by more than aloofness from his fellows – spawned in a laboratory, the culmination of thousands of experiments in the vain hope of circumventing the extremity of the slaughter by manufacturing men. His metabolism was subtly different from that of normal man; he *needed* nicotine in his system for some reason – that was why he chain-smoked – but tobacco was a narcotic; it could not protect protoplasm. *Why can't you die, Carson?* All through the ship, silence, wet clothing, little pools – not even the dead had escaped – nothing moved or lived except this running, half-mad man – or Thing – born in a laboratory, if one could say he *had* been 'born'.

A quick movement of his gloved hands sealed the round helmet on his shoulders. He ran and stumbled and climbed through passageways and down ladders; he fairly flew down the landing-ramp and soon disappeared in the black depths of the tunnel.

And the nighted cavern so recently hacked from the outraged crust was given back to the darkness and the silence it had always known.

# Clifford D. Simak
# Huddling place

The drizzle sifted from the leaden skies, like smoke drifting through the bare-branched trees. It softened the hedges and hazed the outlines of the buildings and blotted out the distance. It glinted on the metallic skins of the silent robots and silvered the shoulders of the three humans listening to the intonations of the black-garbed man, who read from the book cupped between his hands.

'*For I am the Resurrection and the Life –*'

The moss-mellowed graven figure that reared above the door of the crypt seemed straining upward, every crystal of its yearning body reaching towards something that no one else could see. Straining, as it had strained since that day of long ago when men had chipped it from the granite to adorn the family tomb with a symbolism that had pleased the first John J. Webster in the last years he held of life.

'*And whosoever liveth and believeth in Me –*'

Jerome A. Webster felt his son's fingers tighten on his arm, heard the muffled sobbing of his mother, saw the lines of robots standing rigid, heads bowed in respect to the master who now was going home – to the final home of all.

Numbly, Jerome A. Webster wondered if they understood – if they understood life and death – if they understood what it meant that Nelson F. Webster lay there in the casket, that a man with a book intoned words above him.

Nelson F. Webster, fourth of the line of Websters who had lived on these acres, had lived and died here, scarcely leaving, and now was going to his final rest in that place the first of them had prepared for the rest of them – for that long line of shadowy descendants who would live here and cherish the things and the ways and the life that the first John J. Webster had established.

Jerome A. Webster felt his jaw muscles tighten, felt a little tremor run across his body. For a moment his eyes burned and the casket blurred in his sight and the words the man in black was saying were one with the wind that whispered in the pines standing sentinel for the dead. Within his brain remembrance marched – remembrance of a grey-haired man stalking the hills and fields, sniffing the breeze of an early morning, standing, legs braced, before the flaring fireplace with a glass of brandy in his hand.

Pride – the pride of land and life, and the humility and greatness that quiet living breeds within a man. Contentment of casual leisure and surety of purpose. Independence of assured security, comfort of familiar surroundings, freedom of broad acres.

Thomas Webster was joggling his elbow. 'Father,' he was whispering, 'Father.'

The service was over. The black-garbed man had closed his book. Six robots stepped forward, lifted the casket.

Slowly the three followed the casket into the crypt, stood silently as the robots slid it into its receptacle, closed the tiny door and affixed the plate that read:

NELSON F. WEBSTER
2034–2117

That was all. Just the name and dates. And that, Jerome A. Webster found himself thinking, was enough. There was nothing else that needed to be there. That was all those others had. The ones that called the family roll – starting with William Stevens, 1920–99. Gramp Stevens, they had called him, Webster remembered. Father of the wife of the first John J. Webster, who was here himself – 1951–2020. And after him his son, Charles F. Webster, 1980–2060. And his son, John J. II, 2004–86. Webster could remember John J. II – a grandfather who had slept beside the fire with his pipe hanging from his mouth, eternally threatening to set his whiskers aflame.

Webster's eyes strayed to another plate. Mary Webster, the

mother of the boy here at his side. And yet not a boy. He kept forgetting that Thomas was twenty now, in a week or so would be leaving for Mars, even as in his younger days he, too, had gone to Mars.

All here together, he told himself. The Websters and their wives and children. Here in death together as they had lived together, sleeping in the pride and security of bronze and marble with the pines outside and the symbolic figure above the age-greened door.

The robots were waiting, standing silently, their task fulfilled. His mother looked at him.

'You're head of the family now, my son,' she told him.

He reached out and hugged her close against his side. Head of the family – what was left of it. Just the three of them now. His mother and his son. And his son would be leaving soon, going out to Mars. But he would come back. Come back with a wife, perhaps, and the family would go on. The family wouldn't stay at three. Most of the big house wouldn't stay closed off, as it now was closed off. There had been a time when it had rung with the life of a dozen units of the family, living in their separate apartments under one big roof. That time, he knew, would come again.

The three of them turned and left the crypt, took the path back to the house, looming like a huge grey shadow in the mist.

A fire blazed in the hearth and the book lay upon his desk. Jerome A. Webster reached out and picked it up, read the title once again: *Martian Physiology, with Especial Reference to the Brain* by Jerome A. Webster, M.D. Thick and authoritative – the work of a lifetime. Standing almost alone in its field. Based upon the data gathered during those five plague years on Mars – years when he had laboured almost day and night with his fellow colleagues of the World Committee's medical commission, dispatched on an errand of mercy to the neighbouring planet.

A tap sounded on the door.

'Come in,' he called.

The door opened and a robot glided in.

'Your whisky, sir.'

'Thank you, Jenkins,' Webster said.

'The minister, sir,' said Jenkins, 'has left.'

'Oh, yes. I presume that you took care of him.'

'I did, sir. Gave him the usual fee and offered him a drink. He refused the drink.'

'That was a social error,' Webster told him. 'Ministers don't drink.'

'I'm sorry, sir. I didn't know. He asked me to ask you to come to church sometime.'

'Eh?'

'I told him, sir, that you never went anywhere.'

'That was quite right, Jenkins,' said Webster. 'None of us ever go anywhere.'

Jenkins headed for the door, stopped before he got there, turned around. 'If I may say so, sir, that was a touching service at the crypt. Your father was a fine human, the finest ever was. The robots were saying the service was very fitting. Dignified like, sir. He would have liked it, had he known.'

'My father,' said Webster, 'would be even more pleased to hear you say that, Jenkins.'

'Thank you, sir,' said Jenkins, and went out.

Webster sat with the whisky and the book and fire – felt the comfort of the well-known room close in about him, felt the refuge that was in it.

This was home. It had been home for the Websters since that day when the first John J. had come here and built the first unit of the sprawling house. John J. had chosen it because it had a trout stream, or so he always said. But it was something more than that. It must have been, Webster told himself, something more than that.

Or perhaps, at first, it had only been the trout stream. The trout stream and the trees and meadows, the rocky ridge where the mist drifted in each morning from the river. Maybe the rest of it had grown, grown gradually through the years, through years of family association until the very soil was soaked with something that approached, but wasn't quite, tradition. Something that made each tree, each rock, each foot of soil a Webster tree or rock or piece of soil. It all belonged.

John J., the first John J., had come after the breakup of the cities, after men had forsaken, once and for all, the twentieth-century huddling places, had broken free of the tribal instinct to stick together in one cave or in one clearing against a common foe or a common fear. An instinct that had become outmoded, for there were no fears or foes. Man revolting against the herd instinct economic and social conditions had impressed upon him in ages past. A new security and a new sufficiency had made it possible to break away.

The trend had started back in the twentieth century, more than two hundred years before, when men moved to country homes to get fresh air and elbow room and a graciousness in life that communal existence, in its strictest sense, never had given them.

And here was the end result. A quiet living. A peace that could only come with good things. The sort of life that men had yearned for years to have. A manorial existence, based on old family homes and leisurely acres, with atomics supplying power and robots in place of serfs.

Webster smiled at the fireplace with its blazing wood. That was an anachronism, but a good one – something that Man had brought forward from the caves. Useless, because atomic heating was better – but more pleasant. One couldn't sit and watch atomics and dream and build castles in the flames.

Even the crypt out there, where they had put his father that afternoon. That was family, too. All of a piece with the rest of it. The sombre pride and leisured life and peace. In the old days the dead were buried in vast plots all together, stranger cheek by jowl with stranger.

*He never goes anywhere.*

That is what Jenkins had told the minister.

And that was right. For what need was there to go anywhere? It all was here. By simply twirling a dial one could talk face to face with anyone one wished, could go, by sense, if not in body, anywhere one wished. Could attend the theatre or hear a concert or browse in a library halfway around the world. Could transact any business one might need to transact without rising from one's chair.

Webster reached out his hand and drank the whisky, then swung to the dialled machine beside his desk.

He spun dials from memory without resorting to the log. He knew where he was going.

His finger flipped a toggle and the room melted away – or seemed to melt. There was left the chair within which he sat, part of the desk, part of the machine itself and that was all.

The chair was on a hillside swept with golden grass and dotted with scraggly, wind-twisted trees, a hillside that straggled down to a lake nestling in the grip of purple mountain spurs. The spurs, darkened in long streaks with the bluish-green of distant pine, climbed in staggering stairs, melting into the blue-tinged snow-capped peaks that reared beyond and above them in jagged sawtoothed outline.

The wind talked harshly in the crouching trees and ripped the long grass in sudden gusts. The last rays of the sun struck fire from the distant peaks.

Solitude and grandeur, the long sweep of tumbled land, the cuddled lake, the knife-like shadows on the far-off ranges.

Webster sat easily in his chair, eyes squinting at the peaks.

A voice said almost at his shoulder: 'May I come in?'

A soft, sibilant voice, wholly unhuman. But one that Webster knew.

He nodded his head. 'By all means, Juwain.'

He turned slightly and saw the elaborate crouching pedestal, the furry, soft-eyed figure of the Martian squatting on it. Other alien furniture loomed indistinctly beyond the pedestal, half-guessed furniture from that dwelling out on Mars.

The Martian flipped a furry hand toward the mountain range.

'You love this,' he said. 'You can understand it. And I can understand how you understand it, but to me there is more terror than beauty in it. It is something we could never have on Mars.'

Webster reached out a hand, but the Martian stopped him.

'Leave it on,' he said. 'I know why you came here. I would not have come at a time like this except I thought perhaps an old friend—'

'It is kind of you,' said Webster. 'I am glad that you have come.'

'Your father,' said Juwain, 'was a great man. I remember how you used to talk to me of him, those years you spent on Mars. You said then you would come back sometime. Why is it you've never come?'

'Why,' said Webster, 'I just never—'

'Do not tell me,' said the Martian. 'I already know.'

'My son,' said Webster, 'is going to Mars in a few days. I shall have him call on you.'

'That would be a pleasure,' said Juwain. 'I shall be expecting him.'

He stirred uneasily on the crouching pedestal. 'Perhaps he carries on tradition?'

'No,' said Webster. 'He is studying engineering. He never cared for surgery.'

'He has a right,' observed the Martian, 'to follow the life that he has chosen. Still, one might be permitted to wish.'

'One could,' Webster agreed. 'But that is over and done with. Perhaps he will be a great engineer. Space structure. Talks of ships out to the stars.'

'Perhaps,' suggested Juwain, 'your family has done enough for medical science. You and your father—'

'And his father,' said Webster, 'before him.'

'Your book,' declared Juwain, 'has put Mars in debt to you. It may focus more attention on Martian specialization. My people do not make good doctors. They have no background for it. Queer how the minds of races run. Queer that Mars never

thought of medicine – literally never thought of it. Replaced it
with a cult of fatalism. While even in your early history, when
men still lived in caves—'

'There are many things,' said Webster, 'that you thought of
and we didn't. Things we wonder now how we ever missed.
Abilities that you developed and we do not have. Take your own
speciality, philosophy. But different than ours. A science, while
ours never was more than fumbling. An orderly, logical development of philosophy, workable, practical, applicable, an actual
tool.'

Juwain started to speak, hesitated, then went ahead. 'I am
near to something, something that may be new and startling.
Something that will be a tool for you humans as well as the
Martians. I've worked on it for years, starting with certain
mental concepts that first were suggested to me with arrival of
the Earthmen. I have said nothing, for I could not be sure.'

'And now,' suggested Webster, 'you are sure.'

'Not quite,' said Juwain. 'Not positive. But almost.'

They sat in silence, watching the mountains and the lake. A
bird came and sat in one of the scraggly trees and sang. Dark
clouds piled up behind the mountain ranges and the snow-tipped
peaks stood out like graven stone. The sun sank in a welter of
crimson, hushed finally to the glow of a fire burned low.

A tap sounded from a door and Webster stirred in his chair,
suddenly brought back to the reality of the study, of the chair
beneath him.

Juwain was gone. The old philosopher had come and sat an
hour of contemplation with his friend and then had quietly
slipped away.

The rap came again.

Webster leaned forward, snapped the toggle and the mountains vanished, the room became a room again. Dusk filtered
through the high windows and the fire was a rosy flicker in the
ashes.

'Come in,' said Webster.

Jenkins opened the door. 'Dinner is served, sir,' he said.

'Thank you,' said Webster. He rose slowly from the chair.

'Your place, sir,' said Jenkins, 'is laid at the head of the table.'

'Oh, yes,' said Webster. 'Thank you, Jenkins. Thank you very much for reminding me.'

Webster stood on the broad ramp of the space field and watched the shape that dwindled in the sky, dwindled with faint flickering points of red lancing through the wintry sunlight.

For long minutes after the shape was gone he stood there, hands gripping the railing in front of him, eyes still staring up into the steel-like blue.

His lips moved and they said: 'Good-bye, son'; but there was no sound.

Slowly he came alive to his surroundings. Knew that people moved about the ramp, saw that the landing-field seemed to stretch interminably to the far horizon, dotted here and there with hump-backed things that were waiting spaceships. Shooting tractors worked near one hangar, clearing away the last of the snowfall of the night before.

Webster shivered and thought that it was queer, for the noonday sun was warm. And shivered again.

Slowly he turned away from the railing and headed for the administration building. And for one brain-wrenching moment he felt a sudden fear – an unreasonable and embarrassing fear of that stretch of concrete that formed the ramp. A fear that left him shaking mentally as he drove his feet toward the waiting door.

A man walked toward him, briefcase swinging in his hand, and Webster, eyeing him, wished fervently that the man would not speak to him.

The man did not speak, passed him with scarcely a glance, and Webster felt relief.

If he were back home, Webster told himself, he would have finished lunch, would now be ready to lie down for his midday nap. The fire would be blazing on the hearth and the flicker of the flames would be reflected from the andirons. Jenkins would bring him a liqueur and would say a word or two – inconsequential conversation.

He hurried toward the door, quickening his step, anxious to get away from the bare cold expanse of the massive ramp.

Funny how he had felt about Thomas. Natural, of course, that he should have hated to see him go. But entirely unnatural that he should, in those last few minutes, find such horror welling up within him. Horror of the trip through space, horror of the alien land of Mars – although Mars was scarcely alien any longer. For more than a century now Earthmen had known it, had fought it, lived with it, some of them had even grown to love it.

But it had only been utter willpower that had prevented him, in those last few seconds before the ship had taken off, from running out into the field, shrieking for Thomas to come back, shrieking for him not to go.

And that, of course, never would have done. It would have been exhibitionism, disgraceful and humiliating – the sort of thing a Webster could not do.

After all, he told himself, a trip to Mars was no great adventure, not any longer. There had been a day when it had been, but that day was gone forever. He himself, in his earlier days, had made a trip to Mars, had stayed there for five long years. That had been – he gasped when he thought of it – that had been almost thirty years ago.

The babble and hum of the lobby hit him in the face as the robot attendant opened the door for him, and in that babble ran a vein of something that was almost terror. For a moment he hesitated, then stepped inside. The door closed softly behind him.

He stayed close to the one wall to keep out of people's way, headed for a chair in one corner. He sat down and huddled back, forcing his body deep into the cushions, watching the milling humanity that seethed out in the room.

Shrill people, hurrying people, people with strange, unneighbourly faces. Strangers – every one of them. Not a face he knew.

People going places. Heading out for the planets. Anxious to be off. Worried about last details. Rushing here and there.

Out of the crowd loomed a familiar face. Webster hunched forward.

'Jenkins!' he shouted, and then was sorry for the shout, although no one seemed to notice.

The robot moved toward him, stood before him.

'Tell Raymond,' said Webster, 'that I must return immediately. Tell him to bring the 'copter in front at once.'

'I am sorry, sir,' said Jenkins, 'but we cannot leave at once. The mechanics found a flaw in the atomics chamber. They are installing a new one. It will take several hours.'

'Surely,' said Webster, impatiently, 'that could wait until some other time.'

'The mechanic said not, sir,' Jenkins told him. 'It might go at any minute. The entire charge of power—'

'Yes, yes,' agreed Webster, 'I suppose so.'

He fidgeted with his hat. 'I just remembered,' he said, 'something I must do. Something that must be done at once. I must get home. I can't wait several hours.'

He hitched forward to the edge of the chair, eyes staring at the milling crowd.

Faces – faces –

'Perhaps you could televise,' suggested Jenkins. 'One of the robots might be able to do it. There is a booth—'

'Wait, Jenkins,' said Webster. He hesitated a moment. 'There is nothing to do back home. Nothing at all. But I must get there. I can't stay here. If I have to, I'll go crazy. I was frightened out there on the ramp. I'm bewildered and confused here. I have a feeling – a strange, terrible feeling. Jenkins, I—'

'I understand, sir,' said Jenkins. 'Your father had it, too.'

Webster gasped. 'My father?'

'Yes, sir, that is why he never went anywhere. He was about your age, sir, when he found it out. He tried to make a trip to Europe and he couldn't. He got halfway there and turned back. He had a name for it.'

Webster sat in stricken silence.

'A name for it,' he finally said. 'Of course there's a name for it. My father had it. My grandfather – did he have it, too?'

'I wouldn't know that, sir,' said Jenkins. 'I wasn't created until after your grandfather was an elderly man. But he may have. He never went anywhere either.'

'You understand, then,' said Webster. 'You know how it is. I feel like I'm going to be sick – physically ill. See if you can charter a 'copter – anything, just so we get home.'

'Yes, sir,' said Jenkins.

He started off and Webster called him back.

'Jenkins, does anyone else know about this? Anyone—'

'No, sir,' said Jenkins. 'Your father never mentioned it and I felt, somehow, that he wouldn't wish me to.'

'Thank you, Jenkins,' said Webster.

Webster huddled back into his chair again, felt desolate and alone and misplaced. Alone in a humming lobby that pulsed with life – a loneliness that tore at him, that left him limp and weak.

Homesickness. Downright, shameful homesickness, he told himself. Something that boys are supposed to feel when they first leave home, when they first go out to meet the world.

There was a fancy word for it – agoraphobia, the morbid dread of being in the midst of open spaces – from the Greek root for the fear – literally, of the market place.

If he crossed the room to the television booth, he could put in a call, talk with his mother or one of the robots – or, better yet, just sit and look at the place until Jenkins came for him.

He started to rise, then sank back in the chair again. It was no dice. Just talking to someone or looking in on the place wasn't being there. He couldn't smell the pines in the wintry air, or hear familiar snow crunch on the walk beneath his feet or reach out a hand and touch one of the massive oaks that grew along the path. He couldn't feel the heat of the fire or sense the sure, deft touch of belonging, of being one with a tract of ground and the things upon it.

And yet – perhaps it would help. Not much, maybe, but some.

He started to rise from the chair again and froze. The few short steps to the booth held terror, a terrible, overwhelming terror. If he crossed them, he would have to run. Run to escape the watching eyes, the unfamiliar sounds, the agonizing nearness of strange faces.

Abruptly he sat down.

A woman's shrill voice cut across the lobby and he shrank away from it. He felt terrible. He felt like hell. He wished Jenkins would hurry up.

The first breath of spring came through the window, filled the study with the promise of melting snows, of coming leaves and flowers, of north-bound wedges of water-fowl streaming through the blue, of trout that lurked in pools waiting for the fly.

Webster lifted his eyes from the sheaf of papers on his desk, sniffed the breeze, felt the cool whisper of it on his cheek. His hand reached out for the brandy glass and found it empty, put it back.

He bent back above the papers once again, picked up a pencil and crossed out a word.

Critically, he read the final paragraphs:

The fact that, of the two hundred and fifty men who were invited to visit me, presumably on missions of more than ordinary importance, only three were able to come does not necessarily prove that all but those three are victims of agoraphobia. Some may have had legitimate reasons for being unable to accept my invitation. But it does indicate a growing unwillingness for men living under the mode of Earth existence set up following the break-up of the cities to move from familiar places, a deepening instinct to stay among the scenes and possessions which in their mind have become associated with contentment and graciousness of life.

What the result of such a trend will be no one can clearly indicate since it applies to only a small portion of Earth's population. Among the larger families economic pressure forces some

of the sons to seek their fortunes either in other parts of the
Earth or on one of the other planets. Many others deliberately
seek adventure and opportunity in space while still others become associated with professions or trades which make a seden-
tary existence impossible.

He flipped the page over, went on to the last one.

It was a good paper, he knew, but it could not be published,
not just yet. Perhaps after he had died. No one, so far as he
could determine, had even so much as realized the trend, had
taken as a matter of course the fact that men seldom left their
homes. Why, after all, should they leave their homes?

*Certain dangers may be recognized in –*

The televisor muttered at his elbow and he reached out to flip
the toggle.

The room faded and he was face to face with a man who sat
behind a desk, almost as if he sat on the opposite side of Webster's desk. A grey-haired man with sad eyes behind heavy lenses,
eyes that were filled with the sadness and humility of having
looked on death and misery, compassionate eyes.

For a moment Webster stared, memory tugging at him.

'Could it be—?' he asked and the man smiled gravely.

'I have changed,' he said. 'So have you. My name is Clayborne. Remember? The Martian medical commission—'

'Clayborne! I'd often thought of you. You stayed on Mars.'

Clayborne nodded. 'I've read your book, doctor. It is a real
contribution. I've often thought one should be written, wanted
to myself, but I didn't have the time. Just as well I didn't. You
did a better job. Especially on the brain.'

'The Martian brain,' Webster told him, 'always intrigued me.
Certain peculiarities. I'm afraid I spent more of those five years
taking notes on it than I should have. There was other work to
do.'

'A good thing you did,' said Clayborne. 'That's why I'm
calling you now. I have a patient – a brain operation. Only you
can handle it.'

Webster gasped, his hands trembling. 'You'll bring him here?'

Clayborne shook his head. 'He cannot be moved. You know him, I believe. Juwain, the philosopher.'

'Juwain!' said Webster. 'He's one of my best friends. We talked together just a couple of days ago.'

'The attack was sudden,' said Clayborne. 'He's been asking for you.'

Webster was silent and cold – cold with a chill that crept upon him from some unguessed place. Cold that sent perspiration out upon his forehead, that knotted his fists.

'If you start immediately,' said Clayborne, 'you can be here on time. I've already arranged with the World Committee to have a ship at your disposal instantly. The utmost speed is necessary.'

'But,' said Webster, 'but . . . I cannot come.'

'You can't come!'

'It's impossible,' said Webster. 'I doubt in any case that I am needed. Surely, you yourself—'

'I can't,' said Clayborne. 'No one can but you. No one else has the knowledge. You hold Juwain's life in your hands. If you come, he lives. If you don't, he dies.'

'I can't go into space,' said Webster.

'Anyone can go in space,' snapped Clayborne. 'It's not like it used to be. Conditioning of any sort desired is available.'

'But you don't understand,' pleaded Webster. 'You—'

'No, I don't,' said Clayborne. 'Frankly, I don't. That anyone should refuse to save the life of his friend—'

The two men stared at one another for a long moment, neither speaking.

'I shall tell the committee to send the ship straight to your home,' said Clayborne finally. 'I hope by that time you will see your way clear to come.'

Clayborne faded and the wall came into view again – the wall and books, the fireplace and the paintings, the well-loved furniture, the promise of spring that came through the window.

\*       \*       \*

Webster sat frozen in his chair, staring at the wall in front of him.

Juwain, the furry, wrinkled face, the sibilant whisper, the friendliness and understanding that was his. Juwain, grasping the stuff that dreams are made of and shaping them into logic, into rules of life and conduct. Juwain using philosophy as a tool, as a science, as a stepping-stone to better living.

Webster dropped his face into his hands and fought the agony that welled up within him.

Clayborne had not understood. One could not expect him to understand since there was no way for him to know. And, even knowing, would he understand? Even he, Webster, would not have understood it in someone else until he had discovered it in himself – the terrible fear of leaving his own fire, his own land, his own possessions, the little symbolisms that he had erected. And yet not he himself alone, but those other Websters as well. Starting with the first John J. Men and women who had set up a cult of life, a tradition of behaviour.

He, Jerome A. Webster, had gone to Mars when he was a young man, and had not felt or suspected the psychological poison that ran through his veins. Even as Thomas a few months ago had gone to Mars. But twenty-five years of quiet life here in the retreat that the Websters called a home had brought it forth, had developed it without him even knowing it. There had, in fact, been no opportunity to know it.

It was clear how it had developed – clear as crystal now. Habit and mental pattern and a happiness association with certain things – things that had no actual value in themselves, but had been assigned a value, a definite, concrete value by one family through five generations.

No wonder other places seemed alien, no wonder other horizons held a hint of horror in their sweep.

And there was nothing one could do about it – nothing, that is, unless one cut down every tree and burned the house and changed the course of waterways. Even that might not do it – even that—

The televisor purred and Webster lifted his head from his hands, reached out and thumbed the tumbler.

The room became a flare of white, but there was no image. A voice said: 'Secret call. Secret call.'

Webster slid back a panel in the machine, spun a pair of dials, heard the hum of power surge into a screen that blocked out the room.

'Secrecy established,' he said.

The white flare snapped out and a man sat across the desk from him. A man he had seen many times before in televised addresses, in his daily paper.

Henderson, president of the World Committee.

'I have had a call from Clayborne,' said Henderson.

Webster nodded without speaking.

'He tells me you refuse to go to Mars.'

'I have not refused,' said Webster. 'When Clayborne cut off the question was left open. I had told him it was impossible for me to go, but he had rejected that, did not seem to understand.'

'Webster, you must go,' snapped Henderson. 'You are the only man with the necessary knowledge of the Martian brain to perform this operation. If it were a simple operation, perhaps someone else could do it. But not one such as this.'

'That may be true,' said Webster, 'but—'

'It's not just a question of saving life,' said Henderson. 'Even the life of so distinguished a personage as Juwain. It involves even more than that. Juwain is a friend of yours. Perhaps he hinted of something he has found.'

'Yes,' said Webster. 'Yes, he did. A new concept of philosophy.'

'A concept,' declared Henderson, 'that we cannot do without. A concept that will remake the solar system, that will put mankind ahead a hundred thousand years in the space of two generations. A new direction of purpose that will aim toward a goal we heretofore had not suspected, had not even known existed. A brand-new truth, you see. One that never before had occurred to anyone.'

Webster's hands gripped the edge of the desk until his knuckles stood out white.

'If Juwain dies,' said Henderson, 'that concept dies with him. May be lost forever.'

'I'll try,' said Webster. 'I'll try—'

Henderson's eyes were hard. 'Is that the best that you can do?'

'That is the best,' said Webster.

'But, man, you must have a reason! Some explanation.'

'None,' said Webster, 'that I would care to give.'

Deliberately he reached out and flipped up the switch.

Webster sat at the desk and held his hands in front of him, staring at them. Hands that had skill, held knowledge. Hands that could save a life if he could get them to Mars. Hands that could save for the solar system, for mankind, for the Martians an idea – a new idea – that would advance them a hundred thousand years in the next two generations.

But hands chained by a phobia that grew out of this quiet life. Decadence – a strangely beautiful – and deadly – decadence.

Man had forsaken the teeming cities, the huddling places, two hundred years ago. He had done with the old foes and the ancient fears that kept him around the common campfire, had left behind the hobgoblins that had walked with him from the caves.

And yet – and yet –

Here was another huddling place. Not a huddling place for one's body, but one's mind. A psychological campfire that still held a man within the circle of its light.

Still, Webster knew, he must leave that fire. As the men had done with the cities two centuries before, he must walk off and leave it. And he must not look back.

He had to go to Mars – or at least start for Mars. There was no question there at all. He had to go.

Whether he would survive the trip, whether he could perform the operation once he had arrived, he did not know. He wondered vaguely whether agoraphobia could be fatal. In its most exaggerated form, he supposed it could.

He reached out a hand to ring, then hesitated. No use having Jenkins back. He would do it himself – something to keep him busy until the ship arrived.

From the top shelf of the wardrobe in the bedroom, he took down a bag and saw that it was dusty. He blew on it, but the dust still clung. It had been there for too many years.

As he packed, the room argued with him, talked in that mute tongue with which inanimate but familiar things may converse with a man.

'You can't go,' said the room. 'You can't go off and leave me.'

And Webster argued back, half-pleading, half-explanatory. 'I have to go. Can't you understand. It's a friend, an old friend. I will be coming back.'

Packing done, Webster returned to the study, slumped into his chair.

He must go and yet he couldn't go. But when the ship arrived, when the time had come, he knew that he would walk out of the house and toward the waiting ship.

He steeled his mind to that, tried to set it in a rigid pattern, tried to blank out everything but the thought that he was leaving.

Things in the room intruded on his brain, as if they were part of a conspiracy to keep him there. Things that he saw as if he were seeing them for the first time. Old, remembered things that suddenly were new. The chronometer that showed both Earthian and Martian time, the days of the month, the phases of the moon. The picture of his dead wife on the desk. The trophy he had won at prep school. The framed short snorter bill that had cost him ten bucks on his trip to Mars.

He stared at them, half-unwilling at first, then eagerly, storing the memory of them in his brain. Seeing them as separate components of a room he had accepted all these years as a finished whole, never realizing what a multitude of things went to make it up.

Dusk was falling, the dusk of early spring, a dusk that smelled of early pussy willows.

The ship should have arrived long ago. He caught himself listening for it, even as he realized that he would not hear it. A ship, driven by atomic motors, was silent except when it gathered speed. Landing and taking off, it floated like thistledown, with not a murmur in it.

It would be here soon. It would have to be here soon or he could never go. Much longer to wait, he knew, and his high-keyed resolution would crumble like a mound of dust in beating rain. Not much longer could he hold his purpose against the pleading of the room, against the flicker of the fire, against the murmur of the land where five generations of Websters had lived and died.

He shut his eyes and fought down the chill that crept across his body. He couldn't let it get him now, he told himself. He had to stick it out. When the ship arrived he still must be able to get up and walk out the door to the waiting port.

A tap came on the door.

'Come in,' Webster called.

It was Jenkins, the light from the fireplace flickering on his shining metal hide.

'Had you called earlier, sir?' he asked.

Webster shook his head.

'I was afraid you might have,' Jenkins explained, 'and wondered why I didn't come. There was a most extraordinary occurrence, sir. Two men came with a ship and said they wanted you to go to Mars.'

'They are here,' said Webster. 'Why didn't you call me?'

He struggled to his feet.

'I didn't think, sir,' said Jenkins, 'that you would want to be bothered. It was so preposterous.'

Webster stiffened, felt chill fear gripping at his heart. Hands groping for the edge of the desk, he sat down in the chair, sensed the walls of the room closing in about him, a trap that would never let him go.

'I had a rather strenuous time, sir,' said Jenkins. 'They were so insistent that finally, much as I disliked it, I resorted to force. But I finally persuaded them you never went anywhere.'

# Eric Frank Russell

# Hobbyist

The ship arced out of a golden sky and landed with a whoop and a wallop that cut down a mile of lush vegetation. Another half-mile of growths turned black and drooped to ashes under the final flicker of the tail-rocket blasts. That arrival was spectacular, full of verve, and worthy of four columns in any man's paper. But the nearest sheet was distant by a goodly slice of a lifetime, and there was none to record what this far corner of the cosmos regarded as the pettiest of events. So the ship squatted tired and still at the foremost end of the ashy blast-track and the sky glowed down and the green world brooded solemnly all around.

Within the transpex control-dome, Steve Ander sat and thought things over. It was his habit to think things over carefully. Astronauts were not the impulsive dare-devils so dear to the stereopticon-loving public. They couldn't afford to be. The hazards of the profession required an infinite capacity for cautious, contemplative thought. Five minutes' consideration had prevented many a collapsed lung, many a leaky heart, many a fractured frame. Steve valued his skeleton. He wasn't conceited about it and he'd no reason to believe it in any way superior to anyone else's skeleton. But he'd had it a long time, found it quite satisfactory, and had an intense desire to keep it – intact.

Therefore, while the tail tubes cooled off with their usual creaking contractions, he sat in the control seat, stared through the dome with eyes made unseeing by deep preoccupation, and performed a few thinks.

Firstly, he'd made a rough estimate of this world during his hectic approach. As nearly as he could judge, it was ten times the size of Terra. But his weight didn't seem abnormal. Of course, one's notions of weight tended to be somewhat wild when for some weeks one's own weight was shot far up or far down in between periods of weightlessness. The most reasonable estimate had to be based on muscular reaction. If you felt as sluggish as a Saturnian sloth, your weight was way up. If you felt as powerful as Angus McKittrick's bull, your weight was down.

Normal weight meant Terrestrial mass despite this planet's tenfold volume. That meant light plasma. And that meant lack of heavy elements. No thorium. No nickel. No nickel-thorium alloy. Ergo, no getting back. The Kingston-Kane atomic motors demanded fuel in the form of ten-gauge nickel-thorium-alloy wire fed directly into the vaporizers. Denatured plutonium would do, but it didn't occur in natural form, and it had to be made. He had three yards nine and a quarter inches of nickel-thorium left on the feed-spool. Not enough. He was here for keeps.

A wonderful thing, logic. You could start from the simple premise that when you were seated your behind was no flatter than usual, and work your way to the inevitable conclusion that you were a wanderer no more. You'd become a native. Destiny had you tagged as suitable for the status of oldest inhabitant.

Steve pulled an ugly face and said, 'Darn!'

The face didn't have to be pulled far. Nature had given said pan a good start. That is to say, it wasn't handsome. It was a long, lean, nut-brown face with pronounced jaw muscles, prominent cheekbones, and a thin, hooked nose. This, with his dark eyes and black hair, gave him a hawk-like appearance. Friends talked to him about tepees and tomahawks whenever they wanted him to feel at home.

Well, he wasn't going to feel at home anymore; not unless this brooding jungle held intelligent life dopey enough to swap ten-gauge nickel-thorium wire for a pair of old boots. Or unless some dopey search party was intelligent enough to pick this cosmic dust mote out of a cloud of motes, and took him back. He estimated this as no less than a million-to-one chance. Like spitting at the Empire State hoping to hit a cent-sized mark on one of its walls.

Reaching for his everflo stylus and the ship's log, he opened the log, looked absently at some of the entries.

'Eighteenth day: The spatial convulsion has now flung me past rotal-range of Rigel. Am being tossed into uncharted regions. . . .

'Twenty-fourth day: Arm of convulsion now tails back seven parsecs. Robot recorder now out of gear. Angle of throw changed seven times today. . . .

'Twenty-ninth day: Now beyond arm of the convulsive sweep and regaining control. Speed far beyond range of the astrometer. Applying braking rockets cautiously. Fuel reserve: fourteen hundred yards. . . .

'Thirty-seventh day: Making for planetary system now within reach.'

He scowled, his jaw muscles lumped, and he wrote slowly and legibly, 'Thirty-ninth day: Landed on planet unknown, primary unknown, galactic area standard reference and sector numbers unknown. No cosmic formations were recognizable when observed shortly before landing. Angles of offshoot and speed of transit not recorded, and impossible to estimate. Condition of ship: workable. Fuel reserve: three and one-quarter yards.'

Closing the log, he scowled again, rammed the stylus into its desk-grip, and muttered, 'Now to check on the outside air and then see how the best girl's doing.'

The Radson register had three simple dials. The first recorded outside pressure at thirteen point seven pounds, a reading he observed with much satisfaction. The second said that oxygen content was high. The third had a bi-coloured dial, half-white, half-red, and its needle stood in the middle of the white.

'Breathable,' he grunted, clipping down the register's lid. Crossing the tiny control room, he slid aside a metal panel, looked into the padded compartment behind. 'Coming out, Beauteous?' he asked.

'Steve loves Laura?' inquired a plaintive voice.

'You bet he does!' he responded with becoming passion. He

shoved an arm into the compartment, brought out a large, gaudily coloured macaw. 'Does Laura love Steve?'

'Hey-hey!' cackled Laura harshly. Climbing up his arm, the bird perched on his shoulder. He could feel the grip of its powerful claws. It regarded him with a beady and brilliant eye, then rubbed its crimson head against his left ear. 'Hey-hey! Time flies!'

'Don't mention it,' he reproved. 'There's plenty to remind me of the fact without you chipping in.'

Reaching up, he scratched her poll while she stretched and bowed with absurd delight. He was fond of Laura. She was more than a pet. She was a bona fide member of the crew, issued with her own rations and drawing her own pay. Every probe ship had a crew of two: one man, one macaw. When he'd first heard of it, the practice had seemed crazy – but when he got the reasons it made sense.

'Lonely men, probing beyond the edge of the charts, get queer psychological troubles. They need an anchor to Earth. A macaw provides the necessary companionship – and more! It's the space-hardiest bird we've got, its weight is negligible, it can talk and amuse, it can fend for itself when necessary. On land, it will often sense dangers before you do. Any strange fruit or food it may eat is safe for you to eat. Many a man's life has been saved by his macaw. Look after yours, my boy, and it'll look after you!'

Yes, they looked after each other, Terrestrials both. It was almost a symbiosis of the spaceways. Before the era of astronavigation nobody had thought of such an arrangement, though it had been done before. Miners and their canaries.

Moving over to the miniature air lock, he didn't bother to operate the pump. It wasn't necessary with so small a difference between internal and external pressures. Opening both doors, he let a little of his higher-pressured air sigh out, stood on the rim of the lock, jumped down. Laura fluttered from his shoulder as he leaped, followed him with a flurry of wings, got her talons into his jacket as he staggered upright.

The pair went around the ship, silently surveying its condition. Front braking nozzles O.K., rear steering flares O.K., tail propulsion tubes O.K. All were badly scored but still usable. The skin of the vessel likewise was scored but intact. Three months' supply of food and maybe a thousand yards of wire could get her home, theoretically. But only theoretically; Steve had no delusions about the matter. The odds were still against him even if given the means to move. How do you navigate from you-don't-know-where to you-don't-know-where? Answer: you stroke a rabbit's foot and probably arrive you-don't-know-where-else.

'Well,' he said, rounding the tail, 'it's something in which to live. It'll save us building a shanty. Way back on Terra they want fifty thousand smackers for an all-metal, streamlined bungalow, so I guess we're mighty lucky. I'll make a garden here, and a rockery there, and build a swimming-pool out back. You can wear a pretty frock and do all the cooking.'

'Yawk!' said Laura derisively.

Turning, he had a look at the nearest vegetation. It was of all heights, shapes and sizes, of all shades of green with a few tending toward blueness. There was something peculiar about the stuff but he was unable to decide where the strangeness lay. It wasn't that the growths were alien and unfamiliar – one expected that on every new world – but an underlying something which they shared in common. They had a vague, shadowy air of being not quite right in some basic respect impossible to define.

A plant grew right at his feet. It was green in colour, a foot high, and monocotyledonous. Looked at as a thing in itself, there was nothing wrong with it. Near to it flourished a bush of darker hue, a yard high, with green, fir-like needles in lieu of leaves, and pale, waxy berries scattered over it. That, too, was innocent enough when studied apart from its neighbours. Beside it grew a similar plant, differing only in that its needles were longer and its berries a bright pink. Beyond these towered a cactus-like object dragged out of sombody's drunken dreams, and beside it stood an umbrella-frame which had taken root and produced little purple pods. Individually, they were acceptable.

Collectively, they made the discerning mind search anxiously for it knew not what.

That eerie feature had Steve stumped. Whatever it was, he couldn't nail it down. There was something stranger than the mere strangeness of new forms of plant life, and that was all. He dismissed the problem with a shrug. Time enough to trouble about such matters after he'd dealt with others more urgent such as, for example, the location and purity of the nearest water supply.

A mile away lay a lake of some liquid that might be water. He'd seen it glittering in the sunlight as he'd made his descent, and he'd tried to land fairly near to it. If it wasn't water, well, it'd be just his tough luck and he'd have to look some place else. At worst, the tiny fuel reserve would be enough to permit one circumnavigation of the planet before the ship became pinned down forever. Water he must have if he wasn't going to end up imitating the mummy of Rameses II.

Reaching high, he grasped the rim of the port, dexterously muscled himself upward and through it. For a minute he moved around inside the ship, then reappeared with a four-gallon freezocan which he tossed to the ground. Then he dug out his popgun, a belt of explosive shells, and let down the folding ladder from lock to surface. He'd need that ladder. He could muscle himself up through a hole seven feet high, but not with fifty pounds of can and water.

Finally, he locked both the inner and outer air-lock doors, skipped down the ladder, picked up the can. From the way he'd made his landing the lake should be directly bow-on relative to the vessel, and somewhere the other side of those distant trees. Laura took a fresh grip on his shoulder as he started off. The can swung from his left hand. His right hand rested warily on the gun. He was perpendicular on this world instead of horizontal on another because, on two occasions, his hand had been ready on the gun and because it was the most nervous hand he possessed.

The going was rough. It wasn't so much that the terrain was

craggy as the fact that impeding growths got in his way. At one moment he was stepping over an ankle-high shrub, the next he was facing a burly plant struggling to become a tree. Behind the plant would be a creeper, then a natural zareba of thorns, a fuzz of fine moss, followed by a giant fern. Progress consisted of stepping over one item, ducking beneath a second, going around a third, and crawling under a fourth.

It occurred to him belatedly that if he'd planted the ship tail-first to the lake instead of bow-on, or if he'd let the braking rockets blow after he'd touched down, he'd have saved himself much twisting and dodging. All this obstructing stuff would have been reduced to ashes for at least half the distance to the lake – together with any venomous life it might conceal.

That last thought rang like an alarm bell within his mind just as he doubled up to pass a low-swung creeper. On Venus were creepers that coiled and constricted, swiftly, viciously. Macaws played merry hell, if taken within fifty yards of them. It was a comfort to know that, this time, Laura was riding his shoulder unperturbed – but he kept the hand on the gun.

The elusive peculiarity of the planet's vegetation bothered him all the more as he progressed through it. His inability to discover and name this unnameable queerness nagged at him as he went on. A frown of self-disgust was on his lean face when he dragged himself free of a clinging bush and sat on a rock in a tiny clearing.

Dumping the can at his feet, he glowered at it and promptly caught a glimpse of something bright and shining a few feet beyond the can. He raised his gaze. It was then that he saw the beetle.

The creature was the biggest of its kind ever seen by human eyes. There were other things bigger, of course, but not of this type. Crabs, for instance. But this was no crab. The beetle ambling purposefully across the clearing was large enough to give any crab a severe inferiority complex, but it was a genuine twenty-four-carat beetle. And a beautiful one. Like a scarab.

Except that he clung to the notion that little bugs were vicious and big ones companionable, Steve had no phobia about insects. The amiability of large ones was a theory inherited from school-kid days when he'd been the doting owner of a three-inch stag-beetle afflicted with the name of Edgar.

So he knelt beside the creeping giant, placed his hand palm upward in its path. It investigated the hand with waving feelers, climbed on to his palm, paused there ruminatively. It shone with a sheen of brilliant metallic blue and weighed about three pounds. He jogged it on his hand to get its weight, then put it down, let it wander on. Laura watched it go with a sharp but incurious eye.

'*Scarabaeus anderii*,' Steve said with glum satisfaction. 'I pin my name on him – but nobody'll ever know it!'

'Dinna fash y'sel'!' shouted Laura in a hoarse voice imported straight from Aberdeen. 'Dinna fash! Stop chunnerin', wum-man! Y' gie me a pain ahint ma sporran! Dinna—'

'Shut up!' Steve jerked his shoulder, momentarily unbalanc-ing the bird. 'Why d'you pick up that barbaric dialect quicker than anything else, eh?'

'McGillicuddy,' shrieked Laura with ear-splitting relish. 'McGilli-Gilli-Gillicuddy! The great black — !' It ended with a word that pushed Steve's eyebrows into his hair and surprised even the bird itself. Filming its eyes with amazement, it tightened its claw-hold on his shoulder, opened the eyes, emitted a couple of raucous clucks, and joyfully repeated, 'The great black — '

It didn't get the chance to complete the new and lovely word. A violent jerk of the shoulder unseated it in the nick of time and it fluttered to the ground, squawking protestingly. *Scarabaeus anderii* lumbered out from behind a bush, his blue armour glistening as if freshly polished, and stared reprovingly at Laura.

Then something fifty yards away released a snort like the trump of doom and took one step that shook the earth. *Scarabaeus anderii* took refuge under a projecting root. Laura made an agitated swoop for Steve's shoulder and clung there desperately. Steve's gun was out and pointing northward before the bird had found its perch. Another step. The ground quivered.

\*     \*     \*

Silence for a while. Steven continued to stand like a statue. Then came a monstrous whistle more forceful than that of a locomotive blowing off steam. Something squat and wide and of tremendous length charged headlong through the half-concealing vegetation while the earth trembled beneath its weight.

Its mad onrush carried it blindly twenty yards to Steve's right, the gun swinging to cover its course, but not firing. Steve caught an extended glimpse of a slate-grey bulk with a serrated ridge on its back which, despite the thing's pace, took long to pass. It seemed several times the length of a fire ladder.

Bushes were flung roots topmost and small trees whipped aside as the creature pounded grimly onward in a straight line which carried it far past the ship into the dim distance. It left behind a tattered swathe wide enough for a first-class road. Then the reverberations of its mighty tonnage died out, and it was gone.

Steve used his left hand to pull out a handkerchief and wipe the back of his neck. He kept the gun in his right hand. The explosive shells in that gun were somewhat wicked; any one of them could deprive a rhinoceros of a hunk of meat weighing two hundred pounds. If a man caught one, he just strewed himself over the landscape. By the looks of that slate-coloured galloper, it would need half a dozen shells to feel incommoded. A seventy-five-millimetre bazooka would be more effective for kicking it in the back teeth, but probe-ship boys don't tote around such artillery. Steve finished the mopping, put the handkerchief back, picked up the can.

Laura said pensively, 'I want my mother.'

He scowled, made no reply, set out toward the lake. Her feathers still ruffled, Laura rode his shoulder and lapsed into surly silence.

The stuff in the lake was water, cold, faintly green and a little bitter to the taste. Coffee would camouflage the flavour. If anything, it might improve the coffee since he liked his java bitter, but the stuff would have to be tested before absorbing it in any quantity. Some poisons were accumulative. It wouldn't do to guzzle gaily while building up a death-dealing reserve of lead, for instance. Filling the freezocan, he lugged it to the ship in hundred-yard stages. The swathe helped; it made an easier path to within short distance of the ship's tail. He was perspiring freely by the time he reached the base of the ladder.

Once inside the vessel he relocked both doors, opened the air vents, started the auxiliary lighting-set and plugged in the percolator, using water out of his depleted reserve supply. The golden sky had dulled to orange, with violet streamers creeping upward from the horizon. Looking at it through the transpex dome, he found that the perpetual haze still effectively concealed the sinking sun. A brighter area to one side was all that indicated its position. He'd need his lights soon.

Pulling out the collapsible table, he jammed its supporting leg into place, plugged into its rim the short rod which was Laura's official seat. She claimed the perch immediately, watched him beadily as he set out her meal of water, melon seeds, sunflower seeds, pecans and unshelled oleo nuts. Her manners were anything but ladylike and she started eagerly, without waiting for him.

A deep frown lay across his brown, muscular features as he sat at the table, poured out his coffee and commenced to eat. It persisted through the meal, was still there when he lit a cigarette and stared speculatively up at the dome.

Presently, he murmured, 'I've seen the biggest bug that ever was. I've seen a few other bugs. There were a couple of little ones under a creeper. One was long and brown and many-legged, like an earwig. The other was round and black, with little red dots on its wing cases. I've seen a tiny purple spider and a tinier green one of different shape, also a bug that looked like an aphid. But not an ant.'

'Ant, ant,' hooted Laura. She dropped a piece of oleo nut, climbed down after it. 'Yawk!' she added from the floor.

'Not a bee.'

'Bee,' echoed Laura, companionably. 'Bee-ant. Laura loves Steve.'

Still keeping his attention on the dome, he went on, 'And what's cockeyed about the plants is equally cockeyed about the bugs. I wish I could place it. Why can't I? Maybe I'm going nuts already.'

'Laura loves nuts.'

'I know it, you technicoloured belly!' said Steve rudely.

And at that point night fell with a silent bang. The gold and orange and violet abruptly were swamped with deep, impenetrable blackness devoid of stars or any random gleam. Except for greenish glowings on the instrument panel, the control room was stygian, with Laura swearing steadily on the floor.

Putting out a hand, Steve switched on the indirect lighting. Laura got to her perch with the rescued titbit, concentrated on the job of dealing with it and let him sink back into his thoughts.

'*Scarabaeus anderii* and a pair of smaller bugs and a couple of spiders, all different. At the other end of the scale, that gigantosaurus. But no ant, or bee. Or rather, no ants, no bees.' The switch from singular to plural stirred his back hairs queerly. In some vague way, he felt that he'd touched the heart of the mystery. 'No ant – no ants,' he thought. 'No bee – no bees.' Almost he had it – but still it evaded him.

Giving it up for the time being, he cleared the table, did a few minor chores. After that, he drew a standard sample from the freezocan, put it through its paces. The bitter flavour he identified as being due to the presence of magnesium sulphate in quantity far too small to prove embarrassing. Drinkable – that was something! Food, drink and shelter were the three essentials of survival. He'd enough of the first for six or seven weeks. The lake and the ship were his remaining guarantees of life.

Finding the log, he entered the day's report, bluntly, factually, without any embroidery. Partway through, he found himself stuck for a name for the planet. *Ander*, he decided, would cost him dear if the million-to-one chance put him back among the merciless playmates of the Probe Service. O.K. for a bug, but not for a world. *Laura* wasn't so hot, either – especially when you knew Laura. It wouldn't be seemly to name a big, gold planet after an oversized parrot. Thinking over the golden aspect of this world's sky, he hit upon the name of *Oro*, promptly made the christening authoritative by entering it in his log.

By the time he'd finished, Laura had her head buried deep under one wing. Occasionally she teetered and swung erect again. It always fascinated him to watch how her balance was maintained even in her slumbers. Studying her fondly, he remembered that unexpected addition to her vocabulary. This shifted his thoughts to a fiery-headed and fierier-tongued individual named Menzies, the sworn foe of another volcano named McGillicuddy. If ever the opportunity presented itself, he decided, the educative work of said Menzies was going to be rewarded with a bust on the snoot.

Sighing, he put away the log, wound up the forty-day chronometer, opened his folding bunk and lay down upon it. His hand switched off the lights. Ten years back, a first landing would have kept him awake all night in dithers of excitement. He'd got beyond that now. He'd done it often enough to have grown phlegmatic about it. His eyes closed in preparation for a good night's sleep, and he did sleep – for two hours.

What brought him awake within that short time he didn't know, but suddenly he found himself sitting bolt upright on the edge of the bunk, his ears and nerves stretched to their utmost, his legs quivering in a way they'd never done before. His whole body fizzed with the queer mixture of palpitation and shock which follows narrow escape from disaster.

This was something not within previous experience. Sure and certain in the intense darkness, his hand sought and found his gun. He cuddled the butt in his palm while his mind strove to recall a possible nightmare, though he knew he was not given to nightmares.

Laura moved restlessly on her perch, not truly awake, yet not asleep, and this was unusual in her.

Rejecting the dream theory, he stood up on the bunk, looked

out through the dome. Blackness, the deepest, darkest, most impenetrable blackness it was possible to conceive. And silence! The outside world slumbered in the blackness and the silence as in a sable shroud.

Yet never before had he felt so wide awake in this, his normal sleeping time. Puzzled, he turned slowly round to take in the full circle of unseeable view, and at one point he halted. The surrounding darkness was not complete. In the distance beyond the ship's tail moved a tall, stately glow. How far off it might be was not possible to estimate, but the sight of it stirred his soul and caused his heart to leap.

Uncontrollable emotions were not permitted to master his disciplined mind. Narrowing his eyes, he tried to discern the nature of the glow while his mind sought the reason why the mere sight of it should make him twang like a harp. Bending down, he felt at the head of the bunk, found a leather case, extracted a pair of powerful night-glasses. The glow was still moving, slowly, deliberately, from right to left. He got the glasses on it, screwed the lenses into focus, and the phenomenon leaped into closer view.

The thing was a great column of golden haze much like that of the noonday sky except that small, intense gleams of silver sparkled within it. It was a shaft of lustrous mist bearing a sprinkling of tiny stars. It was like nothing known to or recorded by any form of life lower than the gods. But was it life?

It moved, though its mode of locomotion could not be determined. Self-motivation is the prime symptom of life. It could be life, conceivably though not credibly, from the Terrestrial viewpoint. Consciously, he preferred to think it a strange and purely local feature comparable with Saharan sand-devils. Subconsciously, he knew it was life, tall and terrifying.

He kept the glasses on it while slowly it receded into the darkness, foreshortening with increasing distance and gradually fading from view. To the very last the observable field shifted and shuddered as he failed to control the quiver in his hands. And when the sparkling haze had gone he sat down on the bunk and shivered with eerie cold.

Laura was dodging to and fro along her perch, now thoroughly awake and agitated, but he wasn't inclined to switch on the lights and make the dome a beacon in the night. His hand went out, feeling for her in the darkness, and she clambered eagerly on to his wrist, thence to his lap. She was fussy and demonstrative, pathetically yearning for comfort and companionship. He scratched her poll and fondled her while she pressed close against his chest with funny little crooning noises. For some time he soothed her and, while doing it, fell asleep. Gradually he slumped backward on the bunk. Laura perched on his forearm, clucked tiredly, put her head under a wing.

There was no further awakening until the outer blackness disappeared and the sky again sent its golden glow pouring through the dome. Steve got up, stood on the bunk, had a good look over the surrounding terrain. It remained precisely the same as it had been the day before. Things stewed within his mind while he got his breakfast; especially the jumpiness he'd experienced in the night-time. Laura also was subdued and quiet. Only once before had she been like that – which was when he'd traipsed through the Venusian section of the Panplanetary Zoo and had shown her a crested eagle. The eagle had stared at her with contemptuous dignity.

Though he'd all the time in his life, he now felt a peculiar urge to hasten. Getting the gun and the freezocan, he made a full dozen trips to the lake, wasting no minutes, nor stopping to study the still enigmatic plants and bugs. It was late in the afternoon by the time he'd filled the ship's fifty-gallon reservoir, and had the satisfaction of knowing that he'd got a drinkable quota to match his food supply.

There had been no sign of gigantosaurus or any other animal. Once he'd seen something flying in the far distance, bird-like or bat-like. Laura had cocked a sharp eye at it but betrayed no undue interest. Right now she was more concerned with a new fruit. Steve sat in the rim of the outer lock-door, his legs dangling, and watched her clambering over a small tree thirty yards away. The gun lay in his lap; he was ready to take a crack at anything which might be ready to take a crack at Laura.

The bird sampled the tree's fruit, a crop resembling blue-shelled lychee nuts. She ate one with relish, grabbed another. Steve lay back in the lock, stretched to reach a bag, then dropped to the ground and went across to the tree. He tried a nut. Its flesh was soft, juicy, sweet and citreous. He filled the bag with the fruit, slung it into the ship.

Nearby stood another tree, not quite the same, but very similar. It bore nuts like the first except that they were larger. Picking one, he offered it to Laura who tried it, spat it out in disgust. Picking a second, he slit it, licked the flesh gingerly. As far as he could tell, it was the same. Evidently he couldn't tell far enough: Laura's diagnosis said it was not the same. The difference, too subtle for him to detect, might be sufficient to roll him that shape to the unpleasant end. He flung the thing away, went back to his seat in the lock, and ruminated.

That elusive, nagging feature of Oro's plants and bugs could be narrowed down to these two nuts. He felt sure of that. If he could discover why – parrotwise – one nut was not, he'd have his finger right on the secret. The more he thought about those similar fruits the more he felt that, in sober fact, his finger was on the secret already – but he lacked the power to lift it and see what lay beneath.

Tantalizing, his mulling over the subject landed him the same place as before; namely, nowhere. It got his dander up, and he went back to the trees, subjected both to close examination. His sense of sight told him that they were different individuals of the same species. Laura's sense of whatchamacallit insisted that they were different species. Ergo, you can't believe the evidence of your eyes. He was aware of that fact, of course, since it was a platitude of the spaceways, but when you couldn't trust your optics it was legitimate to try to discover just why you couldn't trust 'em. And he couldn't discover even that!

It soured him so much that he returned to the ship, locked its doors, called Laura back to his shoulder and set off on a tail-ward exploration. The rules of first landings were simple and sensible. Go in slowly, come out quickly, and remember that all we want from you is evidence of suitability for human life. Thoroughly explore a small area rather than scout a big one – the mapping parties will do the rest. Use your ship as a base and centralize it where you can live – don't move it unnecessarily. Restrict your trips to a radius representing daylight-reach and lock yourself in after dark.

Was Oro suitable for human life? The unwritten law was that you don't jump to conclusions and say, 'Of course! I'm still living, aren't I?' Cameron who'd plonked his ship on Mithra, for instance, thought he'd found paradise until, on the seventeenth day, he'd discovered the fungoid plague. He'd left like a bat out of hell and had spent three sweaty, swearing days in the Lunar Purification Plant before becoming fit for society. The authorities had vaporized his ship. Mithra had been taboo ever since. Every world a potential trap baited with scientific delight. The job of the Probe Service was to enter the traps and jounce on the springs. Another dollop of real estate for Terra – if nothing broke your neck.

Maybe Oro was loaded for bear. The thing that walked in the night, Steve mused, bore awful suggestion of non-human power. So did a waterspout, and whoever heard of anyone successfully wrestling with a waterspout? If this Oro-spout were sentient, so much the worse for human prospects. He'd have to get the measure of it, he decided, even if he had to chase it through the blank avenues of night. Plodding steadily away from the tail, gun in hand, he pondered so deeply that he entirely overlooked the fact that he wasn't on a pukka probe job anyway, and that nothing else remotely human might reach Oro in a thousand years. Even space-boys can be creatures of habit. Their job: to look for death; they were liable to go on looking long after the need had passed, in bland disregard of the certainty that if you look for a thing long enough ultimately you find it!

The ship's chronometer had given him five hours to darkness. Two and a half hours each way; say ten miles out and ten back. The water had consumed his time. On the morrow, and henceforth, he'd increase the radius to twelve and take it easier.

Then all thoughts fled from his mind as he came to the edge of the vegetation. The stuff didn't dribble out of existence with hardy spurs and offshoots fighting for a hold in suddenly rocky ground. It stopped abruptly, in light loam, as if cut off with a machete, and from where it stopped spread a different crop. The new growths were tiny and crystalline.

He accepted the crystalline crop without surprise; knowing that novelty was the inevitable feature of any new locale. Things were ordinary only by Terrestrial standards. Outside of Terra, nothing was supernormal or abnormal except in so far as they failed to jibe with their own peculiar conditions. Besides, there were crystalline growths on Mars. The one unacceptable feature of the situation was the way in which vegetable growths ended and crystalline ones began. He stepped back to the verge and made another startled survey of the borderline. It was so straight that the sight screwed his brain around. Like a field. A cultivated field. Dead straightness of that sort couldn't be other than artificial. Little beads of moisture popped out on his back.

Squatting on the heel of his right boot, he gazed at the nearest crystals and said to Laura, 'Chicken, I think these things got planted. Question is, who planted 'em?'

'McGillicuddy,' suggested Laura brightly.

Putting out a finger, he flicked the crystal sprouting near the toe of his boot, a green, branchy object an inch high.

The crystal vibrated and said, '*Zing!*' in a sweet, high voice.

He flicked its neighbour, and that said, '*Zang!*' in a lower tone.

He flicked a third. It emitted no note, but broke into a thousand shards.

Standing up, he scratched his head, making Laura fight for a clawhold within the circle of his arm. One zinged and one zanged and one returned to dust. Two nuts. Zings and zangs and nuts. It was right in his grasp if only he could open his hand and look at what he'd got.

Then he lifted his puzzled and slightly ireful gaze, saw something fluttering erratically across the crystal field; it was making for the vegetation. Laura took off with a raucous cackle, her blue-and-crimson wings beating powerfully. She swooped over the object, frightening it so low that it dodged and side-slipped only a few feet above Steve's head. He saw that it was a large butterfly, frill-winged, almost as gaudy as Laura. The bird swooped again, scaring the insect but not menacing it. He called her back, set out to cross the area ahead. Crystals crunched to powder under his heavy boots as he tramped on.

Half an hour later he was toiling up a steep, crystal-coated slope when his thoughts suddenly jelled and he stopped with such abruptness that Laura spilled from his shoulder and perforce took to wing. She beat round in a circle, came back to her perch, made bitter remarks in an unknown language.

'One of this and one of that,' he said. 'No twos or threes or dozens. Nothing I've seen has repeated itself. There's only one gigantosaurus, only one *Scarabaeus anderii*, only one of every danged thing. Every item is unique, original, and an individual creation in its own right. What does that suggest?'

'McGillicuddy,' offered Laura.

'For Pete's sake, forget McGillicuddy.'

'For Pete's sake, for Pete's sake,' yelled Laura, much taken by the phrase. 'The great black—'

Again he upset her in the nick of time, making her take to flight while he continued talking to himself. 'It suggests constant and all-pervading mutation. Everything breeds something quite different from itself and there aren't any dominant strains.' He frowned at the obvious snag in this theory. 'But how the blazes does anything breed? What fertilizes which?'

'McGilli—,' began Laura, then changed her mind and shut up.

'Anyway, if nothing breeds true, it'll be tough on the food problem,' he went on. 'What's edible on one plant may be a killer on its offspring. Today's fodder is tomorrow's poison. How's a farmer to know what he's going to get? Hey-hey, if I'm guessing right, this planet won't support a couple of hogs.'

'No, sir. No hogs. Laura loves hogs.'

'Be quiet,' he snapped. 'Now, what shouldn't support a couple of hogs demonstrably does support gigantosaurus – and any other fancy animals which may be mooching around. It seems crazy to me. On Venus or any other place full of consistent fodder, gigantosaurus would thrive; but here, according to my calculations, the big lunk has no right to be alive. He ought to be dead.'

So saying, he topped the rise and found the monster in question sprawling right across the opposite slope. It *was* dead.

The way in which he determined its deadness was appropriately swift, simple and effective. Its enormous bulk lay draped across the full length of the slope and its dragonhead, the size of a lifeboat, pointed toward him. The head had two dull, lacklustre eyes like dinner plates. He planted a shell smack in the right eye and a sizeable hunk of noggin promptly splashed in all directions. The body did not stir.

There was a shell ready for the other eye should the creature leap to frantic, vengeful life, but the mighty hulk remained supine.

His boots continued to desiccate crystals as he went down the slope, curved a hundred yards off his route to get around the corpse, and trudged up the farther rise. Momentarily, he wasn't much interested in the dead beast. Time was short and he could come again tomorrow, bringing a full-colour stereoscopic camera with him. Gigantosaurus would go on record in style, but would have to wait.

This second rise was a good deal higher, and more trying a climb. Its crest represented the approximate limit of this day's trip, and he felt anxious to surmount it before turning back. Humanity's characteristic urge to see what lay over the hill remained as strong as on the day determined ancestors topped the Rockies. He had to have a look, firstly because elevation gave range to vision, and secondly because of that prowler in the night – and, nearly as he could estimate, the prowler had gone down behind this rise. A column of mist, sucked down from the sky, might move around aimlessly, going nowhere, but instinct maintained that this had been no mere column of mist, and that it was going somewhere.

Where?

Out of breath, he pounded over the crest, looked down into an immense valley, and found the answer.

The crystal growths gave out on the crest, again in a perfectly straight line. Beyond them the light loam, devoid of rock, ran gently down to the valley and up the farther side. Both slopes were sparsely dotted with queer, jelly-like lumps of matter which lay and quivered beneath the sky's golden glow.

From the closed end of the valley jutted a great, glistening fabrication, flat-roofed, flat-fronted, with a huge, square hole gaping in its mid-section at front. It looked like a tremendous oblong slab of polished, milk-white plastic half-buried endwise in a sandy hill. No decoration disturbed its smooth, gleaming surface. No road led to the hole in front. Somehow, it had the new-old air of a house that struggles to look empty because it is full – of fiends.

Steve's back hairs prickled as he studied it. One thing was obvious – Oro bore intelligent life. One thing was possible – the golden column represented that life. One thing was probable – fleshly Terrestrials and hazy Orons would have difficulty in finding a basis for friendship and co-operation.

Whereas enmity needs no basis.

Curiosity and caution pulled him opposite ways. One urged him down into the valley while the other drove him back, back, while yet there was time. He consulted his watch. Less than three hours to go, within which he had to return to the ship, enter the log, prepare supper. That milky creation was at least two miles away, a good hour's journey there and back. Let it wait. Give it another day and he'd have more time for it, with the benefit of needful thought betweentimes.

Caution triumphed. He investigated the nearest jellyblob. It was flat, a yard in diameter, green, with bluish streaks and many tiny bubbles hiding in its semi-transparency. The thing pulsated slowly. He poked at it with the toe of his boot, and it contracted, humping itself in the middle, then sluggishly relaxed. No amoeba, he decided. A low form of life, but complicated withal. Laura didn't like the object. She skittered off as he bent over it, vented her anger by bashing a few crystals.

This jellyblob wasn't like its nearest neighbour, or like any other. One of each, only one. The same rule: one butterfly of a kind, one bug, one plant, one of these quivering things.

A final stare at the distant mystery down in the valley, then he retraced his steps. When the ship came into sight he speeded up like a gladsome voyager nearing home. There were new prints near the vessel, big, three-toed, deeply impressed spoor which revealed that something large and two-legged had wandered past in his absence. Evidently an animal, for nothing intelligent would have meandered on so casually without circling and inspecting the nearby invader from space. He dismissed it from his mind. There was only one thingummybob, he felt certain of that.

Once inside the ship, he relocked the doors, gave Laura her feed, ate his supper. Then he dragged out the log, made his day's entry, had a look around from the dome. Violet streamers once more were creeping upward from the horizon. He frowned at the encompassing vegetation. What sort of stuff had bred all this in the past? What sort of stuff would this breed in the future? How did it progenerate, anyway?

Wholesale radical mutation presupposed modification of genes by hard radiation in persistent and considerable blasts. You shouldn't get hard radiation on lightweight planets – unless it poured in from the sky. Here, it didn't pour from the sky, or from any place else. In fact, there wasn't any.

He was pretty certain of that fact because he'd a special interest in it and had checked up on it. Hard radiation betokened the presence of radioactive elements which, at a pinch, might be usable as fuel. The ship was equipped to detect such stuff. Among the junk was a cosmiray counter, a radium hen, and a gold-leaf electroscope. The hen and the counter hadn't given so much as one heartening cluck, in fact the only clucks had been Laura's. The electroscope he'd charged on landing and its leaves still formed an inverted vee. The air was dry, ionization negligible, and the leaves didn't look likely to collapse for a week.

'Something wrong with my theorizing,' he complained to Laura. 'My think-stuff's not doing its job.'

'Not doing its job,' echoed Laura faithfully. She cracked a pecan with a grating noise that set his teeth on edge. 'I tell you it's a hoodoo ship. I won't sail. No, not even if you pray for me, I won't, I won't, I won't. Nope. Nix. Who's drunk? That hairy Lowlander Mc—'

'Laura!' he said sharply.

'Gillicuddy,' she finished with bland defiance. Again she rasped his teeth. 'Rings bigger'n Saturn's I saw them myself. Who's a liar? Yawk! She's down in Grayway Bay, on Tethis. Boy, what a torso!'

He looked at her hard and said, 'You're nuts!'

'Sure! Sure, pal! Laura loves nuts. Have one on me.'

'O.K.,' he accepted, holding out his hand.

Cocking her colourful pate, she pecked at his hand, gravely selected a pecan and gave it to him. He cracked it, chewed on the kernel while starting up the lighting-set. It was almost as if night were waiting for him. Blackness fell even as he switched on the lights.

With the darkness came a keen sense of unease. The dome was the trouble. It blazed like a beacon and there was no way of blacking it out except by turning off the lights. Beacons attracted things, and he'd no desire to become a centre of attraction in present circumstances. That is to say, not at night.

Long experience had bred fine contempt for alien animals, no matter how whacky, but outlandish intelligence was a different proposition. So filled was he with the strange inward conviction that last night's phenomenon was something that knew its onions that it didn't occur to him to wonder whether a glowing column possessed eyes or anything equivalent to a sense of sight. If it had occurred to him, he'd have derived no comfort from it. His desire to be weighed in the balance in some eerie, extrasensory way was even less than his desire to be gaped at visually in his slumbers.

An unholy mess of thoughts and ideas was still cooking in his mind when he extinguished the lights, bunked down and went to sleep. Nothing disturbed him this time, but when he awoke with the golden dawn his chest was damp with perspiration and Laura again had sought refuge on his arm.

Digging out breakfast, his thoughts began to marshal themselves as he kept his hands busy. Pouring out a shot of hot coffee, he spoke to Laura.

'I'm durned if I'm going to go scatty trying to maintain a three-watch system single-handed, which is what I'm supposed to do if faced by powers unknown when I'm not able to beat it. Those armchair warriors at headquarters ought to get a taste of situations not precisely specified in the book of rules.'

'Burp!' said Laura contemptuously.

'He who fights and runs away lives to fight another day,' Steve quoted. 'That's the Probe Law. It's a nice, smooth, lovely law – when you can run away. We can't!'

'Burrup!' said Laura with unnecessary emphasis.

'For a woman, your manners are downright disgusting,' he told her. 'Now, I'm not going to spend the brief remainder of my life looking fearfully over my shoulder. The only way to get rid of powers unknown is to convert 'em into powers known and understood. As Uncle Joe told Willie when dragging him to the dentist, the longer we put it off the worse it'll feel.'

'Dinna fash y'sel',' declaimed Laura. 'Burp-gollop-bop!'

Giving her a look of extreme distaste, he continued, 'So we'll try tossing the bull. Such techniques disconcert bulls sometimes.' Standing up, he grabbed Laura, shoved her into her travelling compartment, slid the panel shut. 'We're going to blow off forthwith.'

Climbing up to the control seat, he stamped on the energizer stud. The tail rockets popped a few times, broke into a subdued roar. Juggling the controls to get the preparatory feel of them, he stepped up the boost until the entire vessel trembled and the rear venturis began to glow cherry-red. Slowly the ship commenced to edge its bulk forward and, as it did so, he fed it the take-off shot. A half-mile blast kicked backward and the probe ship plummeted into the sky.

Pulling it round in a wide and shallow sweep, he thundered over the borderline of vegetation, the fields of crystals and the hills beyond. In a flash he was plunging through the valley, braking rockets blazing from the nose. This was tricky. He had to co-ordinate forward shoot, backward thrust and downward surge, but like most of his kind he took pride in the stunts performable with these neat little vessels. An awe-inspired audience was all he lacked to make the exhibition perfect. The vessel landed fairly and squarely on the milk-white roof of the alien edifice, slid halfway to the cliff, then stopped.

'Boy,' he breathed, 'am I good!' He remained in his seat, stared around through the dome, and felt that he ought to add, 'And too young to die.' Occasionally eyeing the chronometer, he waited a while. The boat must have handed that roof sufficient to wake the dead. If anyone were in, they'd soon hotfoot out to see who was heaving hundred-ton bottles at their shingles. Nobody emerged. He gave them half an hour, his hawk-like face strained, alert. Then he gave it up, said, 'Ah, well,' and got out of the seat.

He freed Laura. She came out with ruffled dignity, like a dowager who's paraded into the wrong room. Females were always curious critters, in his logic, and he ignored her attitude, got his gun, unlocked the doors, jumped down on to the roof. Laura followed reluctantly, came to his shoulder as if thereby conferring a great favour.

Walking past the tail to the edge of the roof, he looked down. The sheerness of the five-hundred-feet drop took him aback. Immediately below his feet, the entrance soared four hundred feet up from the ground and he was standing on the hundred-foot lintel surmounting it. The only way down was to walk to the side of the roof and reach the earthy slope in which the building was embedded, seeking a path down that.

He covered a quarter of a mile of roof to get to the slope, his eyes examining the roof's surface as he went, and failing to find one crack or joint in the uniformly smooth surface. Huge as it was, the erection appeared to have been moulded all in one piece – a fact which did nothing to lessen inward misgivings. Whoever did this mighty job weren't Zulus!

From the ground level the entrance loomed bigger than ever. If there had been a similar gap the other side of the building, and a clear way through, he could have taken the ship in at one end and out at the other as easily as threading a needle.

Absence of doors didn't seem peculiar. It was difficult to imagine any sort of door huge enough to fill this opening yet sufficiently balanced to enable anyone – or anything – to pull open or shut. With a final, cautious look around which revealed nothing moving in the valley, he stepped boldly through the entrance, blinked his eyes, found interior darkness slowly fading as visual retention lapsed and gave up remembrance of the golden glow outside.

There was a glow inside, a different one, paler, ghastlier, greenish. It exuded from the floor, the walls, the ceiling, and the total area of radiation was enough to light the place clearly, with no shadows. He sniffed as his vision adjusted itself. There was a strong smell of ozone mixed with other, unidentifiable odours.

To his right and left, rising hundreds of feet, stood great tiers of transparent cases. He went to the ones on his right and examined them. They were cubes, about a yard each way, made of something like transpex. Each contained three inches of loam from which spouted a crystal. No two crystals were alike; some small and branchy, others large and indescribably complicated.

Dumb with thought, he went around to the back of the monster tier, found another ten yards behind it. And another behind that. And another and another. All with crystals. The number and variety of them made his head whirl. He could study only the two bottom rows of each rack, but row on row stepped themselves far above his head to within short distance of the roof. Their total number was beyond estimation.

It was the same on the left. Crystals by the thousands. Looking more closely at one especially fine example, he noticed that the front plate of its case bore a small, inobtrusive pattern of dots etched upon the outer surface. Investigation revealed that all cases were similarly marked, differing only in the number and arrangement of the dots. Undoubtedly, some sort of cosmic code used for classification purposes.

'The Oron Museum of Natural History,' he guessed, in a whisper.

'You're a liar,' squawked Laura, violently. 'I tell you it's a hoodoo—' She stopped, dumfounded, as her own voice roared through the building in deep, organ-like tones, 'A hoodoo – a hoodoo –'

'Holy smoke, will you keep quiet!' hissed Steve. He tried to keep watch on the exit and the interior simultaneously. But the voice rumbled away in the distance without bringing anyone to dispute their invasion.

Turning, he paced hurriedly past the first blocks of tiers to the next batteries of exhibits. Jellyblobs in this lot. Small ones, no bigger than his wristwatch, numberable in thousands. None appeared to be alive, he noted.

Sections three, four and five took him a mile into the building as nearly as he could estimate. He passed mosses, lichens and shrubs, all dead but wondrously preserved. By this time he was ready to guess at section six – plants. He was wrong. The sixth layout displayed bugs, including moths, butterflies, and strange, unfamiliar objects resembling chitinous humming-birds. There was no sample of *Scarabaeus anderii*, unless it were several hundred feet up. Or unless there was an empty box ready for it – when its day was done.

Who made the boxes? Had it prepared one for him? One for Laura? He visualized himself, petrified forever, squatting in the seventieth case of the twenty-fifth row of the tenth tier in section something-or-other, his front panel duly tagged with its appropriate dots. It was a lousy picture. It made his forehead wrinkle to think of it.

Looking for he knew not what, he plunged steadily on, advancing deeper and deeper into the heart of the building. Not a soul, not a sound, not a footprint. Only that all-pervading smell and the unvarying glow. He had a feeling that the place was visited frequently but never occupied for any worthwhile period of time. Without bothering to stop and look, he passed an enormous case containing a creature faintly resembling a bison-headed rhinoceros, then other, still larger cases holding equally larger exhibits – all carefully dot-marked.

Finally, he rounded a box so tremendous that it sprawled across the full width of the hall. It contained the grand-pappy of all trees and the great-grand-pappy of all serpents. Behind, for a change, reared five-hundred-feet-high racks of metal cupboards, each cupboard with a stud set in its polished door, each ornamented with more groups of mysteriously arranged dots.

Greatly daring, he pressed the stud on the nearest cupboard and its door swung open with a juicy click. The result proved disappointing. The cupboard was filled with stacks of small, glassy sheets each smothered with dots.

'Super filing-system,' he grunted, closing the door. 'Old Prof Heggarty would give his right arm to be here.'

'Heggarty,' said Laura, in a faltering voice. 'For Pete's sake!'

He looked at her sharply. She was ruffled and fidgety, showing signs of increasing agitation.

'What's the matter, Chicken?'

She peeked at him, returned her anxious gaze the way they had come, side-stepped to and fro on his shoulder. Her neck feathers started to rise. A nervous cluck came from her beak and she cowered close to his jacket.

'Darn!' he muttered. Spinning on one heel, he raced past successive filing blocks, got into the ten-yards space between the end block and the wall. His gun was out and he kept watch on the front of the blocks while his free hand tried to soothe Laura.

She snuggled up close, rubbing her head into his neck and trying to hide under the angle of his jaw.

'Quiet, Honey,' he whispered. 'Just you keep quiet and stay with Steve, and we'll be all right.'

She kept quiet, though she'd begun to tremble. His heart speeded up in sympathy though he could see nothing, hear nothing to warrant it.

Then, while he watched and waited, and still in absolute silence, the interior brightness waxed, became less green, more golden. And suddenly he knew what it was that was coming. He *knew* what it was!

He sank on one knee to make himself as small and inconspicuous as possible. Now his heart was palpitating wildly and no coldness in his mind could freeze it down to slower, more normal beat. The silence, the awful silence of its approach was the unbearable feature. The crushing thud of a weighty foot or hoof would have been better. Colossi have no right to steal along like ghosts.

And the golden glow built up, drowning out the green radiance from floor to roof, setting the multitude of case-surfaces afire with its brilliance. It grew as strong as the golden sky, and stronger. It became all-pervading, unendurable, leaving no darkness in which to hide, no sanctuary for little things.

It flamed like the rising sun or like something drawn from the heart of a sun, and the glory of its radiance sent the cowering watcher's mind awhirl. He struggled fiercely to control his brain, to discipline it, to bind it to his fading will – and failed.

With drawn face beaded by sweat, Steve caught the merest fragmentary glimpse of the column's edge appearing from between the stacks of the centre aisle. He saw a blinding strip of burnished gold in which glittered a pure white star, then a violent effervescence seemed to occur within his brain and he fell forward into a cloud of tiny bubbles.

Down, down he sank through myriad bubbles and swirls and sprays of iridescent froth and foam which shone and changed and shone anew with every conceivable colour. And all the time his mind strove frantically to battle upward and drag his soul to the surface.

Deep into the nethermost reaches he went while still the bubbles whirled around in their thousands and their colours were of numberless hues. Then his progress slowed. Gradually the froth and the foam ceased to rotate upward, stopped its circling, began to swirl in the reverse direction and sink. He was rising! He rose for a lifetime, floating weightlessly, in a dream-like trance.

The last of the bubbles drifted eerily away, leaving him in a brief hiatus of non-existence – then he found himself sprawled full length on the floor with a dazed Laura clinging to his arm. He blinked his eyes, slowly, several times. They were strained and sore. His heart was still palpitating and his legs felt weak. There was a strange sensation in his stomach as if memory had sickened him with a shock from long, long ago.

He didn't get up from the floor right away; his body was too shaken and his mind too muddled for that. While his wits came back and his composure returned, he lay and noted all the invading goldness had gone and that again the interior illumination was a dull, shadowless green. Then his eyes found his watch and he sat up, startled. Two hours had flown.

That fact brought him shakily to his feet. Peering around the end of the bank of filing cabinets, he saw that nothing had changed. Instinct told him that the golden visitor had gone and that once more he had this place to himself. Had it become aware of his presence? Had it made him lose consciousness or, if not, why had he lost it? Had it done anything about the ship on the roof?

Picking up his futile gun, he spun it by its stud guard and looked at it with contempt. Then he holstered it, helped Laura on to his shoulder where she perched groggily, went around the back of the racks and still deeper into the building.

'I reckon we're O.K., Honey,' he told her. 'I think we're too small to be noticed. We're like mice. Who bothers to trap mice when he's got bigger and more important things in mind?' He pulled a face, not liking the mouse comparison. It wasn't flattering either to him or his kind. But it was the best he could think of at the moment. 'So, like little mice, let's look for the cheese. I'm not giving up just because a big hunk of something has sneaked past and put a scare into us. We don't scare off, do we, Sweetness?'

'No,' said Laura unenthusiastically. Her voice was still subdued and her eyes perked apprehensively this way and that. 'No scare. I won't sail, I tell you. Blow my sternpipes! Laura loves nuts!'

'Don't you call me a nut!'

'Nuts! Stick to farming – it gets you more eggs. McGillicuddy, the great—'

'Hey!' he warned.

She shut up abruptly. He put the pace on, refusing to admit that his system felt slightly jittery with nervous strain or that anything had got him bothered. But he knew that he'd no desire to be near the sparkling giant again. Once was enough, more than enough. It wasn't that he feared it, but something else, something he was quite unable to define.

Passing the last bank of cabinets, he found himself facing a machine. It was complicated and bizarre – and it was making a crystalline growth. Near it, another and different machine was manufacturing a small, horned lizard. There could be no doubt at all about the process of fabrication because both objects were half-made and both progressed slightly even as he watched. In a couple of hours' time, perhaps less, they'd be finished, and all they'd need would be . . . would be—

The hairs stiffened on the back of his neck and he commenced to run. Endless machines, all different, all making different things, plants, bugs, birds and fungoids. It was done by electroponics, atom fed to atom like brick after brick to build a house. It wasn't synthesis because that's only assembly, and this was assembly plus growth in response to unknown laws. In each of these machines, he knew, was some key or code or cipher, some weird master-control of unimaginable complexity, determining the patterns each was building – and the patterns were infinitely variable.

Here and there a piece of apparatus stood silent, inactive, their tasks complete. Here and there other monstrous layouts were in pieces, either under repair or readied for modification. He stopped by one which had finished its job. It had fashioned a delicately shaded moth which perched motionless like a jewelled statue within its fabrication jar. The creature was perfect as far as he could tell, and all it was waiting for was . . . was—

Beads of moisture popped out on his forehead. All that moth needed was the breath of life!

He forced a multitude of notions to get out of his mind; it was the only way to retain a hold on himself. Divert your attention – take it off this and place it on that! Firmly, he fastened his attention on one tremendous, partly disassembled machine lying nearby. Its guts were exposed, revealing great field-coils of dull grey wire. Bits of similar wire lay scattered around on the floor.

Picking up a short piece, he found it surprisingly heavy. He took off his wristwatch, opened its back, brought the wire near to its works. The Venusian jargoon bearing fluoresced immediately. V-jargoons invariably glowed in the presence of near radiation. This unknown metal was a possible fuel. His heart gave a jump at the mere thought of it.

Should he drag out a huge coil and lug it up to the ship? It was very heavy, and he'd need a considerable length of the stuff – if it was usable as fuel. Supposing the disappearance of the coil caused mousetraps to be set before he returned to search anew?

It pays to stop and think whenever you've got time to stop and think; that was a fundamental of Probe Service philosophy. Pocketing a sample of the wire, he sought around other disassembled machines for more. The search took him still deeper into the building and he fought harder to keep his attention concentrated solely on the task. It wasn't easy. There was that dog, for instance, standing there, statue-like, waiting, waiting. If only it had been anything but indubitably and recognizably an Earth-type dog. It was impossible to avoid seeing it. It would be equally impossible to avoid seeing other, even more familiar forms – if they were there.

He'd gained seven samples of different radioactive wires when he gave up the search. A cockatoo ended his peregrinations. The bird stood steadfastly in its jar, its blue plumage smooth and bright, its crimson crest raised, its bright eye fixed in what was not death but not yet life. Laura shrieked at it hysterically and the immense hall shrieked back at her with long-drawn roars and rumbles that reverberated into dim distances. Laura's reaction was too much: he wanted no cause for similar reaction of his own.

He sped through the building at top pace, passing the filing cabinets and the mighty array of exhibition cases unheedingly. Up the loamy side-slopes he climbed almost as rapidly as he'd gone down, and he was breathing heavily by the time he got into the ship.

His first action was to check the ship for evidence of interference. There wasn't any. Next, he checked the instruments. The electroscope's leaves were collapsed. Charging them, he watched them flip open and flop together again. The counter showed radiation aplenty. The hen clucked energetically. He'd blundered somewhat – he should have checked up when first he landed on the roof. However, no matter. What lay beneath the roof was now known; the instruments would have advised him earlier but not as informatively.

Laura had her feed while he accompanied her with a swift meal. After that, he dug out his samples of wire. No two were the same gauge and one obviously was far too thick to enter the feed holes of the Kingston-Kanes. It took him half an hour to file it down to a suitable diameter. The original piece of dull grey wire took the first test. Feeding it in, he set the control to minimum warming-up intensity, stepped on the energizer. Nothing happened.

He scowled to himself. Someday they'd have jobs better than the sturdy but finicky Kingston-Kanes, jobs that'd eat anything eatable. Density and radioactivity weren't enough for these motors; the stuff fed to them had to be right.

Going back to the Kingston-Kane, he pulled out the wire, found its end fused into shapelessness. Definitely a failure. Inserting the second sample, another grey wire not so dull as the first, he returned to the controls, rammed the energizer. The tail rockets promptly blasted with a low, moaning note and the thrust dial showed sixty per cent normal surge.

Some people would have got mad at that point. Steve didn't. His lean, hawk-like features quirked, he felt in his pocket for the third sample, tried that. No soap. The fourth likewise was a flop. The fifth produced a peculiar and rhythmic series of blasts which shook the vessel from end to end and caused the thrust-dial needle to waggle between one hundred per cent and zero. He visualized the Probe patrols popping through space like outboard motors while he extracted the stuff and fed the sixth sample. The sixth roared joyously at one hundred and seventy per cent. The seventh sample was another flop.

He discarded all but what was left of the sixth wire. The stuff was about twelve-gauge and near enough for his purpose. It resembled deep-coloured copper but was not as soft as copper nor as heavy. Hard, springy and light, like telephone wire. If there were at least a thousand yards of it below, and if he could manage to drag it up to the ship, and if the golden thing didn't come along and ball up the works, he might be able to blow free. Then he'd get some place civilized – if he could find it. The future was based on an appalling selection of 'ifs'.

The easiest and most obvious way to salvage the needed treasure was to blow a hole in the roof, lower a cable through it, and wind up the wire with the aid of the ship's tiny winch. Problem: how to blow a hole without suitable explosives. Answer: drill the roof, insert unshelled pistol ammunition, say a prayer and pop the stuff off electrically. He tried it, using a hand drill. The bit promptly curled up as if gnawing on a diamond. He drew his gun, bounced a shell off the roof; the missile exploded with a sharp, hard crack and fragments of shell casing whined shrilly into the sky. Where it had struck, the roof bore a blast smudge and a couple of fine scratches.

There was nothing for it but to go down and heave on his shoulders as much loot as he could carry. And do it right away. Darkness would fall before long, and he didn't want to encounter that golden thing in the dark. It was fateful enough in broad light of day, or in the queer, green glow of the building's interior, but to have it stealing softly behind him as he struggled through the night-time with his plunder was something of which he didn't care to think.

Locking the ship and leaving Laura inside, he returned to the building, made his way past the mile of cases and cabinets to the machine section at the back. He stopped to study nothing on his way. He didn't wish to study anything. The wire was the thing, only the wire. Besides, mundane thoughts of mundane wire didn't twist one's mind around until one found it hard to concentrate.

Nevertheless, his mind was afire as he searched. Half of it was prickly with alertness, apprehensive of the golden column's sudden return; the other half burned with excitement at the possibility of release. Outwardly, his manner showed nothing of this; it was calm, assured, methodical.

Within ten minutes he'd found a great coil of the coppery metal, a huge ovoid, intricately wound, lying beside a dis-assembled machine. He tried to move it, could not shift it an inch. The thing was far too big, too heavy for one to handle. To get it on to the roof he'd have to cut it up and make four trips of it – and some of its inner windings were fused together. So near, so far! Freedom depended upon his ability to move a lump of metal a thousand feet vertically. He muttered some of Laura's words to himself.

Although the wire cutters were ready in his hand, he paused to think, decided to look farther before tackling this job. It was a wise decision which brought its reward, for at a point a mere hundred yards away he came across another, differently shaped coil, wheel-shaped, in good condition, easy to unreel. This again was too heavy to carry, but with a tremendous effort which made his muscles crack he got it up on its rim and proceeded to roll it along like a monster tyre.

Several times he had to stop and let the coil lean against the nearest case while he rested a moment. The last such case trembled under the impact of the weighty coil and its shining, spidery occupant stirred in momentary simulation of life. His dislike of the spider shot up with its motion; he made his rest brief, bowled the coil onward.

Violet streaks again were creeping from the horizon when he rolled his loot out of the mighty exit and reached the bottom of the bank. Here, he stopped, clipped the wire with his cutters, took the free end, climbed the bank with it. The wire uncoiled without hindrance until he reached the ship, where he attached it to the winch, wound the lot in, rewound it on the feed spool.

Night fell in one ominous swoop. His hands were trembling slightly but his hawk-like face was firm, phlegmatic as he carefully threaded the wire's end through the automatic injector and into the feed hole of the Kingston-Kanes. That done, he slid open Laura's door, gave her some of the fruit they'd picked off the Oron tree. She accepted it morbidly, her manner still subdued, and not inclined for speech.

'Stay inside, Honey,' he soothed. 'We're getting out of this and going home.

Shutting her in, he climbed into the control seat, switched on the nose beam, saw it pierce the darkness and light up the facing cliff. Then he stamped on the energizer, warmed the tubes. Their bellow was violent and comforting. At seventy per cent better thrust he'd have to be a lot more careful in all his adjustments: it wouldn't do to melt his own tail off when success was within his grasp. All the same, he felt strangely impatient, as if every minute counted, aye, every second!

But he contained himself, got the venturis heated, gave a discreet puff on his starboard steering flare, watched the cliff glide sidewise past as the ship slewed around on its belly. Another puff, then another, and he had the vessel nose-on to the front edge of the roof. There seemed to be a faint aura in the gloom ahead and he switched off his nose beam to study it better.

It was a faint yellow haze shining over the rim of the opposite slope. His back hairs quivered as he saw it. The haze strengthened, rose higher. His eyes strained into the outer pall as he watched it fascinatedly, and his hands were frozen on the controls. There was dampness on his back. Behind him, in her travelling compartment, Laura was completely silent, not even shuffling uneasily as was her wont. He wondered if she were cowering.

With a mighty effort of will which strained him as never before, he shifted his control a couple of notches, lengthened the tail blast. Trembling in its entire fabric, the ship edged forward. Summoning all he'd got, Steve forced his reluctant hands to administer the take-off boost. With a tearing crash that thundered back from the cliffs, the little vessel leaped skyward on an arc of fire. Peering through the transpex, Steve caught a fragmentary and foreshortened glimpse of the great golden column advancing majestically over the crest; the next instant it had dropped far behind his tail and his bow was arrowing for the stars.

An immense relief flooded through his soul though he knew not what there had been to fear. But the relief was there and so great was it that he worried not at all about where he was bound or for how long. Somehow, he felt certain that if he swept in a wide, shallow curve he'd pick up a Probe beat-note sooner or later. Once he got a beat-note, from any source at all, it would lead him out of the celestial maze.

Luck remained with him, and his optimistic hunch proved correct, for while still among completely strange constellations he caught the faint throb of Hydra III on his twenty-seventh day of sweep. That throb was his cosmic lighthouse beckoning him home.

He let go a wild shriek of, 'Yippee!' thinking that only Laura heard him – but he was heard elsewhere.

Down on Oro, deep in the monster workshop, the golden giant paused blindly as if listening. Then it slid stealthily along the immense aisles, reached the filing system. A compartment opened, two glassy plates came out.

For a moment the plates contacted the Oron's strange, sparkling substance, became etched with an array of tiny dots. They were returned to the compartment, and the door closed. The golden glory with its imprisoned stars then glided quietly back to the machine section.

Something nearer to the gods had scribbled its notes. Nothing lower in the scale of life could have translated them or deduced their full purport.

In simplest sense, one plate may have been inscribed, 'Biped, erect, pink, homo intelligens type P.739, planted on Sol III, Condensation Arm BDB – moderately successful.'

Similarly, the other plate may have recorded, 'Flapwing, large, hook-beaked, vari-coloured, periquito macao type K.8, planted on Sol III, Condensation Arm BDB – moderately successful.'

But already the sparkling hobbyist had forgotten his passing notes. He was breathing his essence upon a jewelled moth.

# Philip Latham
# The Xi effect

For a week the team of Stoddard and Arnold had met with nothing but trouble in their solar infra-red exploration programme. First the lead sulphide photo-conductive cell had refused to function. Next an electrical storm – practically unknown in September – had put a crimp in the power line to the mountain observatory. And now for some wholly inexplicable reason the automatic recorder stubbornly refused to register a single quantum of radiation beyond 20,000A.

'Here's the end of the atmospheric carbon dioxide band at sixteen thousand,' said Arnold, indicating a point on their last record sheet. 'You can see everything's all right out to there. But beyond twenty thousand we aren't getting a thing.'

Stoddard grunted. 'That's what comes of our big economy drive. Trying to cut expenses by buying from the dime store.' He walked over to the spectrometer and regarded it gloomily. It was the product of his own mind, an impressive series of slits and parabolic mirrors fed by a beam of sunlight from the top of the tower. When the optical set-up was in perfect adjustment the apparatus would bring just the desired band of infra-red radiation on to the sensitive surface of the photo-conductive cell. But obviously all was not in perfect adjustment.

'Maybe it's in the amplifier this time,' Arnold suggested hopefully.

'Well, that's the only part of this contraption that hasn't balked on us so far,' said Stoddard. 'Suppose you look it over while I check the cell again.'

For the next hour the astronomers probed the interior of the spectrometer as intently as two surgeons performing an exploratory laparotomy, passing tools back and forth and generally anticipating each other's wants with scarcely a word spoken. For fifteen years they had thus worked together, one of the oddest-looking scientific teams at the Western Institute of Technology, but one that had also proven itself amazingly productive. Stoddard at forty had the general shape of an old-fashioned beer-barrel, with big hands, big feet and a big protruding stomach. His half-closed eyes gave him a perpetually sleepy expression, a highly effective mask for one of the keenest minds in the business. Arnold, although nearly as old as his partner, somehow still gave the impression of youth. He was small and slight with an eager boyish expression that often caused visitors to mistake him for a graduate student embarking on his first research problem. Stoddard was the practical man of the firm who designed the apparatus for their various investigations and took the bulk of the observations. Arnold was the one who reduced the observations and discussed their theoretical significance.

'Find anything wrong?' Stoddard inquired at length, straightening up and replacing the cover that housed the cell assembly.

'Nothing worth mentioning,' said Arnold. 'Think there's time for another run?'

'Yeah, I guess so. Put the sun back on the slit and we'll take another crack at her anyhow.'

But the second run proved no better than the first; in fact, if anything, the cut-off occurred a trifle farther in toward the violet than before.

'I might as well take the whole works down to the laboratory for a complete overhaul,' Stoddard declared, looking at his brain-child as if he would have liked to heave it over the side of the mountain. He watched a cloud drift lazily across the disc of the sun projected against the slit. 'Get any weather predictions on the radio this morning?'

Arnold gave him a quizzical glance. 'Haven't you heard yet? All the radio stations have been dead for more than a week.'

'What's the matter with 'em?'

'Well, it's really quite mysterious. Last Monday KLX faded out right in the middle of a programme, and then stations farther up the dial began to be hit one after the other. For a while all you could get were the amateurs and the police department. Now they're dead, too.'

Stoddard, who regarded the radio as one of the major threats to his peace of mind, took the news philosophically. 'Well, I'm glad to hear we aren't the only ones having trouble these days. But I'll bet my wife was sore when she couldn't hear what happened to Priscella Lane, Private Secretary, last night.'

Stoddard was in his laboratory in the basement of the Astrophysics Building at Western Tech hard at work on the wiring diagram for the amplifier system when Arnold came breezing in, his bright, young face aglow with enthusiasm.

'Guess what?' he exclaimed. 'Friedmann's in town. He's agreed to give a talk this afternoon in Dickinson Hall on his theory of the Xi effect. You know Friedmann, don't you?'

Stoddard shook his head. 'Never heard of him.'

Arnold hooked one leg over the corner of the desk. 'Well, in my opinion he's the foremost cosmologist in the world today. He had so much trouble getting published at first that his reputation isn't as big as it should be. Everybody thought his first paper was written by some crank until Eddington saw it and recognized its value immediately. Now Friedmann won't send his articles to any of the regular journals. You've got to dig his stuff out of all sorts of queer places, like the *Proceedings of the Geophysical Society of Venezuela* or the *Annals of the Portuguese Meteorological Union.*'

'I know how he feels,' said Stoddard sympathetically.

'Well, I thought we should hear him because his theory might possibly have some bearing on our infra-red observations last week.'

'Think I could understand him if I did hear him?'

'Oh, probably not, but that goes for a lot of the rest of us, too.'

Stoddard reached for the wiring diagram. 'Well, I'll see if I can manage it. But you know what I think of these high-powered theoretical fellows.'

Arnold laughed. 'I've been briefed on that before.' He got up and started for the door. 'Room 201 at four-thirty. I'll have a seat for you.'

The meeting was already in progress when Stoddard opened the door and slipped to his seat without creating any more commotion than a horse backing into a stall. As usual, the front rows were occupied by the hardened campaigners among the faculty, the grizzled veterans of a thousand seminars: Fosberg and Ballantyne from the maths department, Blacker and Tinsdale from the radiation laboratory, and Denning the nuclear physicist. The remainder of the audience in the rear was composed of a miscellaneous rabble of graduate students and professors from neighbouring institutions of learning and culture.

'Who's ahead?' asked Stoddard, sinking into the chair beside his partner.

'You should have heard Friedmann put old Blacker in his place a minute ago,' Arnold whispered with evident relish. 'He sure slapped him down plenty that time.'

To Stoddard, all theoretical physicists were strange creatures far removed from the rest of mankind. It was his experience that they could be divided with remarkable uniformity into two types, A and B. A typical specimen of Type A, for example, is mentally accessible only with the greatest difficulty. As a general rule, he moves through life with the vague detached air of a confirmed somnambulist. Should you summon the courage to ask his opinion on a paper, he regards it with much the same expression of critical disapproval that a secondhand-car dealer instinctively assumes when inspecting a battered automobile brought in for sale. Everything is in a pretty bad state. It is possible, however, that a little progress may be made along the following lines, et cetera. A pure Type B, on the other hand, gives the impression of being always on the point of boiling over. He trembles with suppressed excitement. One of his former pupils has just proposed a theory that constitutes a tremendous advance. Where there was only darkness before now all is sunshine and light. As soon as a few odds and ends are cleared up the whole problem will be practically solved, et cetera, et cetera.

Stoddard classified Friedmann as predominantly Type A with a few overtones of Type B thrown in. He was a tall, thin man of about thirty, with sharp angular features, and a way of looking at you as if his eyes were focused on a point ten feet behind your back. His voice was dry and flat with the barest trace of foreign accent.

Stoddard had not listened for more than five minutes before he began to experience the same sense of bewilderment that little Dorothy must have felt on her first trip to the land of Oz. As nearly as he could gather, Friedmann considered the familiar everyday world to constitute merely a tiny corner or 'clot' in a vastly higher order of space-time or 'Xi space'. Ordinarily, events in the Xi space are on too gross a scale to exert a sensible effect on the fine-grained clot space. On rare occasions, however, a clot might be seriously disturbed by events of an exceptional nature in the Xi space, in somewhat the same way that the atoms on the surface of a stick of amber may be disturbed by rubbing it vigorously. When events in the super-cosmos happen to intrude upon an individual clot extraordinary results ensue; for example, angular momentum is not strictly conserved, and Hamilton's equations require modification, to mention only a few.

'Thus for a properly oriented observer the universe must at all times have a radius equal to tau times the velocity of light,' said Friedmann, by way of conclusion. 'Hence, if tau increases uniformly we must of necessity have the expanding universe as shown by the general recession of the extragalactic nebulae.

'But this increase in tau time is not really uniform but a statistical effect. Local fluctuations in the Xi space may attain such magnitude as to become distinctly perceptible in clot space. Evidence for the Xi effect in our vicinity is shown by the behaviour of the Andromeda nebula, which instead of sharing in

the general recession is approaching the Earth at three hundred
kilometers per second. Again, certain anomalies in the motion
of the inner planets, notably the secular variation in the node of
Venus,* clearly indicate encroachment of the Xi effect within the
confines of our own solar system. Further anomalies of increasing magnitude may be anticipated.'

With a curt nod he gathered together his papers and sat down
abruptly, scarcely bothering to acknowledge the prolonged applause from the student section. The secretary of the Astronomy
and Physics Club thanked Dr Friedmann for his address, which
he was sure they had all enjoyed, and inquired if there were any
questions. This announcement was followed by the customary
minute of awkward silence. Finally the spell was broken by
Fosberg, an authority on the theory of numbers and uncrowned
king of the faculty's eccentric characters.

'As I get it, this postulated Xi effect started a shrinkage in our
sector about ten-to-the-ninth years ago. Now then, I've just been
doing some figuring on the back of this envelope and if I haven't
made a mistake the present diameter of the solar system out to
Pluto is $3.2 \times 10^8$ kilometers, or about two hundred million miles.
Is that right?' Everyone looked expectantly at the speaker.

'I work entirely with the generalized formulae; never with
numerical values,' Friedmann replied with cold dignity. 'However, I do not question the accuracy of Dr Fosberg's arithmetic.
Naturally the shrinkage would be quite imperceptible with
ordinary measuring rods. It would be necessary to make some
observation involving explicitly the velocity of light.'

'I'm willing to grant you that,' Fosberg returned, 'but aren't

---

*The outstanding difference between gravitational theory and
observation is the well-known discrepancy of 43″ per century in
the motion of the perihelion of Mercury. Einstein's explanation
of this discrepancy was considered a triumph for relativity.

The next largest difference between gravitational theory and
observation is the secular variation of 13″ per century in the node
of Venus, which has not been explained by relativity. See *Journal
of the Optical Society of America*, vol. 30 (1930), p. 225.

you going to get into serious trouble with the law of gravitation due to all this shrinkage? Why, in a few more years the congestion in the solar system will be worse than the campus parking problem!' It was a remark that was always good for a laugh and one of the principal reasons he had asked the question in the first place.

'The gravitational difficulties that so worry Dr Fosberg did not follow as a necessary consequence,' said Friedmann, entirely unruffled. 'As I have demonstrated, the laws of Newtonian mechanics may fail to hold even as a first approximation. At these extreme limits, however, the integration of the equations becomes quite insuperable by ordinary methods. One of my pupils at the University of Pennsylvania plans to explore these regions next year with the EDVAC.'

Fosberg wagged his bald head. 'Just the same, all this crowding together still worries me,' he declared. 'And I don't like the idea of being reduced to the size of a microcosmic midget either.'

Friedmann's shrug plainly indicated that it was a matter of complete indifference to him if Fosberg were reduced to the dimensions of a neutrino, and as there were no more questions the meeting broke up. Stoddard, who had grown thoroughly bored with the whole proceedings, made a bolt for the door, but Arnold was only a few lengths behind.

'Wasn't Friedmann good,' he demanded. 'Don't you think it's the most satisfying cosmological theory you ever heard?'

'No doubt about it,' said Stoddard, continuing on down the hall.

'You know, I was thinking,' Arnold went on, falling into step beside him, 'why couldn't we test the Xi effect ourselves?'

'Test it ourselves!'

'Why not? After all, it shouldn't be too difficult. As Friedmann said, we would only need to make some observation that depends explicitly on the velocity of light.'

Stoddard snorted. 'Bet he's never made a bona fide observation in his whole life.'

They stopped on the steps outside Dickinson Hall before

wending their separate ways homeward. The sun had set and a slight breeze was beginning to stir the leaves of the giant oak tree at the entrance.

'Well, the next time you're in my office we'll have a long talk about it,' said Stoddard, edging down the steps. 'But right now I've got to get home for dinner.'

'The observation would consist simply in determining whether some distant event occurred at the time predicted,' Arnold mused. 'Let's see, what would be the easiest thing to observe?'

At that instant his eye was attracted to a star faintly visible near the eastern horizon. 'I've got it!' he cried. 'We could observe an eclipse of one of Jupiter's satellites. If the solar system has really shrunk as much as the Xi effect predicts, it should occur way ahead of time.'

'You mean do a kind of repeat on Roemer's work,' said Stoddard, 'only with a light time corresponding to the whole distance to Jupiter instead of the diameter of the Earth's orbit?'

'Exactly!'

Stoddard could feel the net closing around him. He knew that once his partner in crime became infatuated with an idea it was useless to try to discourage him. 'Well, I guess we've looked for less hopeful things. Only I can't seem to remember what they were.'

'Listen,' said Arnold, his eyes shining, 'is there a class at the ten-inch tonight?'

Stoddard considered. 'This is Wednesday, isn't it? Nope, don't think there will be one.'

'Then what's to stop us from making the observation right now – tonight?'

'Nothing, so far as I know, except maybe a nice thick fog.' He heaved a sigh of resignation. 'Come on, let's take a look at the *Ephemeris*. Maybe there *aren't* any eclipses tonight.'

But the *American Ephemeris* said otherwise. An occultation of Jupiter I was scheduled for Thursday, 5 October, at four hours eight minutes and ten seconds of Greenwich Civil Time.

Arnold was delighted. 'I'll meet you at the ten-inch at seven-fifteen tonight. O.K.?'

'O.K.'

'We can stop in at my house for a drink afterwards.'

'We'll probably need one,' was Stoddard's grim comment, 'after we find out how much the universe has shrunk.'

The lamp over the desk threw grotesque shadows around the circular room making the telescope and pier look like some giant insect flattened against the curving walls of the dome. At that moment, however, Stoddard was in no mood to appreciate the projective geometry of shadow pictures. Like all other manually operated observatory domes in the world, the one on the ten-inch at Western Tech opened only with the utmost reluctance. At length, in response to an effort worthy of Superman, Stoddard forced the shutter back, revealing the constellation of Cygnus sprawling across the meridian. Breathing heavily, he turned the dome until Jupiter came into the centre of the opening, a gleaming yellow stoplight among the faint stars of Aquarius. Then, swinging the telescope around on the pier as if it were an anti-aircraft gun, he sighted along the tube until the planet came darting into the field of view.

'How's the seeing?' asked Arnold, a formless black shape by the desk. He twisted the shade over the lamp until the light illuminated the chronometer and pad of paper at his elbow, but left the end of the telescope in shadow.

Stoddard gave the focusing screw another touch. 'Not so good,' he muttered. Removing the eyepiece from the end of the telescope he substituted a longer one in its place from the box beside him. 'There – that's better.'

'How do the satellites look?'

'Well, just about the way the *Ephemeris* predicted. Callisto and Ganymede are over on the west. Europa's about a diameter of Jupiter to the east. Io doesn't seem to be anywhere around.'

He lowered the seat on the observing platform a couple of notches, thus enabling him to look into the telescope with less strain on his vertebrae. 'Wait a minute – caught a glimpse of her at the limb just then.'

Arnold shot a glance at the chronometer. 'Gosh, don't tell me it's going into occultation already!'

'Well, it sure looks like it.'

'But it can't be that much ahead of time.'

'Why not? That's what you were hoping for, wasn't it? Keep an eye on the chronometer, anyhow. I'll give you the time as close as I can in this bum seeing.'

For several minutes the dome was silent except for the steady ticking of the chronometer and the low hum of traffic from Los Feliz Boulevard far below. Stoddard concentrated his every faculty on the tiny point of light projecting from the planet's disc. Sometimes he felt sure it must be gone only to have it flash into view again. He waited until it had remained out of sight for an unusually long interval. 'All right, get ready,' he warned. 'Now!'

'Seven-thirty-three-zero-zero,' said Arnold, writing down the numbers at the top of the record sheet. Stoddard rose painfully from his cramped position at the end of the telescope and began cautiously exercising one leg. His partner continued figuring busily for another five minutes. Presently he leaned back and began tapping the desk thoughtfully with the tip of his pencil.

'What's the answer?' said Stoddard, limping across the room.

'Well, according to these figures,' Arnold replied, speaking with elaborate casualness, 'the occultation occurred just thirty-five minutes and ten seconds ahead of time.'

For a moment neither spoke. Then Stoddard let out a belly laugh that shattered the peaceful calm that had hitherto enveloped Observatory Hill. 'That puts Jupiter right in our backyard. It's so close the light gets here in nothing flat.'

Arnold gazed up at the planet riding so serenely among the stars. There were Vega and Altair over in the west, with Cygnus flying close behind, and the great square of Pegasus wheeling upward in the north, precisely as he had seen them a thousand times before. Could it be possible that some catastrophe from Outside had warped their little corner of space until the giant Jupiter had been brought to what would once have been an arm's length, so close you might have reached out and seized it between your thumb and forefinger like a cherry? As a boy he had loved to read tales of time travel and flights to other planets, and the feeling that something transcendental was lurking around the corner had never entirely left him. In their seminars they talked of world lines and a space of *n* dimensions, but did any of them really believe it? Now perhaps it was here at last. He shivered in the damp night air. The ocean breeze blowing in through the dome certainly felt real enough.

Mechanically he began helping Stoddard put the telescope to bed for the night, replacing the cap on the objective and swinging the telescope over the polar axis, where he clamped it in declination.

'What do you say we go down in the darkroom for a smoke?' said Stoddard, when everything was ship-shape. 'I'd like to take a look at those figures of yours myself.'

The darkroom in the basement below was a welcome relief from the windy dome. Stoddard threw off his jacket, pulled a stool up to the bench that ran down one side of the room, and began stoking his pipe from a can of tobacco in one of the drawers. Not until the operation was completed to his entire satisfaction, and the bowl glowing brightly, did he turn his attention to Arnold's reduction. Then with exasperating deliberation he started checking off the figures, pausing occasionally between puffs to compare them with those in the *Ephemeris*. Arnold leaned against the wall watching him nervously.

'Well, I can't seem to find anything wrong,' he admitted grudgingly, 'but, of course, that doesn't mean it's right either.'

Taking careful aim, he blew a smoke ring at the girl on the calendar over the sink, watching it swirl around her plunging neckline with moody satisfaction. 'A dozen times in my life I've got results almost as crazy as this one. Every time I couldn't help saying to myself, "Stoddard, maybe you've discovered something at last. Maybe you've stumbled on to something big.' So far I've never made a single scientific discovery.

'Now, you take this observation tonight. Sure, it would be exciting to suppose the solar system has shrunk to the size of a dime, but first I want to be absolutely sure there isn't some perfectly natural commonplace explanation. It's a depressing fact that most of the exciting results a scientist gets can eventually be traced to errors of observation. Think of all the times Mira Ceti at maximum has been mistaken for a nova.'

'Everybody knows that,' Arnold objected. 'But where's the chance for error in this observation? It's so simple.'

'Maybe not so simple as you think. Remember the seeing was terrible. That time I gave you might have been off by a couple of minutes – maybe more.'

'That still leaves thirty minutes to explain.'

'All right. Now the question is how much faith can we put in the *Ephemeris*? It wouldn't surprise me if the predicted time itself was way off.'

'As much as that?'

'Well, I know the predictions for Jupiter's four great satellites are based on Sampson's tables of 1910, and they certainly must require some kind of correction by this time. I don't know how often the Naval Observatory checks up on things like that. But until we do know – and have a lot more observations – we really don't know a thing.'

'O.K., O.K.,' said Arnold impatiently. 'All the same, I still think it's a whale of an error.'

'It's a king-size one, I'll admit,' said Stoddard, relighting his pipe. 'And now there's something I wish you'd explain to me. After all that palaver this afternoon I still don't understand how this so-called Xi effect ties in with our infra-red observations.'

Arnold reached for the pencil and a pad of yellow scratch-paper. 'Assume that this line represents the boundary of our local universe or "clot",' he said, drawing an irregular closed figure with a dot near the centre. 'According to Friedmann, occasionally some disturbance in the outer supercosmos or Xi space becomes sufficiently violent to affect a particular clot. Now there are several things that can happen as a result, but by far the most probable is that the clot will begin to shrink, very slowly at first and then more rapidly. But for a long time now nobody would be aware of the shrinkage because everything within the clot shrinks in proportion, with one exception. That exception is the wavelength of electromagnetic radiation.

'Suppose the boundary has shrunk until it has an average radius of a thousand kilometers.' He drew a line from the central dot to a point on the boundary. 'Obviously nothing can exist within the boundary bigger than the boundary itself. Therefore, this means that all electromagnetic radiation exceeding a thousand kilometers is eliminated. That accounts for the fadeout in radio transmission. As the boundary continues to shrink shorter wavelengths keep being cut out all the time.'

'I think I'm beginning to get it,' said Stoddard, studying the diagram. 'We didn't get any transmission beyond twenty thousand angstroms because there wasn't any radiation to transmit.'

'That's it! Our universe only had a diameter of twenty thousand angstroms. All radiation of longer wavelength was cut out.'

'About one ten-thousandth of an inch,' said Stoddard, doing some fast mental arithmetic. He chuckled. 'No wonder old Fosberg was worried!'

'You see the Xi effect does give a consistent explanation of all the phenomena,' said Arnold triumphantly. 'In any case, we can't be in doubt much longer.'

'How's that?'

'Why, because the universe will have shrunk so much the optical spectrum will be affected. The landscape will change colour.'

'Well, maybe you're right,' Stoddard agreed reluctantly, 'but so far everything looks just the same to me as it always has.' Absently he began doodling a series of circles and squares across Arnold's diagram. 'What I wish,' he said with a yawn, 'is that somebody would find a way to shorten the time from one payday till the next.'

Arnold waved his arms in a helpless gesture and walked to the other end of the room. Stoddard sat motionless as if half-asleep. Presently he took a briefcase from one of the drawers and began exploring its contents. 'Here're those snapshots we took at the zoo the other day,' he said. 'Haven't had time to develop 'em yet.'

His partner eyed the rolls of film without interest. 'My wife was asking about them at dinner. She wants to see that one where she's feeding the eagle.'

'If you want to wait, I can develop 'em now.'

Arnold glanced at his wristwatch. 'Sure, go ahead. It's only eight-thirty.'

Stoddard turned off the overhead light, plunging the little room into total darkness. Arnold could hear him searching for the switch that operated the safelight, but when he snapped it on there was no result. He snapped it several times but still without result.

'Globe's probably burnt out,' said Arnold.

Stoddard jerked the screen back revealing the light inside burning brightly. 'Now what?' he muttered.

They stood staring at the light in puzzled silence. Suddenly Arnold leaped forward, his face tense in the white glare from the lamp.

'Stoddard.'

'Yeah?'

'*Put the screen back over the lamp.*'

His partner hesitated then obediently shoved the screen back in place until not a chink of white light was visible. Gradually as their eyes gained sensitivity in the dark the oblong shape of the safety screen became faintly visible.

But the screen was no longer ruby red. It was a dull colourless grey.

No scientific theory ever became accepted as fact so quickly as Friedmann's theory of the Xi effect, but then no other theory before ever had such a convincing array of scientific evidence to support it. The change in the tint of the landscape that Arnold had foreseen eventually developed, but for several weeks it was too slight to be readily obvious. The effect was the same as if everyone had gone colour-blind to an effective wavelength of about 6500A. It was disconcerting to find that your hedge of geraniums was black instead of scarlet, and the absence of stoplights was nearly disastrous. Some women became violently hysterical when they first beheld the inky fluid oozing from their veins. But after the novelty had worn off the public soon lost interest. They had lived through the invasion from Mars, the flying saucers and other scientific gags, and doubtless in time this, too, would pass. Besides, how could you expect people to work up any enthusiasm over something when they weren't even sure how to pronounce it?

But as orange and yellow followed red into the grey there came a change in the public attitude, a kind of half-credulous belief mingled with misgiving and dismay. Men still laughed and joked about the Xi effect over their old-fashioneds at the country club, but just when everybody was feeling happy and secure again someone was sure to spoil it all. 'You know, this thing may turn out to be more serious than we think,' he would say. 'I've got a nephew teaches out at the university. Hasn't got a dime but smart as the devil. Well, he told me confidently it's getting worse instead of better. No telling where it may end, in fact.'

Rather curiously, women had much more awareness of the Xi effect than men, for it struck at their most vulnerable point – their appearance. Golden hair could turn grey in a matter of weeks. A complexion drained of its warm flesh tints looked dead. Cosmetics were of no avail against it. For of what use was lipstick if it only turned the lips from grey to black? Or of rouge if it left only deeper shadows on the cheeks? The radiant beauty of a short time past anxiously examining her face in her mirror at night might see an old woman staring back at her out of the glass. Deaths from sleeping-pills became a commonplace.

Not until late in November, however, did the situation reach such a critical stage that government officials felt compelled to recognize the Xi effect as a definite world menace. Previously its encroachment had been dismissed by the ingenious process of studiously minimizing its existence. It was true that the papers printed the censored reports from scientific institutions but always under captions that were misleading and with the significant news buried near the bottom of the column. A few scientists who refused to be muzzled soon found themselves out of a job or called up before an investigation committee.

Eventually, however, the clamour became so loud that announcement was made of a series of mass meetings to be held across the country in which all the facts in so far as they were known would be discussed without reservation. The first in the series was scheduled for the Los Angeles Coliseum for Monday, 27 November, with the great Dr Friedmann as the feature speaker of the evening. Public sentiment changed almost overnight. The personal appearance of Friedmann alone did much to restore confidence. He was the fellow who had discovered this Xi effect, wasn't he? Well, then, he could probably control it, too. Man had never met a problem that man was unable to solve.

By the evening of the twenty-seventh public curiosity over what Friedmann would say had been excited to such a degree that it was necessary to keep the man's whereabouts a profound secret to prevent him from being mobbed on sight. By five o'clock every street leading toward the coliseum was blocked solid with cars for miles around, and by seven o'clock more than a hundred thousand people had jammed themselves into the vast structure, while thousands more milled around the walls outside seeking entrance. Although the Los Angeles Police Department had every man available on duty in addition to two hundred special officers hired from outlying districts, they were able to maintain order only with considerable difficulty. An attitude of reckless abandon was manifest even among ordinarily well-behaved individuals. It was a holiday crowd without the holiday spirit.

'I'm not at all sure Friedmann is the best man to talk to these people tonight,' said Arnold, standing up and gazing uneasily around him at the throngs still climbing up and down the aisles in search of seats. 'They've come here confidently expecting to be told something that sounds nice and reassuring, and instead Friedmann will simply hand them the hard, cold facts. We scientists have known the truth for weeks and had a chance to become reconciled to it. But what about the average man whose cosmic outlook is limited to his job and the mortgage on his home out in Brentwood?'

'Be quite a blow to 'em probably,' said Stoddard, biting into his hot dog. 'Trouble with these theoretical fellows is they act as if the Xi effect had been invented for the sole purpose of letting them test out all their screwy ideas on nuclear structure.'

Arnold sat down and began studying his programme. 'I see Atchison Kane is going to speak, too.'

'Atchison Kane. Who's he?'

'Shakespearean actor,' Arnold replied. Long ago he had become accustomed to his partner's splendid state of isolation from the world of the stage and screen. 'Made a big hit in *Richard III* recently. I heard him at the Philharmonic last August.'

'That so?' said Stoddard. For the tenth time he looked at the great clock over the archway at the east entrance. 'What's holding up the procession, anyhow? They were supposed to kick off half an hour ago.'

Others beside Stoddard were getting impatient. So far the crowd had been fairly well behaved but now it was growing decidedly restless. Someone yelled, 'We want Friedmann!' and in an instant thousands of voices were repeating the words over and over in a kind of savage chant. When this failed to produce results, a mob of boys, acting as if upon signal, leaped over the parapet on to the field toward the speakers' stand. Before the police could intervene they began tearing down the decorations and smashing the chairs and railing. The dozen or so officers in the vicinity were overwhelmed at first but reinforcements soon gained the upper hand. The crowd was delighted, following every incident of the struggle with fascinated attention. Several men were knocked down and trampled in the mêlée, or sent reeling from the battle bleeding from lacerations around the head. Suddenly a great shout went up. The speakers, surrounded by a husky squad of police, were spotted emerging from the south entrance. Interest in the fight evaporated immediately. The floodlights were dimmed and an expectant hush fell over the assemblage.

After the usual preliminaries, to which no one paid the slightest attention, the chairman of the National Scientific Security Council finally got around to introducing the main speaker.

'In the brief span that this committee has been in existence, citizens from all parts of the southland have been besieging us with questions concerning this effect which has been uppermost in the thoughts of each and every one of us during these last troubled days. Unfortunately, no funds were appropriated for the purpose of answering these questions. And yet as representatives of the people we felt in all sincerity that they could not and must not be ignored.'

The burst of applause at this point forced him to halt briefly until quiet reigned again and he was able to gather himself together for another effort.

'In view of this situation, my colleagues and I, after due deliberation, have asked our distinguished speaker if in lieu of a formal address he would consent to answer a set of representative questions selected by the committee. To this request I am happy to say that our speaker has most willingly and graciously given his consent.

'And now, without further ado, it is my great pleasure and privilege this evening to present to you a man who I am sure needs no introduction from me, that renowned scientist and scholar, Dr Karl Gustav Friedmann.'

From the uproarious applause that greeted Friedmann as he stepped to the front of the platform, it might have been supposed that he had discovered another Santa Claus instead of an effect that was relentlessly extinguishing the light of the world.

He shook hands with the chairman, bowed a few degrees in the general direction of the crowd, and then stood quietly waiting for the tumult to subside. The chairman nervously riffled through the cards in his hand, selected one and peered at it through his bifocals.

'Our first question is from a housewife in Long Beach,' he announced. 'She says, "My husband has lost his job as radio salesman on account of the Xi effect. How soon will it be over so he can go back to work again?"'

Friedmann's voice was as unemotional as if he were lecturing half a dozen sleepy students rather than a crowd of a hundred thousand that were hanging on his every word. 'I think that question may be answered by reading a message from the National Bureau of Standards which was handed to me as I entered the coliseum here tonight. Here is the message: "Spectroscopic laboratory reports sudden marked acceleration Xi effect. Cut-off 5500 at 0000 GCT." Now in plain language what does this mean? It means that at four o'clock this afternoon the extinction of radiation extended nearly to the green.' He hesitated. 'I regret to inform the lady that her husband will never be able to return to his work. Why? Because so little while is left to us that no time remains for either work or play.'

An excited, uneasy murmur swept around the coliseum that rose to a sharp peak then hastily died away as the chairman selected another card. 'Our second question is from a man in Pomona who signs himself "Taxpayer". His letter is too long to read in full so that I must confine myself to his inquiry at the end. "If scientists knew light was going to be extinguished, then why didn't they get busy and do something about it a long time ago? The Government makes me pay taxes so scientists can sit in their laboratories and hatch these wild theories. But when danger comes along they're just as helpless as the rest of us."'

The letter provoked a good deal of laughter mingled with a surprising amount of handclapping. The humour of the situation, however, was wholly lost on Friedmann. 'What would Mr Taxpayer have the scientists do?' he demanded in a voice that was openly contemptuous. 'Does he think they deliberately create the lightning that destroys a tree? Or the earthquake that engulfs a city? Well, I can assure him that these are nothing compared to the force that threatens us now. But before he criticizes science let him first learn something about it – go back to grammar school or read some little children's book.'

There was a timid scattering of applause that was soon drowned in a chorus of boos and catcalls from all sides. One could sense the rising tide of resentment and frustration underneath.

'What did I tell you?' Arnold shouted. 'They aren't going to take it.'

Stoddard hunched down farther in his seat. 'If you ask me all hell's going to break loose here in another minute.'

Two members of the committee could be seen apparently expostulating with Friedmann, who stood listening to them indifferently with folded arms. The chairman was doing his best to restore order but it was nearly a minute before he was able to proceed. 'Quiet, please. Quiet,' he entreated. 'We have many more questions on the programme of vital interest which I am sure you are all anxious to hear. Now, here is one from a schoolteacher in Lynwood which goes straight to the point. "Dear Dr Friedmann, can you tell us what course of events we may expect from the Xi effect in the immediate future?"'

'There can be no doubt as to the course of events up to a certain point,' Friedmann replied, speaking more slowly than usual and evidently weighing his words with care. 'Beyond that point there is no knowledge, only speculation and conjecture.

'But in the immediate future the course of events is very clear. The extinction of radiation will continue at a rapidly increasing pace. Soon the world will be completely devoid of the quality of radiation that excites the sensation of visible light. As it disappears, the sensation will be similar to that of watching a scene in a play in which the lights are gradually dimmed until finally the stage and players are utterly blotted out.'

There was so much noise now that Arnold was able to hear only with the greatest difficulty. Some people stood yelling and shaking their fists at Friedmann while others shouted for them to sit down and let him proceed.

'After the visible radiation there remains the spectrum of the X-radiation and gamma rays,' Friedmann continued, apparently unmindful that he had lost his audience. 'Especially significant will be the nature of the reaction upon cosmic rays, a subject upon which scientists have been wholly unable to agree. At present there is no hope of securing records of this vitally important phenomenon. Furthermore, there is no hope—'

A whisky bottle crashed against the stand, showering Friedmann with glass. Another followed and another until the air was filled with them. A dozen fights were in progress within the coliseum, while without a mob was attempting to break through the gate at the east entrance. In the distance could be heard the rising wail of police sirens.

Suddenly the floodlights blinked, wavered uncertainly, then slowly faded out to a chorus of anguished wails and frantic howls for lights. Whether the fadeout was by accident or intent the result was the same. A terrified panic-stricken hush descended upon the multitude.

It was at that instant a new voice was heard in the darkness; a voice calm and powerful, yet withal tender and reassuring.

'*The Lord is my Shepherd; I shall not want.*'

In the dim light men and women looked at each other fearful and bewildered as if a miracle were about to happen.

Again the voice came crying in the darkness. '*He maketh me to lie down in green pastures; He leadeth me beside the still waters.*'

Arnold grabbed his partner by the shoulder. 'It's Atchison Kane! If he can hold this crowd tonight, he's a wonder.'

Men who were shouting and cursing a moment before now stood awed and irresolute. Here and there a few were beginning to kneel while others sobbed openly and unashamed.

'*He restoreth my soul; He leadeth me in the paths of righteousness for His name's sake.*'

Many were beginning to repeat the familiar words after him. Now the voice swelled to a mighty climax in its message of faith and hope.

*'Yea, though I walk through the valley of the shadow of death I will fear no evil—'*

And then more softly,

*'For Thou art with me; Thy rod and Thy staff they comfort me—'*

From directly behind Arnold there came a woman's shriek with piercing intensity. It was a shriek filled with despair. A shriek that meant something was terribly wrong. Others around her began shouting and screaming too, pointing toward the great archway at the east entrance.

The low fog that had hung over the city all evening had broken momentarily, revealing the rising moon. But it was a moon that no one there had ever seen before, a moon out of a nightmare, swollen and elongated as if viewed through a cylindrical lens. But even more unnatural than its shape was its *colour* – a deep transparent blue.

Arnold was so intent upon the moon that he scarcely noticed when the floodlights came on again. Gradually he became aware of some change in the aspect of the coliseum itself; there seemed to be a soft waviness spreading everywhere warping some portions of the scene but leaving others untouched, like gelatin melting and flowing down a photographic plate. His eyes were unable to bring the mass of humanity banked against the opposite wall of the coliseum into sharp focus. The tiers of seats kept blurring and shimmering as if the light were coming from a great distance through layers of heated air.

With a sickening sensation he perceived that the distortion in space-time was beginning to affect objects right around him. The faces were undergoing some subtle alteration, noticeable particularly in the irregular position of the mouth with respect to the nose and eyes together with an apparent thickening and bending of the jaw and forehead, such as he had once seen in patients whose bony structure had undergone prolonged softening from osteitis deformons.

The night was deepening rapidly now, closing in like the folds of a vast purple curtain. Simultaneously people were gripped by that primitive wholly unreasoning fear that is felt at a total solar eclipse the instant before totality, when the shadow of the moon suddenly looms on the horizon, advancing with terrifying speed. Men and women clung to each other or ran frantically this way and that way as if by fleeing they could escape a fate from which no escape was possible.

Stoddard and Arnold sat huddled together watching the groping figures grow dimmer and dimmer until the last ray of light was extinguished in the dense impenetrable blackness. But hours later they knew from the sound of voices and the pressure of hands and bodies that thousands were still crouching in their seats waiting hopefully for the light that had always returned.

Arnold dozing against Stoddard's shoulder found himself repeating a phrase from Friedmann's last remark: 'There is no hope— There is no hope—'